THE VISCOUNT'S CHRISTMAS BRIDE

BRONWYN SCOTT

If you purchased this book without a cover you should be aware that this book is stolen property. It was reported as "unsold and destroyed" to the publisher, and neither the author nor the publisher has received any payment for this "stripped book."

ISBN-13: 978-1-335-53980-9

The Viscount's Christmas Bride

Copyright © 2024 by Nikki Poppen

All rights reserved. No part of this book may be used or reproduced in any manner whatsoever without written permission.

Without limiting the author's and publisher's exclusive rights, any unauthorized use of this publication to train generative artificial intelligence (AI) technologies is expressly prohibited.

This is a work of fiction. Names, characters, places and incidents are either the product of the author's imagination or are used fictitiously. Any resemblance to actual persons, living or dead, businesses, companies, events or locales is entirely coincidental.

For questions and comments about the quality of this book, please contact us at CustomerService@Harlequin.com.

TM and ® are trademarks of Harlequin Enterprises ULC.

Harlequin Enterprises ULC
22 Adelaide St. West, 41st Floor
Toronto, Ontario M5H 4E3, Canada
www.Harlequin.com

Printed in U.S.A.

Her gloved hand stroked his jaw and he caught her wrist, caution exerting its last defense.

"Aurelia, we said no more kisses."

"We said no more *impetuous* kisses. We decided nothing about planned kisses, and I've been planning this one for quite some time today." She leaned in and feathered his lips with hers. His body rocketed to attention as she whispered against his mouth, "Truth be told, Julien, I think you have been, too." And damn it if she wasn't right.

He let her be right, let his choice be ruled by his body, let his mouth take the kiss from her, deepening it as his hand sank into the thick coil of hair at her nape, where the winter bonnet exposed it. He tasted the sweet cider and the spice of ginger on her tongue, a lovely, apt metaphor for the woman in his arms, who tempted him to taste and to take, and to travel a path his common sense forbade him.

Author Note

Julien's story was inspired by Washington Irving's Christmas essays found in his work *Old Christmas*, which is a collection of essays he wrote as he traveled through England at Christmastime. Notably, Irving did as much for Christmas in America as Dickens did for Christmas in England. If you know Tristan's story (*The Captain Who Saved Christmas*), you know that Dickens's essay "Christmas as We Grow Older" inspired his homecoming, just as Irving's essays inspired Julien's homecoming. As I wrote every chapter, I found a line from each of his essays that spoke to facets of that chapter, whether it be a reflection on the feelings of home evoked by the holidays or a recollection of old holiday traditions.

Particularly, the feelings of home and friendliness are important to Julien and Aurelia's story, which is a tale of broken hearts, trust, second chances, leaps of faith and forgiveness, all important elements at the heart of the holiday season.

Bronwyn Scott is a communications instructor at Pierce College and the proud mother of three wonderful children—one boy and two girls. When she's not teaching or writing, she enjoys playing the piano, traveling—especially to Florence, Italy—and studying history and foreign languages. Readers can stay in touch via Facebook at Facebook.com/bronwyn.scott.399 or on her blog, bronwynswriting.blogspot.com. She loves to hear from readers.

Books by Bronwyn Scott

Harlequin Historical

The Art of Catching a Duke
The Captain Who Saved Christmas
Cinderella at the Duke's Ball

Enterprising Widows

Liaison with the Champagne Count
Alliance with the Notorious Lord
A Deal with the Rebellious Marquess

Daring Rogues

Miss Claiborne's Illicit Attraction
His Inherited Duchess

The Peveretts of Haberstock Hall

Lord Tresham's Tempting Rival
Saving Her Mysterious Soldier
Miss Peverett's Secret Scandal
The Bluestocking's Whirlwind Liaison
"Dr. Peverett's Christmas Miracle"
in *Under the Mistletoe*

Visit the Author Profile page
at Harlequin.com for more titles.

This story is for the Reed family and Jordan,
who helped brainstorm the duck-boxes.
Merry Christmas.

Chapter One

Hemsford Village, Sussex—
November 27th, 1850

There was no place like home for Christmas. Especially when home was Brentham Woods, just outside Hemsford Village, on a crisp, dusky evening in early winter. Julien Lennox, the newly minted Viscount Lavenham, drew his horse to a halt at the fork in the road and inhaled deeply of the fresh night air. To the left was Heartsease, home of his infant niece and rumbustious three-year-old nephew, home of his brother, Tristan, and his wife, Elanora, a place aptly named because of the love it was wrapped in. He would be welcome there. Or he could continue on to the right, to Brentham Woods, the Lennox family home where his parents expected him, where supper would be waiting for him punctually at seven of the clock.

Julien smiled to himself. His father was as well known for his appreciation of punctuality as his mother was for always setting a table with a full complement of silver and china. And he loved them for it. He chuckled and turned his horse, a big, pure-bred Cleveland Bay, to the right and headed for Brentham Woods. Far be it from him to upset the clockwork precision of his father's house. *His father's house.* A place where he was welcomed, but a place that was not quite his. Just like the town house, which was also not his, but his father's.

Well, that at least would change. He smiled a little to himself at the thought. This time next year, he would have his own place not far from here. He'd closed the deal right before he'd left town. His stay would be punctuated by several visits to the estate. There would be renovations to plan. He would need to enlist his mother's and Elanora's help on decorating. He could hardly wait to show them the property.

A mile later, Brentham came into view, soft lamplight emanating from each of his mother's lace-curtained windows, each lamp casting its golden glow into the indigo night like the welcoming beacon of a lighthouse calling ships to the safe harbour of home. This was the home he'd come of age in. They'd moved to Hemsford when he was thirteen and Tristan, ten, his father in search of a more genteel life for the family than the one they'd lived in Bloomsbury amid the bustle of London. That house, the house of Julien's extreme youth, was long gone now. Traded in by the Lennoxes for their country estate and a more upscale town house in Mayfair where Julien spent most of the year carrying out the family investment business.

Julien paused just beyond the gate to privately savour his homecoming before announcing his return. He let his gaze rove over the house with its many lamp-lit windows, let his lungs breathe in the cold, fresh country air, let his mind admit to the bittersweetness of the homecoming. The sweetness was in Christmas, in them all being together, celebrating the end of another year full of achievement: his father's aspirations for the family were alive and well. The coffers were full, business was growing, as was the family's name.

Julien had seen to it, devoting his time in London not only to business but to philanthropy. He'd seen a new foundling home established, a new school opened, and he socialised with the likes of the Dukes of Cowden and Creighton and their sons. Earlier in the year, he'd been bestowed the title Viscount Lavenham in recognition of his philanthropic efforts. It should be enough for any man—official recognition, wealth, a sense of purpose, a family who cared for him. Therein lay the bitterness. It should be enough, but he wanted more.

Specifically, he wanted a home of his own, a family of his own. The viscountcy had not come with any land, which was why it had been bestowed on him—the son of a banker. The family—his parents, his brother, his brother's wife and children—was not Julien's own. Whenever he saw his young nephew and little niece, the craving for family grew.

Once, he never would have dreamed he'd attain his thirty-eighth year without a wife and family beside him. Yet, despite the best efforts of his sister-in-law and the relentless matchmaking of the *ton*, here he was—thirty-eight and *sans* wife. He had only himself to blame for that, he supposed. He'd given his heart away in his youth and never quite got it back.

The sound of a dog's far-off bark drawing nearer cut through Julien's thoughts, recalling him from his ruminations as the dark blur of a black-and-tan hound barrelled towards him. Julien gave a joyful shout and dismounted to greet it, the hound's exuberance nearly knocking him to the ground. 'I'm home, boy. I'm home.' He laughed and ruffled the dog's short fur, to which the dog gave a happy, deep-chested bark. The house would surely be alerted to his arrival now.

Still, Julien lingered in the dark, playing with the hound. Benjamin was his in a way no one or nothing else was. When Julien had found him, Ben had been a stray puppy barely twelve weeks old, wandering the Hemsford countryside lost, alone and on a collision course with death, the little pup gallantly struggling to hunt and feed himself. The same desire that prompted Julien to fund orphanages and found schools had prompted him to scoop the pup up and warm him in the folds of his greatcoat.

Now Benjamin was five, the best hound in the field when it came to the Hemsford Hunt Club, and loyal. That's what Julien liked best about Benjamin. When he was home, Benjamin followed him everywhere. Ben slept on the floor beside his bed and lay at his feet, waiting patiently while he worked, or ran beside him when Julien went riding. Julien knew the rarity of such devotion and he did not take it lightly in animals or in people.

Julien gathered the reins of his horse in one hand and gestured for Benjamin to fall in beside him for the short journey to the house. The head groom, Joseph, waited for him there to take his horse. No sooner had the horse been led away than the front door opened, his mother and father coming out to welcome him. A sense of peace fell over him as his mother hugged him and his father asked the usual questions: How was the trip down? Was the train on time? What did he think of the new branch line straight into Hemsford? Didn't it make the trip from London so much more efficient?

Amid the questions and conversation of homecoming, he was ushered into the cosy front parlour, a drink pressed into his hand, Benjamin lying at his feet, a fire in the grate to take off the evening chill. Julien let the peace engulf him, let the sweetness of arrival sweep over him, and he pushed away the sadness that lingered on the edges. There was no place for it when one was home for Christmas.

The sweetness of homecoming sustained him right up until the cheese plate was served at the end of supper—a meal which had featured all of his favourites. His mother and Cook had no doubt deliberately laboured over the menu quite intentionally to please him, and Julien had been effusive in his thanks. 'Food always tastes better at home.' He smiled at his mother, who beamed with pleasure. She was a born hostess who could put even a stranger at ease in her home and who loved nothing more than her grown sons at her table even if only in temporary doses.

'Are you not happy with your cook at the town house?' she asked. 'I could make enquiries.'

'Cook is fine, I think it's the eating alone that gets tiresome,' Julien confessed. If he wasn't eating alone at home, he was eating out in the company of others for business or for pleasure and he'd learned that the joy of eating at home was only in part the food one ate. The other part was whom one ate the meal with. In London he seemed unable to put those two parts together.

His father smiled. 'Well, it's Christmas, so there's no risk of eating alone at Brentham. In fact, we shall have a full table starting tomorrow night.' He divulged the information with a twinkle in his eye that had Julien on edge. These were plans and guests that he'd not been apprised of.

'For business or pleasure?' Julien enquired, splitting his gaze between his parents. He'd heard nothing of guests visiting at Brentham for Christmas, neither in his mother's letters to London nor in his father's weekly business missives. Perhaps he'd missed it? He had been busy these past weeks in London, what with the Duchess of Cowden's Christmas charity ball and other festivities ramping up in town while he tried to ramp business down long enough to depart for a month in the country. November had passed in a whirlwind of parties and calls as he wrapped up the year.

'A bit of both, I suppose,' his father said jovially. Truth be told, Julien didn't share that joviality. He was disappointed to hear it. He'd been hoping for some quiet and for some privacy in which to plan for his new home. Hemsford was a special place during Christmas. He'd wanted to enjoy it with his family.

His mother rose with a soft smile for his father. 'I'll leave you two to discuss the business of our visitors. I have a long overdue letter to my sister to write.' Julien watched his mother depart with growing trepidation. She'd used the word 'business' and that was the last thing he wanted to do over Christmas. He'd worked all month to avoid it.

His father poured himself a glass of port and passed the decanter to him. 'First order of business is a toast. Cheers to my son. Welcome home.' Their eyes met over their glasses as they drank the toast, his father's gaze punctuated by the lateral canthal lines fanning out from the corners of his eyes, and grey dominated his temples these days rather than teased at them, all reminders that his father had turned sixty-three this year—something Julien did not spare much thought for until he was forced to, as he was in this moment when reality was staring back at him. His father was getting older. Time was passing.

His father set down his tumbler. 'Now, to discuss our visitors. The Earl of Holme and his family are coming.'

The Earl of Holme, his sworn enemy, was coming *here*? Julien's usually organised thoughts were a riot of disarray as he tried to make sense of this illogical association. His father held up the decanter, the gesture silently asking the question, *More?* Julien shook his head. He didn't think there was enough brandy in the world to handle his father's news. Of all the people in the world he would have chosen to spend Christmas with, Holme would have been last. Dead last. And he rather thought the Earl of Holme would think the same. On that one item at least they would both be agreed.

'I'm counting on your new title to smooth the way for both parties, given that you're a viscount now.'

'Have you forgotten he refused my suit for his daughter's hand?' Julien asked with all the sangfroid he could muster.

'No, I have not,' his father answered, but did not elaborate. It made Julien wonder what he was playing at, what sort of plan he was hatching.

'Why are they coming?' His father didn't know them except through him, and the impressions he'd passed on had hardly been favourable. There was no reason for the Earl to spend the intimate season of a family Christmas with them—the family of the man who'd been turned away, deemed not worthy enough for Holme's esteemed daughter.

His father gave a wry smile wrapped in smug humility. 'The same reason anyone comes to the Lennox Consolidated Trust. He is in need of funds.' Desperately so if he was willing to come to the father of the son he'd refused. Cynicism crept in. Or was it that Holme thought the Lennoxes would *beg* for his business? That they'd be so glad for the chance to loan money to a 'real' aristocrat that they'd give him more favourable terms than what he'd receive elsewhere? And there was an 'elsewhere', which prompted the question of why he'd chosen them if it wasn't because he thought they'd beg.

'There *are* banks for gentlemen with financial needs,' Julien posited his hypothesis. 'Holme does not need to come to us. We're business people.' An important point indeed. Bad blood or not, it seemed odd that the Earl *would* come to them.

Coutts was the bank of the peerage and there were others as well that had long histories of discreetly handling the financial concerns of Britain's aristocracy. Lennox Consolidated Trust was a business investment firm before it was anything else. It wasn't even in truth a bank. The money they lent was primarily for business investments and joint ventures.

His father leaned in. 'I think that's where the Earl's story gets interesting. His coffers are empty to the degree that the usual avenues are closed to him. Coutts will not advance him any further funds and his lands are mortgaged to the hilt. Between the mortgages and the entailment, he has nothing the banks perceive as collateral.' His father gave a shrug of one shoulder. 'Not even a son to secure an heiress and the promise of future wealth.' No, but the old man had a daughter. Lady Aurelia Ripley, as exquisitely beautiful as she was coldhearted. Julien had experienced both up close and personal seven years ago.

Julien gave a harsh chuckle. 'The Earl of Holme does not sound like a good investment. No funds, no collateral. Why ever would we loan him money? He'll just sink it into the never-ending pit of failing estates and mounting debt.' It was an unfortunate pattern card for the aristocracy these days. If one did what one always did, the results did not vary, no matter how much money was thrown at the problem.

'On the contrary, I do think he is an investment in the future. He might not have money to offer us, but I think he offers us inroads into the next level of society. You've made progress there with your title. I suspect your new title is the reason he's sought us out. He feels comfortable doing business with a peer, someone like him.'

'We are *not* like him,' Julien cut in sharply. 'The man embodies the height of snobbery. He is not a kind man.' Especially when rejecting a young man's sincere suit. Julien had believed he loved Aurelia and that she'd loved him, too. Worse, he'd honestly and perhaps naively believed love would be enough to overcome any opposition to their union. After seven years, he still felt the sting of those moments.

His father waited patiently before continuing. 'He is a desperate man, Julien. Desperate enough to ask for a loan from us and we can name our terms. There's more than one way to claim interest on an investment. We can ask him to open doors for us. If others see the business association, they will come to us with their needs as well. We may not currently be a bank to the aristocracy, but we could become one.'

Julien grimaced. 'Why would we want that? They're broke and, within a few generations, they'll be obsolete, defeated by their own avarice.' It was no less than what the man deserved for his arrogance.

His father arched a brow. 'Who is the snob now?' he said pointedly. 'I thought I'd taught you better than that. It can't hurt to have an earl or a duke in one's pocket. One can never have too many friends.'

Julien chuckled, sensing the true direction of his father's thoughts. 'That's the moral of "The Quackling", the French folk tale about the duck who undoes a king. I remember it. So that's the game, is it? You want to be financiers to the Queen.' Not just the aristocracy. He should have known his father wouldn't stop at earls and dukes. His father hadn't simply been rusticating in the country, building his image as a country gentleman. He'd been thinking and plotting.

His father gave a nonchalant shrug. 'Well, why not, Julien? You're a viscount now. You've found favour with her. Why shouldn't we aim for the throne? With the rate the empire is expanding, we're the sort of money the Queen needs.' There was no arguing that. Julien knew his father's reasoning was sound, as always. The empire didn't need just money, but the expertise of men like himself and his father who knew how to invest and spend that money wisely.

But first, one had to prove their worth, cut their teeth on other aristocrats before being allowed access to the throne. That's where his father obviously saw Holme come into it. Doing business with Holme was a chance for the Lennoxes to pay their dues, put in their time and prove their worth. He understood the reasons, but that didn't make him like the idea any better.

Julien pressed the bridge of his nose with his thumb and forefinger. 'If Holme thinks we'll beg for his poor business, he'll be disappointed.' Holme was not a friend Julien needed or wanted in his arsenal of social contacts. It was the larger concept of what Holme represented. In that, Holme was merely a placeholder. 'I may not do your cause any good,' he cautioned his father. 'Holme did not approve of me once upon a time.' The history between them shadowed and shaped the present. It could not be ignored.

'You weren't a viscount then and he wasn't desperate. Seven years is a long time. Things have changed.' His father smiled. 'We have the upper hand now. If you're willing to humour me, my son, and allow me to extend on the fowl metaphors, I might say his situation is such that he is willing to eat a little crow.'

Julien laughed at his father's humour in spite of his need for caution. 'Well, if so, it sounds to me as though *he* ought to be the one currying favour, not us. Yet, *we* are hosting *him*.' *And* the man's family. Which meant Lady Aurelia Ripley, Julien's very own ghost of Christmases past—a reminder of the one time he'd given his heart, only to have it thrown back at him.

Seven years on and his gut still twisted with the memory. An upwardly mobile financier had not been good enough for the daughter of the Earl of Holme to consider as more than a dance partner. And now she was coming here, invading his home during Christmas, the season he loved. Julien didn't like it one bit.

Chapter Two

Aurelia didn't like it one bit. She wanted to be home for Christmas at Moorfields, amid the familiar, surrounded by the traditions she loved: the yule log crackling in the fire, the bells at midnight pealing from the village church, greenery draping the mantels and lintels of the hall, the rooms bursting with good cheer and villagers even if those rooms were bursting a little less these days with other things like art and paintings.

She peered out the train window at the grey landscape speeding past, each mile carrying her further from Moorfields and closer to facing a spectre of her past. The prospect of seeing Julien Lennox again raised reminders from a complicated time and concerns about what her future might hold if her father were given free rein to decide.

'You should be thankful the journey is just a long day by train from York to Sussex instead of nearly a week on insufferable winter roads by carriage.' Her father looked up from his newspapers with a quelling stare.

'I didn't say a thing,' Aurelia countered, but the knot in her stomach tightened. Despite the first-class luxury of their surroundings, the train seemed more like a tumbril to her, the infamous conveyance that had brought thousands to the guillotine. If needed, she was to be bartered in order to secure the loan, her own preferences of no consequence. She might not see Moorfields, her beloved horse, her little reading school or the people she cared about again for a very long time.

Her father wagged an irate finger in her direction. He was always angry. She couldn't recall a time when he wasn't. 'No, but you were thinking it, gel. This is not a season for ungratefulness, especially when one is packing a trunk full of new clothes bought at great personal expense to your mother and me.' That was a lie, in Aurelia's opinion. They'd been bought at her mother's expense, not his.

Her mother set aside her book, ready to act the peacemaker as always. 'I hear Hemsford has a reputation for its Christmas festivities. You might enjoy it if you give it a chance, my dear.' She smiled apologetically. Aurelia had seen her make that smile countless times. Her father was angry, her mother was sorry and it was all Aurelia's fault. Everything had been her fault since the day she was born—the twin that lived. That she'd been a girl and the other a boy had only added salt to the wound of her father's disappointment.

'I'm sure I will enjoy it since I don't have a choice.' Aurelia ignored her mother's silent plea for peace and fixed her father with a stoic stare. She wouldn't pretend to know what he'd done. He'd contrived an invitation from the Lennoxes to spend Christmas in Sussex to discuss a loan that could have been discussed in a matter of a few hours in London. The moment he had the invitation, he'd rented out Moorfields for cash to an American businessman eager to embrace British Christmas. What her father had done bordered on sacrilege. Medieval witches had been burnt for less. Christmas was for hearth and home, not for travelling and living among strangers.

Only the Lennoxes weren't strangers, not quite. At least not Julien Lennox. Viscount Lavenham, now. That made her father's posturing all the worse. He was giving himself airs when everyone, Julien Lennox included, knew the Earl was the beggar at this particular feast. Her father had no shame, asking for money from a man he'd shunned seven years prior when fortunes were a bit reversed, when it was impossible to believe the Earl of Holme would fall so far or that a common financier would rise so high that now they met somewhere in the middle.

Her father had misjudged Julien Lennox all those years ago, dismissing him as a fortune hunter looking to buy his way into the peerage, but Aurelia was not surprised by Julien's continued success. From a distance, she'd watched his star rise. It was hard not to. His name was etched on every orphanage and hospital in the city. He was a determined man who knew how to get what he wanted. Except for her.

Did he want her still? Once, he'd wanted her desperately. Now, did he even think on her? The last time they'd been together, she'd not been kind. She'd refused his proposal. She'd hurt him and it had hurt her to do it, although she doubted he would believe that.

What would it be like to see him again? Would there be anything left of the old thrill she used to feel? Would her skin tingle where he touched her? Or was all that entirely buried beneath the well-deserved hatred he must feel for her? Did she *want* there to be anything? Perhaps it would be best if there wasn't anything. Feelings could be...well, expensive, as she'd once learned. She'd been careful with her feelings since then, keeping them under wraps and closely guarded. She was not interested in paying such a price again.

The real question was whether or not he would make her and her family suffer for that past set down. Had that been the motive for the invitation? Revenge? Did he mean to lead them on, make them grovel for the loan her father desperately needed? Would he make her beg on her father's behalf? Determined men were often vengeful men.

If so, she could not blame him. It would be no less than what she and her family deserved. Was he laughing at her already, knowing that she'd once been the toast of the *ton* and now she was twenty-five and unwed? Her father's misfortunes had become hers when it came to the marriage mart. People were not interested in marrying an impoverished earl's daughter.

Too many gentlemen of rank needed an heiress with money, not bloodlines, if they had to choose and her father had been too proud to let her go to a cit with funds. Then, by the time her father might have relented on his standards, her dowry was gone, sacrificed to the never-ending money pit of keeping up appearances. The cits were gone, too. It turned out that even they expected a dowry.

Her father leaned forward and glanced out the window. 'We're nearly there.' A hundred nightmares played through her mind. Would Julien meet them at the station or would she have a little longer to gather herself before seeing him? Her father's gaze gave her a quick perusal. 'Look smart. Pinch your cheeks or some trick you women do. You look pale. I didn't pawn your mother's tiara to not have you do justice to those new clothes.'

Her mother's jaw clenched. The Rose of York tiara was a sore subject between them. It had been in her family for centuries and had joined Aurelia's dowry in service to the Holme debt. 'You look lovely, my darling, just as you are. The blue brings out your eyes.' She reached over and made a little show of adjusting the gold pin Aurelia wore. 'There, now it's perfect. You are more beautiful than ever.'

'She'd better be. She's all the collateral we've got left,' her father muttered, 'if it comes to that.'

Aurelia stiffened. Her father couldn't possibly think Julien Lennox would offer for her after how he'd been treated. Julien had too much pride for that. As a matter of fact, so did she. Too much pride between them to go back and address old wrongs. 'I won't be bartered like chattel.'

If her parents' marriage was an example of what constituted the inner workings of marital bliss, she wanted none of it. Every year she remained single, the more the state recommended itself to her, although it came with a cost—there'd be no family, no loving husband like she'd dreamed of in the days of Julien's courtship. Still, she would not give that freedom up idly. She had new dreams now: the little school she was building, ways to serve the village at Moorfields.

'You will do your duty to this family. You will do your part to see we are not sunk in poverty.'

'What is that part, may I ask?' She was being impertinent on purpose, wanting him to say the words out loud.

'To ensure we are not turned down.' He gave her a dark, gimlet stare full of implicit meaning. 'The young Viscount liked you well enough once. Enchant him again.'

'That was before you and I threw him over because he didn't have a title,' Aurelia reminded him, her gaze going to the window as the train slowed. They were pulling into the station. Her eyes scanned the little crowd on the platform, nervously looking for him, a knot tying itself tight in her stomach. Would he be there? Would she have to face him immediately? Despite her father's edict, she did not think Julien Lennox would charm so easily a second time.

Luck was with her—a little. Julien Lennox had not come to the station. No one had—only a carriage and a driver were waiting with a separate wagon for their trunks. It was all handled efficiently and expertly. The Lennoxes were used to entertaining. Of course, it upset her father, who wasted no time expressing his disapproval to her and her mother the moment the carriage door shut behind them.

'It's a damn slap in the face not to meet us. Certainly Lennox or the Viscount could have come. It suggests they're embarrassed to be seen with us, that they didn't want to acknowledge us as their guests. And it's a plain carriage. There's no coat of arms. What sort of viscount has a carriage without his arms on it?'

A viscount who valued frugality and discretion, Aurelia thought. Not just his own discretion, but that of his guests. She did not need a coat of arms on a coach trumpeting to everyone where she was going. But she also had to admit that it might be a subtle reminder of who held the upper hand now.

'It was quite thoughtful of the Lennoxes to think of our privacy,' her mother tried to reframe the scenario in a positive light. 'This allows us a few moments to get our bearings between travelling and arriving.' In other words, it saved them from the public awkwardness of meeting people they didn't know well and needing to make small talk all the way back to the house as if they were old friends come for Christmas instead of strangers.

Aurelia was less kind. 'It's nonsense to think they're embarrassed to be seen with us. They're hosting a Christmas ball in a few weeks and we'll be sitting with them at church.' Mrs Lennox had sent a rather detailed itinerary of activities, none of which indicated any desire to see them hidden away. 'Perhaps you're overthinking it too much. Maybe they were simply too busy to come themselves, or too polite.'

In the time she'd known Julien, she'd never seen him idle. He believed every minute of the day should be accounted for. There was always so much to do, so much life to live in both work and pleasure. Julien Lennox worked hard but he also knew how to have a good time, a man who was disciplined but not necessarily straitlaced. She'd liked that balance about him.

So many of the young men she'd met were driftless idlers with no more purpose to their days than waiting to inherit. Then and only then would their lives start. Given that many of them wouldn't inherit until their middle years, she thought their attitude of waiting a waste of prime decades. Julien Lennox and his ambition had been a breath of fresh air.

Too fresh, it turned out, for her father: *'This is how the aristocracy dies, infiltrated, and polluted by commoners with money.'*

When Julien had been made a viscount at the Queen's annual announcement of New Year's honours last January, her father had said, *'Lennox will never really be one of us. His family will always be new.'* As in, the Lennoxes hadn't held a title that could be traced back to the Conqueror, or even to the Glorious Revolution. It had been positively galling for her father to have to revisit those opinions now that the Lennoxes were the only ones willing to lend him money.

The station was not far from the estate and Aurelia couldn't decide if she was grateful for the short journey so that she was no longer confined to the close quarters of a carriage with her irascible father, or if this was a case of out of the frying pan and into the fire. If Julien hadn't been at the station, the likelihood increased that he'd be here. Meeting him again was becoming inevitable.

'Well, at least Brentham Woods isn't entirely disappointing,' her father offered by way of begrudging compliment as the carriage came to a halt and the coach step was set.

'No.' Her mother smiled, letting a footman hand her down. 'It's quite charming, grand and yet comfortable.'

Aurelia might have appreciated her mother's assessment more if she hadn't been so nervous, so on edge, prepared to fight, to protect. Brentham was pleasing with its redbrick façade and white trim around the windows—and, oh, there were a lot of windows.

Aurelia could imagine how it might look all lit up night, a lamp in every window. It would be beautiful and serene, a welcome brought to life, a refuge at dusk for the weary traveller. But not for her. This was not a place of welcome or refuge for her. This was a battleground, a place where she might be ambushed at any moment and revenge extracted. She must be on her guard here. How much easier it would be if this were a cold Gothic castle or draughty medieval manse.

Easy and obvious was not going to be the order of the day. Aurelia saw that immediately. Inside, Brentham Woods was an homage to elegant comfort. The dark hardwood floors were polished to a sheen, the sage-and-cream wallpaper in the wide entrance hall was fresh, unmarred by signs of wear where art had once been hung and then later moved or, in the Ripleys' case, *re*moved. The rug beneath the round pedestal table in the centre of the hall was Thomas Whitty and it was *not* frayed at the edges. The vase on top of the table was filled with deep pink cyclamen and wintergreens. New. Fresh. When had such adjectives described anything at Moorfields with its antiques and worn carpets?

'Welcome, I'm so pleased you've arrived.' A striking dark-haired woman in her late fifties, dressed in a deep-maroon afternoon gown with a bodice done in the latest open jacket style, stepped forward from one of the rooms off the hall, a smile on her face, her hands outstretched in greeting as if she were genuinely glad to see them, as if they'd not all but invited themselves to be interlopers in her home and come to beg her husband for money.

'I hope the journey wasn't too arduous. I'm Mrs Lennox, but please call me Caroline, or Caro, even. Everyone does.' Such warmth was far too familiar for greeting an earl. On purpose? Aurelia wondered, to set the tone, or because it was simply this woman's way—this woman who might have been her mother-in-law if the world had been a different place.

Aurelia hazarded a quick glance at her father. This was not the fashion in which her father was used to being greeted. There was no curtsy, no deference. What would he make of that? She saw his jaw tighten and, for a moment, she was unsure whose side to be on. She liked seeing him thwarted. Yet the Lennoxes were not her friends and were no doubt out for a little revenge of their own. She rooted for them at her peril.

Her father took one of Mrs Lennox's hands and made a small bow over it. 'How good of you to invite us. We are looking forward to sharing Christmas with you. Allow me to introduce my wife, Lady Holme, and my daughter, Lady Aurelia Ripley.'

Caroline Lennox turned her smile on them, a twinkle of mischief in her warm brown gaze—a gaze that was joltingly familiar even after seven years. Those were Julien's eyes, dark and warm like hot chocolate from the pot on a cold morning. 'And does Lady Holme have a name?'

A set down didn't get any subtler than that. Women would not be objectified in Caroline Lennox's home even if they were the mother of the daughter who'd rejected her son.

Aurelia saw her mother hesitate, perhaps as torn as she was about whose side to be on. Then, she took Caroline Lennox's hands and smiled her courage. 'You may call me Elizabeth if you like.'

'Winter travel can be tiresome even with the trains.' Caroline Lennox gestured towards the room she'd come from. 'I've asked for tea to be set up in my private parlour. My husband will join us shortly. He's been delayed at the stables. He's the master of the local hunt and in charge of the hunt club string. There's always something to take care of with the horses.'

She led the way into a cheery room done in pink-and-cherry chintz overstuffed furniture that had a decidedly comfortable and feminine quality to it. Aurelia divined at once that this was *her* room, Mrs Lennox's private domain: part-sitting room, part-writing room and lady's office and, best of all, part-library. The woodwork was all painted white to brighten the space and bookcases lined the wall opposite the fireplace.

'Are you a reader as well?' Caroline Lennox asked, catching her drifting eye as they took seats by the fire. 'We have a larger library, of course, but this is my personal collection. I keep my novels here and my gardening books for quick reference. Please feel free to borrow anything that takes your fancy while you're here.' Julien was a reader, too. So, he'd got his eyes *and* his love of books from his mother.

There were bootsteps in the hall and Aurelia tensed. Would this be the moment she saw him? But in the next moment, the worry was eased. It was only Cameron Lennox, returned from the stables, followed by the arrival of tea, both of which led to a bit of upheaval as introductions were made and the tea was laid out.

'Will the Viscount be joining us?' her mother asked in deceptively casual tones once everyone was settled again.

'I do not know.' Caroline Lennox looked up from pouring the tea. 'We'll see him at dinner, of course. But when he's out on a ramble it's hard to say when he'll be back. Do you prefer sugar, Elizabeth?'

Caroline Lennox could not know how much her words put Aurelia at ease. There was peace in knowing when she would have to face Julien. She could set her guard aside. For now, she was safe. She could afford to take comfort in the tea and the warm atmosphere of the room. Her mother could benefit greatly from such a space, a place where her mother could have her own things and interests on display. She ought to encourage her mother to replicate this room at Moorfields.

Aurelia was already decorating the room in her mind when she realised her mistakes—both of them. She should never have set aside her guard. And she should never have allowed herself to be lulled by this room or by Caroline Lennox's kind smile and hospitality. Otherwise, she would have heard the front door open, the low tones of the footman greeting the new arrival, the quick tread of boots on the polished hardwoods. She would have had valuable seconds in which to steel herself for the encounter. As it was, she looked up from her tea, her gaze randomly drifting to the doorway, and there *he* was: all tight breeches, boots, and windblown hair. The man she'd almost married.

Her breath caught. For the briefest of moments, she had him all to herself—hers to look upon in frank enquiry. In those moments his gaze was unguarded, his smile open and inviting. Here was a man who was content, happy. Had she'd ever seen *this* man? It was as if she was looking upon Julien Lennox unmasked. Then he saw her and the moment was gone. The mask slid into place. The smile faded, the light in his dark eyes dimmed.

'I beg your pardon for barging in, Mother. I was unaware our guests had arrived.' Julien was all proper decorum, perhaps conscious of the mud on his boots and the informality of his attire. His dark gaze swept the room, his eyes colder, more calculating than they had been seconds ago. Those eyes rested on her only briefly, perhaps to show her his indifference. She was no more than a guest of his parents, someone he need not be bothered with beyond the merest of civilities.

'Please, sit, have some tea with us,' his mother invited, and her mother nodded encouragingly in support of the idea.

'No, thank you. I am not fit company.' His gaze lingered on hers long enough for the innuendo of his words to strike home. 'I've been setting out duck boxes for the winter and tramping through all nature of mud and dirt.' He gave the room a bow. 'Excuse me, I must get cleaned up.'

At least the room seemed a few degrees warmer when he left, or perhaps that was just her blood. Aurelia took a contemplative sip of her tea. She'd expected such a cool reception. He had not disappointed in that regard. Well, so be it. The battle was officially joined.

Chapter Three

It was to be full armour tonight for supper. That meant evening wear fit for London. It meant the dark, formal suit from Henry Poole, tailor to England's finest and Europe's as well. It meant the gold-and-topaz cufflinks at his wrists, the topaz discreetly winking, the matching stickpin fastened in the folds of his pristine white cravat while the bronze-and-maroon paisley-patterned silk waistcoat sported a thin chain tethering the elegant watch from Phillips on Bond Street in his pocket. It meant the cologne and aftershave from Harris's, uniquely mixed for him—a scent no one else was allowed to purchase.

Julien flexed his hand, stretching his fingers as his valet opened the ring case. Most all, it meant adorning the little finger of his left hand with the solid gold signet ring sporting its lion's head, the symbol of the Lavenham viscountcy. It would be a subtle reminder to their guests that he was in possession of a title now. To Aurelia, the ring was a rebuke. She should have trusted him seven years ago. She should have believed in him, in them.

Kymm slid the ring on, the gold cool against Julien's skin. Julien curled his hand into a fist and flexed.

'Thank you, Kymm.' His brother made a habit of teasing him over having a valet, but it was for occasions like this when he absolutely had to look his best that a valet was essential. Tristan might have been a soldier, but Julien's battlefields were ballrooms and billiards tables. He closed deals over drinks, acquired information on new clients during quadrilles. To make those things possible, one had to look the part, *be* the part. London society could scent an impostor at a hundred yards, like Benjamin hunting a rabbit. No one had thought him an impostor for six years.

'Remember, sir...' Kymm smoothed the shoulders of his evening jacket '...they have come to you. You are the feast. They are the beggars and they are not fit to wipe your boots. They never were.' Kymm had been with him a while, privy to the tragedy of his failed pursuit of Lady Aurelia Ripley.

Julien gave a wry smile as he headed for the door. 'Thank you, Kymm, for your validation.' He checked the expensive but simple gold pocket watch on his way downstairs. Half past six. Everyone would be gathered in the drawing room. Waiting for dinner. Waiting for him.

The drawing-room doors were open and voices in the throes of conversational small talk drifted up to him. From the direction of the sounds, he could tell his father was with the Earl, perhaps standing by the fireplace. The women were together, likely on the other side of the room. He could hear the rise and fall of their gentle tones. The light, airy laugh that sounded like bells on a crisp, snowy evening belonged to Aurelia. He'd been led on by that laugh once, had thought it meant...something. He would not be led on by it again. Only a fool allowed the same knife to cut him twice.

Julien gave a final tug at the hem of his waistcoat and shot his cuffs, fully armed in his Bond Street best, every item designed to display his authority. He was in control here. This was his territory, his money, his decision. He stepped into the room, his arrival drawing all eyes in his direction, but his gaze went immediately to her. To Aurelia. One should always know the position of one's enemy at all times. And because there simply seemed nowhere else to look.

He was not the only one who'd come dressed for battle. She wore a gown of deep, lush midnight blue, made from the new camayeux silk that had the ladies scouring the Bond Street drapers for its exquisite expensive lengths. The neckline, trimmed in a fall of cream-coloured Brussels lace, was scooped and off the shoulder, exposing the delicate elegance of her collarbones and the queenly slenderness of her neck. The skirt was plain, falling unadorned without tiers and flounces over the crinoline cage beneath, allowing an unobstructed view of her trim waist and the hint of curving hips.

Simple. Elegant. Expensive. Too expensive given the state of the Earl's finances. Julien had seen the files, read them this morning before going out. To say the Earl's pockets were to let was an understatement and a gown like that would cost two hundred pounds. That fabric was of the highest quality. He'd invested in enough silk shipments over the years to know.

Julien approached the women and made a bow to the group. 'Good evening, ladies.' He let his gaze drift to Lady Holme. Hmm. *She* was dressed neatly, but not in camayeux silk, or even in the first stare of fashion. These were gowns from a few years ago. Then again, Lady Holme could not catch a viscount. The thought put Julien on the defensive. Was Holme here for more than a loan? Did he think to secure himself a permanent route to funds? It bore thinking about.

Due to his past failures in that department, it had not crossed Julien's mind that Holme might be rethinking that option as well. He glanced at Aurelia, with her midnight-blue gown and golden curls, her good looks on obvious display, prompting the question—how was it that such a beauty was still unwed after seven Seasons? Not that *he* was tempted. He saw behind that beauty to the coldness, to the calculation in her gaze when she looked his way. Another man might see a coy invitation, might be taken in by those blue eyes. Julien knew better. Her gaze wasn't an invitation as much as it was an interrogation. In her own way, Lady Aurelia Ripley was a skilled huntress.

'Tell me about your duck boxes, Lord Lavenham.' Lady Holme fixed him with a polite smile designed to draw him into the conversation. 'I've never heard of them.'

He offered her a polite recitation. 'They're places where ducks can nest. Wood ducks particularly prefer to nest in holes in the ground or in trees. They don't make their own nests, so they rely on whatever cavities or depressions currently exist. Sometimes, there are no places to nest within a mile or more of water. In those cases, the boxes can be a necessary substitute for the absence of natural habitats.'

'So, they become sitting ducks, quite literally.' The razor-edged reply came from Aurelia, emphasised by the snap of her ivory fan. 'How convenient. Easy prey.' Her gaze was sapphire-sharp with accusation.

Julien answered with a cool stare of his own. 'On the contrary, Lady Aurelia. The boxes actually offer protection from predators and the purpose of the boxes is to help grow the duck population in areas where there aren't enough natural cavities for the population to grow on its own.'

'So, you're not a hunter?' she queried, looking to trap him.

'Only when population control requires it.' He gave a cold, polite smile, his gaze tracking her response, taking in the little tic in her jaw at having been foiled in her attempt to bait him into an argument.

That tic still jumped. How funny to notice such a little thing after all this time.

The butler announced dinner and Julien's mother wasted no time in seeing everyone paired up, not that it took a genius to figure out how it was all going to work. His mother went in with the Earl, his father with Lady Holme, leaving him to bring up the rear the Aurelia on his arm. Once, the merest touch from her would heat his blood, once he'd resented the layers of cloth and silk that had kept them from one another. Tonight, he was glad for them as she laid her white gloved hand on his sleeve.

'You're looking well, Julien,' she murmured. 'Still patronising Harry Poole and Co., I see.'

'And you're still keeping Madame Devy's in the black.' Madame Devy was one of the most sought-after modistes on Bond Street and one of the most expensive.

She gave a cool laugh. 'I had forgotten how you could dress a woman down to the very pence.' It was meant to be unkind, a reminder of how gauche it was in her circles to admit to the existence of money, even if it was the very thing that made her world possible.

'Occupational hazard, I suppose,' Julien replied frostily with an emphasis on *occupational*. Occupations were nearly as taboo a subject as money. 'Although I do find myself surprised Madame Devy deigns to dress you, given your father's current circumstances. She'll expect to be paid.' It did make him wonder what sort of promises Holme had traded on to get such a gown. It certainly added credence to the nascent thought that Holme was hunting a husband for his daughter along with a handout for himself.

'My dress bill is hardly any of your business,' she snapped at the offence, her chin tipping upwards in her trademark show of defiance—yet another of her motifs. Another little thing he'd apparently not forgotten despite the years.

'I must disagree. Everything where your father is concerned is my business. That's why you're here, after all, for *my* business.' He ushered her into the dining room, pleased to see the table was laid to discreetly reinforce that lesson. His mother might be a warm hostess, but she did not miss any opportunity to assist her husband and son in their endeavours.

She understood the merits of a well-set table: the Bloor Derby plates with Thomas Steel fruit paintings at their centres done in muted golds, greens and plum shades to highlight the winter season, the Baccarat Parme crystal, the polished English silver all laid out in honour of the season and in homage to the extent of the Lennox wealth—an extent that said quietly: *This is how we can afford to set the table for a quiet night in among the six of us.* It also implied: *Just think what we can do if it were a formal occasion for twenty.* And that was before his father rolled out the wine, which would no doubt feature the Duke of Cowden's favourite red from France, which only a few could afford.

Julien held Aurelia's chair for her, taking the opportunity to lean near and whisper in low tones as she arranged her skirts, 'That's twice you've been wrong tonight, Lady Aurelia. It's very unlike you.' It may also have been a mistake to get that close. The scent of her, all rose and amber with an undernote of vanilla, ambushed him with memories. How many evenings had he held her chair like this? Sat beside her? Danced with her, breathing in that sultry sweet scent?

Those were better times, to be sure. Happy times. No, not better times, he was quick to correct, taking the seat beside her. Not better or happier times, just *other* times when he was not as well educated about the dangers of her charms. But he had her measure now. He knew empirically she wasn't the girl he'd fallen for seven years ago. She never had been. That girl was a fantasy. He would not charm so easily a second time.

* * *

Charm him, her father mouthed over his wine glass from across the table, a scold in his eyes.

They were halfway through supper and Julien hadn't offered a single comment in her direction. That was probably her fault. She ought not have baited him about the ducks. She'd been out of her depth. She'd thought to make him admit to using the boxes to trap the ducks and increase his own pleasure of simply sport hunting, something she did not agree with. One could not live in Yorkshire without being attuned to the dynamics of grouse hunting, but those rules had not readily applied to the situation Julien described and he'd put her in her place. Not once, but twice.

Aurelia sipped her wine, a delicious red that paired brilliantly with the jugged hare. She'd deserved the first set-down, but not the second. It had been bad form of him to mention the dressmaker's bill and the obvious reason for their visit. No one liked to be reminded of their unfortunate circumstances even if those circumstances were an open secret. But Julien wasn't pulling his punches tonight. Well, she'd expected as much, hadn't she? He despised her. Time had not softened his heart as much as it had hardened it. Against her. Her father could not expect her to overcome Julien's resistance in the space of a night. Except that he would. Her father was not a man for patience and she'd already tried his for years now.

'Tell me about the wine.' She set her glass down and turned to Julien, making it clear this was a question for him alone. 'It must be French, but from where?'

'Cumières, which is usually Champagne country.' Julien offered a short answer.

She tried again, this time with a smile. He'd always liked her smile, had always indulged it. 'Which doubly intrigues me. How does a fine red wine come from such a region? One would expect the quality from Bordeaux or Burgundy, but not Cumières.'

'It's a *couteau champenois* from a small, private winery. The gentleman who runs it tells me it's the soil that makes all the difference.'

'Do you believe him?' She took another sip and tried a little light flirtation. 'Perhaps it makes a good story.'

'Yes, absolutely. I make it my practice to only do business with those whose word I can rely on. Loyalty is a precious commodity. Once it is lost with me, it is difficult to regain.'

The lesson was not even subtle. Aurelia felt the twin stabs of anger and guilt prick at her. She'd not been loyal to him, although she might argue, if given the chance, that she'd not had a choice, that it hadn't entirely been up to her. To be a woman alone was a frightening prospect. The wealthier the woman the more frightening the prospect, the further she fell if her judgement should fail her. To put all of her faith in him had been too daunting for an eighteen-year-old girl. None the less, he had condemned her as much as he condemned her father for what had happened.

'Do you mean to say inviting us here is all folly, then? That you've already made up your mind?' she parried, dropping all attempts at warmth. She couldn't resist needling him a bit. She desperately wanted to win at least one argument with him tonight. 'Perhaps there's room to win back your loyalty after all? Or at least to buy it.'

His dark eyes hardened to obsidian. 'My loyalty is not for sale. It cannot be purchased. It must be earned.'

She offered a tiny smile. 'Then one can hope they'll be given the chance to earn it.' She picked up her wine glass and tapped it gently against his. 'Here's to loyalty, Julien, and here's to earning yours.' Across the table, her father gave the merest of nods, pleased with the little show she'd worked hard to put on for him. If her father thought it was going to be easy to win over Julien with a few smiles and pretty dresses, he'd sorely underestimated the man Julien Lennox was. Indeed, her father hardly understood him.

Chapter Four

'You don't seem to understand the gravity of our situation, Daughter.' Her father lounged uninvited in the chair set in the corner of her large, prettily appointed guest chamber, where a fire warmed the entire space, an absolute luxury compared to her room at Moorfields where coal was meticulously meted out and monitored daily. 'You squandered your opportunity at dinner tonight, hardly saying a word to him until the end.'

'He wasn't talkative.' Aurelia snapped from the dressing vanity where she took down her hair and began to brush it. They'd not brought a maid. She'd have to call for one to help her undress once her parents left the room.

'*Make* him talkative. That's your job. What's a pretty girl worth if she won't use her charms to entice a man?'

She didn't need to glance in his direction to know how livid her father was. Her mother stirred from the window seat. 'It's just the first night. They need time to reacquaint themselves with each other,' she placated.

'Our time is limited,' her father reminded.

'We have five weeks,' she soothed, flashing a smile in Aurelia's direction. 'I have every confidence in our daughter.' Aurelia wished she shared that confidence.

But her mother hadn't sat beside Julien at supper and felt the chill of him, hadn't had him whisper her mistakes in her ear before he'd even sat down, or turn each conversational offering into a verbal fencing match that ended with him imparting reminders of her betrayal. He was prepared for a siege and well fortified behind the high walls of his pride.

'Five weeks,' her father scoffed. 'I want this settled before Christmas. Compromise him if you need to. I'll play the righteous, wronged father to the hilt and see him marched to the altar in penance.'

'Absolutely not!' Aurelia's head whipped in her father's direction, temper flaring. 'I am to charm him, not wed him, not compromise him. That was the deal.' She was to charm the money out of him, nothing more. And in return, she'd have Elspeth and her freedom.

'If charming proves impossible, we may need to up the stakes.' Her father feigned benign idleness. 'You said yourself he's proving difficult. Charming may be too subtle, too indirect to get the results we want.'

'The results *you* want,' Aurelia replied sharply.

Her father smiled coldly. 'You rise and fall on the merits of my success. What do you think happens to you if we fail here? Do you relish going back to Moorfields to cull the house for silver and art, expendable furniture like your pianoforte and luxuries like your horses? Like Elspeth?'

Not Elspeth. Not her mare. Real fear thrilled through her. Jewels and artwork were one thing. Her mare was quite another. She'd grown up with Elspeth, learned every path and trail of Moorfields on the mare's back.

Elspeth was a best friend. 'You would not dare,' Aurelia countered.

He held up empty hands. 'I won't have a choice. The jewels are gone. Your mother's heirloom tiara is gone. Most of the silver is gone. We're down to last things. If we lose the Lennox money, we're rolled up.'

'Charles, stop. You're frightening her.' Her mother crossed the room and put a hand on her father's shoulder.

'The girl should be frightened.' Her father glared in her direction. 'Perhaps if my daughter can't sleep tonight, she'll go down to the library and find a book to read or a viscount to charm.' His face was turning red as he worked up a full head of steam. 'My son would not have allowed it to come to this.' His son who'd only existed in this world for a handful of minutes, but for whom her father had designed a whole history, a whole life of might-have-beens.

Her mother intervened swiftly. 'Come now, there's no need to be worked up. We are not desperate yet. Come to bed, it's been a long day and we're none of us ourselves.' Her mother took her father's hand as he stood and Aurelia envied her father in that moment. She'd have liked her mother's comfort, too, to feel someone's arms about her, to hear soothing words and promises that all would come out right. But her mother couldn't be in two places at once. It was enough, perhaps, that her mother was getting him out of the room.

Still, the damage was done. Aurelia's hands were shaking. She couldn't hold the hairbrush. The threat of selling Elspeth had real teeth. She closed her eyes and drew a deep breath. She couldn't call for a maid in this state. She would not let it happen. She would not lose Elspeth. She would run away with the mare if it came to that, join the Gypsies, or a circus show like Astley's. A couple of years ago, she'd seen Pablo Fanque, the black equestrian, perform there. Perhaps she could do the same, not in London of course, it would be too easy to find her... It wouldn't come to that, to running away. She wouldn't let it. She opened her eyes and slowly let out her breath. If she must, she would throw herself on Julien's mercy.

Surely she would find a way past his dislike. Surely his hate did not run so deeply it could not be overcome? Yet he'd never looked at her the way he had looked at her tonight, with guarded gaze and eyes dark with wariness.

Tonight, he'd been in full control of himself and his surroundings. Everything about him had been calculated for best effect. The windblown woodsman was safely tucked away but, oh, what she wouldn't give for another look at *him*, free and relaxed, unencumbered. In truth, she'd not been immune either to the calculated banker-cum-Viscount in his immaculate, tailored dark evening clothes and carefully combed hair.

All that manly perfection only tempted her to want to mess him up, to run her fingers through that thick hair, to keep him talking late into the night so that she might see dark stubble take root along that strong jaw. She wanted his chocolate gaze to melt with laughter, to twinkle with the secrets of a private joke, his mouth to curve in a smile of pure joy. She'd had those things once before. Once, he'd shown himself to her and in his authenticity, he'd been like no other. It had been the reward of her loyalty and losing those things had been the price, a very high price for her betrayal.

'My loyalty needs to be earned.'

However would she earn it? How could she reclaim the trust she'd thrown away? She had to find a way. Day by day, slowly and steadily she had to prove herself to him. She had to show him that she was worthy. Not just because her family needed the money, but because she wanted to prove that he was wrong about her. It might be too late to undo the past, but she had her pride, as well as he, and she wasn't exactly the villain he made her out to be.

'She's as much the villain as her father.' Julien sat down heavily in one of the matching leather chesterfield chairs beside the library fire.

'How do you rationalise that?' His father took the other, a tumbler of 'thinking brandy' in his hand. The house was still, everyone having retired an hour ago. He and his father had shot a few rounds of billiards to take the edge off the evening. They'd invited the Earl, but Holme had refused. That was fine with Julien. He'd had quite enough of the Ripleys for the night. His own emotions were high. Despite his coolness at dinner, his anger was running hot, not all of that anger was for the Ripleys.

Julien gave his brandy a swirl. 'It wasn't just Holme who refused my suit. *She* refused me, too.' He had never discussed that unsavoury detail with his father. At the time it had hurt too badly and after that, it only mattered that he'd been refused. He'd had no interest in resurrecting such hurt, such shame, so he'd buried it deep. If it had just been Holme's refusal, he might have come to grips with it the way one comes to grips with a balance sheet. But her refusal had not been about pounds and pence. She simply hadn't loved him, hadn't shared the feelings he'd thought were there.

'I see now why you're angry at me for inviting them,' his father surmised after a swallow.

Julien looked into the depths of his own glass. 'Yes. I am angry with you, too. It feels like a betrayal to have you invite them into our home when I was so looking forward to a moment's peace during Christmas.' He glanced up, studying his father. 'Which leads me to think there's more at play here than becoming the favourite financier of the aristocracy and the Crown. What's the game?' He and his father were close, close enough to speak hard truths and ask hard questions. He'd always valued that about their relationship.

His father shook his head. 'There's no game. I must apologise to you. I misread the situation. I didn't know, Julien, about the other... It's true I thought there was an opportunity for us to gain entry into higher circles. I still think that. But it wasn't my entire motive. I thought perhaps there might be opportunity for a second chance for you, that the Earl might reconsider your suit. You have the title now. It softens the reality that you have a fortune you've worked for. You have overcome his initial opposition to you.' His father sighed. 'I see now that isn't the only opposition. I had hoped to kill two birds with one stone.' He gave a self-deprecatingly wry smile.

'What two birds would that be?'

'Taking the next step into society, building on the foundations you've so well laid with your work in London, and to see my son settled with a wife and eventually the children I know he desires.' His father's eyes shimmered with emotion as they held his. 'She's the one you wanted all those years ago and I thought it was a stroke of luck that she'd not married, that you had a title and her father needed our money. I thought perhaps she had waited all these years for you. There were too many coincidences to be overlooked.'

'Coincidences? Luck?' Julien chuckled. He would not have taken his father for a matchmaker. 'My father, the most efficient, practical man I know, is a hopeless romantic at heart. Do you really believe in such things?'

His father gave a cryptic smile. 'I believe in love and the power it wields.' He paused. 'But I didn't know, Son. I didn't know.'

Julien's anger vanished in the wake of his father's confession. 'Well, I must bear some of the blame. I didn't tell you. I didn't want you worrying over me.' But his father had worried anyway just for different reasons.

'Tristan was always the wild one, the one who spent the summers running and riding pell-mell with Teddy Grisham, the one who had the wanderlust,' his father mused. 'I worried about him, but it turns out he's the one who is settled now with Elanora at Heartsease, two children trailing in his wake.' His father's eyes turned soft. 'And my practical son, the one who has stayed with me and seen the family business exceed expectations, seen us take our place in Hemsford society and got us a foothold among the peerage, counting the Dukes of

Cowden and Creighton among his friends, is still alone. You deserve a family, Julien.'

'I deserve a woman who loves me. I do not think love is something Lady Aurelia Ripley is capable of. She is capable of many things, but not that.' And no wonder, given the family she came from. There was no love there. How did one learn love if they didn't see it at home? He'd come to understand that even if he wasn't ready to forgive the consequences. It did not excuse how she'd treated him at the end.

His father nodded thoughtfully. 'I appreciate the need for wariness. One must learn from mistakes, not repeat them. But one should not let anger cloud their judgement.'

'I'm not,' Julien assured his father. 'I saw the Earl's files this morning. I see him clear. What he wants, what he needs. And again, I would counsel you against the investment. I'll find another way to further our presence in the peerage. You should refuse him.'

His father was pensive for a long moment. 'Have you thought about what happens to Lady Aurelia and her mother if we refuse the Earl?'

'No, not particularly,' Julien confessed honestly. 'I try hard not to think about Lady Aurelia at all.' He tried not to think about her being in his house in the present, tried not to think about her in his arms in the past and he certainly didn't spend time thinking about her in the future—his or hers.

'Perhaps you should,' his father prompted.

Julien finished his drink. He could say no to the Earl of Holme as Holme had said no to him all those years ago. There would be vengeful satisfaction in that: to shatter a desperate man's hopes the way Holme had shattered his own dreams. Julien's would be the larger victory, though. Holme's rejection had affected one man. His rejection would affect an entire family. There was no brother. When Holme died, his heir, a distant cousin, would take possession of the estates. The women, should Aurelia not marry, would lose their home. They would have little income to live on. Aurelia would go from living a life of luxury in expensive silk gowns to living in mean circumstances. She would no longer be an earl's pampered daughter. She would be a nobody with seven Seasons and nothing to show for them.

'Is that what you want?' his father asked quietly. 'Vengeance? You can choose to ruin her life or you can toss her a lifeline. She may not deserve it, but are you sure she deserves the other?' When his father put it like that, his conscience began to prick. Ruining people was Holme's method. Did he want to put himself in that same category? He was a man who built orphanages and hospitals. He did not ruin women.

His father rose and put a hand on his shoulder as he passed. 'I'm not asking you to give her a second chance. But I am asking you to consider that this is the season of love and forgiveness and new beginnings. Perhaps if you can forgive her, you can heal yourself and move on.'

'Thank you, Father. You always know how to frame things in a new light.' He clasped his father's hand briefly in gratitude.

Julien stayed in the library long after his father left. Perhaps he could find it in his heart to forgive Aurelia for her betrayal, but that didn't mean he had to spend time with her. This evening at dinner had raised complicated emotions and reactions there was no purpose in exploring.

He would make himself scarce. He would ride out early in the mornings, check his duck boxes, visit his new property, spend afternoons at Heartsease with Tristan and the children. His actions would make it clear that he was entirely neutral and that his consideration of the Earl's application for a loan was completely objective. He was above being influenced by a blonde beauty in an expensive gown with a laugh like Christmas bells.

Chapter Five

Aurelia gave Julien three days in which to indulge his disappearing act. His absence was not subtle, nor did she think it was intended to be. Instead, it was intended to be a very overt reminder as to what he thought of her and what he thought of her family being in his home over Christmas. Which was not much.

They were to be invisible to him, just as he made himself invisible to them, joining them only for dinner and then retiring at the first opportunity decency allowed with a never-ending supply of excuses: he had duck boxes to ride out and check at dawn, he had a string of horses to exercise for the hunt club, he had business in town, business at Heartsease with his brother—the list went on. She thought he'd ride to London in the frigid cold if it meant avoiding her family, most particularly her. And she simply couldn't have that.

Aurelia dressed quickly in the dreary grey half-light of an early morning winter, donning a warm, hollyberry-red riding habit of finest Italian wool with black frogging on the jacket. She smoothed her skirts and took a glance in the mirror. It was a rather dashing ensemble and a rather daring one, too. But red could be excused on the grounds of the Christmas season and her age.

At twenty-five, with a record seven Seasons to her tally, she couldn't be expected to limit her wardrobe to pastels. This morning, she needed a bit of daring along with a bit of luck. She let the maid pin on her hat, a jaunty red cap with a black feather, and she was off, hoping she was early enough to catch him. Julien's avoidance had to end today.

Her father had been unrelenting last night in what had become his nightly visit to her rooms for an update on her progress with the Viscount. She hated the intrusion, knowing it for what it was—a jailer checking in on his charge, a reminder that she was his hostage, that for her, life was going to change regardless of the outcome of this visit. There was no going back. The life she'd known at Moorfields was over. All she could do was protect Elspeth and attempt to manoeuvre the outcome of this visit to benefit her favourably. So, she was on her way to the stables for herself even though her father would no doubt benefit from it.

Aurelia pulled on her riding gloves and rubbed her hands against the chill. The cold in Sussex was a different kind of cold than the cold at Moorfields. It was damper, wetter, on account of being closer to the sea. Its fingers reached through one's clothes. In the stable, a big Cleveland Bay stood patiently in the cross ties as a groom tacked him up. Aurelia let out a frosty breath of relief. She was in time. Julien hadn't arrived yet. The groom acknowledged her with a nod.

'I'm riding out with Lord Lavenham. I'll need a horse

readied,' Aurelia ordered with friendly assertiveness. If one was confident but polite, one was less likely to be gainsaid.

'Yes, right away, milady.' The groom hurried off to the give the order and Aurelia took the opportunity to step up to the Cleveland Bay. She stroked the horse's velvety nose and fed him a bit of apple, talking in low tones.

'Are you trying to steal my horse?' Low gruff tones announced Julien's arrival. He was dressed for winter riding in tall boots and a dark greatcoat that looked quite sombre next to her red riding habit. She wondered for a moment if she'd overdone it. Then, his gaze swept her and something moved in the depths of his eyes—an appreciation, perhaps, that he'd never admit to. It was a start, something to build on.

'No, I'm just waiting for the groom to bring my horse,' she offered with a smile. 'We haven't had much time together and I thought this would be a good opportunity to speak away from the families. Just us.' Another smile. 'Besides, I admit to some curiosity over the duck boxes. I thought you might show me.'

Julien lifted the saddle flap to check the buckles on the girth. Ignoring her. 'Do we *need* time together?' His tone was as cool as the morning. 'I was under the impression the first night that we would be happiest if we kept our distance. I've been trying to ensure that. I was not aware there was a "just us."'

She stroked the horse's nose, giving the horse all of her attention. She would not allow herself to be distracted by the broad shoulders beneath the capes of the greatcoat, or the enigmatic flicker in his eyes that might denote myriad emotions. That was not a guessing game she wanted to play. 'That first night you also spoke of proving loyalty. I'd like to earn a bit of that. There are things we should speak of, but not here.' A groom brought out her horse, the clop of hooves on the stone floor of the stable interrupting their conversation.

Julien glanced between her and the saddled mare. 'All right, but I am taking a chaperon. Joseph, saddle up, you'll come with us.' He gave her a strong stare as Joseph left to saddle another horse. 'I will not be compromised into marriage, if you had plans in that direction.'

'Isn't it usually the other way around? It's the woman who needs the chaperon.' Aurelia laughed—it was rather comical to think of the gentleman standing before her being in any sort of danger he couldn't handle. She dropped her voice to a conspiratorial whisper. 'Marriage is the last thing on my mind, that's what I wanted to tell you. But we'll need a better plan than mere avoidance if either of us want to get out of this snare alive, as it were.'

'The enemy of my enemy, my friend?' Julien was all cool wariness as Joseph returned with a hardy country cob.

'Something like that.' Aurelia replied with equal coolness, leading her mare to the mounting block before Julien felt compelled to offer to help her mount. She might need a reason to see him, but she did not need a reason to touch him, or vice versa. It would only encourage more wariness on his part. He would think she was taking advantage and she hated the idea of him thinking she was the sort of woman who would manipulate a man.

No matter what he thought, and no matter how badly they'd ended, she'd never once deceived him.

They rode out of the stable, Joseph maintaining an appropriately private distance behind them. She waited until they were on a bridle path, the stable far behind them, before she began, bringing the mare up beside him so that they rode two abreast.

'My father brought me to act as bait,' she offered without preamble, the shocking statement earning only the briefest of nods from Julien. His eyes remained fixed on the path. 'But perhaps you've already surmised that for yourself,' she continued undeterred. 'I am to charm you to ensure he is granted the loan and, if possible, I am to coax you into a proposal by any means possible. He's decided that a more permanent access to your funds would suit him better than a one-time loan.'

She gave a shake of her head. 'I do not wish for the latter and I don't think you do either. But it may not be up to us. If my father suspects I am not doing my part to charm you, he may manufacture something on his own, something beyond my control. I'd prefer things stay in my control as much as possible. And for that, I need you to...'

'You need me to soften.' Julien interrupted with a chuckle that bordered on a disbelieving snort. 'So, I am to grant the loan in order to spare you from marriage. I see how this works. Your father gets the money, which he's wanted all along, and you and I don't have to worry about spirited matchmaking efforts.'

'To spare *you* from a marriage you don't want. I think you're missing that part.' Aurelia furrowed her brow.

'You're missing the part where I am trying to save you. I am trying to *earn* your loyalty.'

'And yet your father gets what he wants. You say you're warning me, but in reality you're advocating for him, ensuring that he gets what he wants.' Julien did turn to look at her then, his dark eyes sharp. 'And you get what you want by extension.'

'What do you know about what I want?'

'I don't need to know anything to know that your fate is tied to his as long you remain under his care. You made that very clear several years ago, I believe.'

She felt her cheeks burn at the reminder. She could see that moment, hear those words as if they'd happened yesterday.

'It's just down to us now. Come away with me.'

'I couldn't possibly leave my family, leave my life. You don't know what you're asking me to walk away from, from all I've ever known.'

'Yes, I do. I am asking you to trust me.'

And she had not. She'd had her reasons, her defence. What did a well-bred eighteen-year-old girl fresh from the schoolroom know of taking chances?

'Perhaps there is someone else waiting to marry you back home in Yorkshire?' He reached a hand up to push a low-hanging branch out of the way as they passed.

'I do not wish marry *anyone*. In another year or two, I'll officially be a spinster. I'll be twenty-seven. I can access a modest trust a great-aunt left for me. I'll be completely free.' Free of her father. Free of his threats which had kept her bound to him when she was eighteen. The trust had not come her way until she was twenty-one.

Since then, it had been her one hope, the light at the end of a very long tunnel.

'Do not wish to marry or cannot marry?' Julien probed mercilessly. 'I have seen your father's financial files. They are devastating. It is no wonder you are unwed after seven Seasons. These days, you would be a liability to any man who took you on. Many titled gentlemen whom your father would deem appropriate don't have the funds. They need an heiress, not a pauper. Perhaps now your father is more open to approaching a commoner with wealth in order to trade his title for money.'

'Then you know I speak the truth when I say you are at risk.' And perhaps she was at more risk than she thought. Simply charming him might not be enough to stop her father.

'I perceived the depth of my danger the moment I saw you in that midnight-blue gown of camayeux silk and every gown since affirms my assessment. You are hunting me—'

'Not me. My father,' Aurelia interrupted. 'That's why we need a plan. I want my freedom. I have to survive two more years and I can't do that if I am married to you or if my father goes under financially.' Her voice cracked.

Hearing the words out loud from her own lips made it all too real—what her father was asking her to do, what would happen if she failed and, despite her private promises to herself that she wouldn't allow those consequences come to pass, she didn't honestly know how she'd prevent them. She had no power to stop her father. Nothing belonged to her. Everything belonged to him, including her. He could do with her things and with her as he wished, and the law would not stop him. It would, in fact, support him and she was overwhelmed.

At the tremble in her voice, Julien drew his horse to a halt and reached for Aurelia's reins. He should not. He should leave this alone. He didn't want to ask the question, didn't want to know the answer. Would the answer even be true? But she was in distress and he could not ignore it on the off chance that the distress was real. It was not what a gentleman did. Everything she'd shared this morning had been real so far. 'You seem very concerned about what could happen to me, but what happens to you if I don't give your father the money?' Julien asked in the quiet of morning. Somewhere in the bushes the winter wren warbled.

He detected the slight set of her shoulders beneath her red jacket. She was gathering herself, putting back together the bravado that had been on display in the stables. 'He will go home and continue to sell what assets and objects we have left, which is not many. Everything non-essential has been sold already.'

Julien nodded. He'd seen those reports as well. The art was gone, the jewels gone except for those entailed by the estate. The rare book collection was gone. The rest of the library would follow. Aurelia would hate that. She loved to read, play the pianoforte and ride. His gaze narrowed. 'The books, the horses,' he said softly. Holme had an expensive stable, full of horses too good for a man who didn't ride seriously although his daughter did.

'Yes,' she replied tightly. 'The books, the horses. The pianoforte, too.' All the things she cared for. Anger began to burn, a slow licking flame in his stomach for how the Earl treated his family with callous disregard. A man was supposed to protect his family.

A thought came to him. 'Elspeth, your mare.' To say she loved that mare did not do her feelings justice. And rightly so. Elspeth had come to London with her that first Season. He'd seen them gallop on the Lady's Mile in the park, and he had been at a house party with her. She'd brought Elspeth for the ride the party was famed for. Together, they were unstoppable—hedges, hurdles, or just plain speed on the flat.

She flashed him a blue-fire stare full of fear-driven determination. 'I won't let him take her.' Ah, so that was what the Earl was holding over her. This was what had driven her out into the morning to beg him to stop playing his avoidance game. She was being made to pay for his absence. That had not been his intention. He'd meant only to foil her pursuit, seeing her in league with the Earl. Instead, she was fighting her own battle.

If she could be believed.

'What can you do to stop him?' Perhaps it was a cruel reminder.

'I'll run away if I have to. Ride off in the night,' she said with the staunchness of one who'd given such a plan much thought.

'And have him bring you up on charges of horse theft?' Julien cautioned. Holme would do it, too, to ensure that he had one more piece of leverage over his daughter. She said nothing and he felt guilty for puncturing whatever bit of hope she'd managed to cobble together. 'What do you propose, then?' If he knew Aurelia, she'd not asked him out here to simply inform him of a risk he already perceived. She had a plan.

'I must look like I'm trying with you and that I am gaining ground. It would be in your best interest to offer the loan sooner rather than later. He wants the deal set before Christmas. If you are quick to agree, perhaps he'll give up the notion of marriage if terms are amenable. My father has a tendency to see what is right in front of him instead of what lies down the road. With money in his hand, he'll be less likely to push for other things.'

'If I grant the loan tonight, you could all leave tomorrow.' How pleasant that would be. He could have his Christmas back.

'No, that's too fast. He'll just be back for more. That speed will see you blackmailed into another loan. If he thinks you'll pay him to get rid of him, he'll play that card again and again.' Aurelia looked horrified at the notion. 'Besides, we can't go home. He's rented Moorfields out to an American for Christmas. You're stuck with us.'

Too bad. But it did give Julien an idea about terms. He did not want this happening again and there was something he could do about that although he'd need time. He could show the Earl how to actually run his estate. He could show the Earl how to safely invest his funds so that there would always be passive income. The aristocracy didn't know a thing about money, they truly thought it grew on trees to be picked at any time they desired. But money was only a renewable resource if one knew how to use it.

He urged his horse into a walk and they continued on the path. The duck boxes were just up ahead and he wanted this settled before they reached them. 'So, you're suggesting that we pretend to get along, to act as if interest in each other has kindled anew?' Her idea was as daring as that red habit.

'Yes.'

He thought for a long moment. She had broken his heart, shown no regard for his feelings. He would not, could not let her do it a second time. Her ploy was just begging to slip past his guard, to let her get under his skin and into his heart again. Perhaps this was a game within the game? Where she pretended to not want a marriage in order to get close to him, to convince him they were on the same side, both of them allied against her father, that she was protecting him, trying to earn a bit of the loyalty she'd squandered years ago, and then trap him into a proposal she'd wanted all along.

This was the devious depths to which his mind had sunk in the years since she'd denied him, the level of wariness he carried within himself as a result. 'Even if I agree to this, I am not your friend, Aurelia.' He couldn't be her friend. He would not willingly walk that path again.

'But you were once. Please believe me when I say I am trying to protect you as much as I'm trying to protect myself. Perhaps in some small way I can make up for what passed between us all those years ago.' His father's conversation rang clearly in his conscience. Could he not forgive her? Perhaps he needed to forgive in order to heal his own wounds? Now, here was his chance and yet he baulked at the leap of faith she was asking him to take. Just as she'd once baulked at the leap he'd asked of her. The irony was not lost on him.

'All right then, we shall flirt and play at courtship in public, but in private the game ends. The moment your father has his money, the game ends. When Christmas is over, the game ends.' She would be on her own then.

'Agreed.' She stuck out her gloved hand in businesslike fashion and he shook it, a moment of connection passing between them as she gave him a small, satisfied smile. There'd been moments like this before, moments when being in accord with her had been intoxicating, when he had felt as if he could conquer the world if she was beside him.

'If we are together, nothing can stop us,' she'd whispered once in the dark of a summer night.

He'd believed her, but she hadn't meant it. Did she mean it now? He would have to walk this path with care so that old feelings and old emotions didn't rise to overwhelm what he knew was real—that Aurelia Ripley did what was best for her first and foremost, no matter what she said.

He was doing this now because the Earl was a complete bastard to his daughter, not because his heart might not be as hard as he thought when it came to Aurelia Ripley. He was too smart for that.

They reached the edge of a meadow and he turned to her. 'This a good place for a gallop. The duck boxes are across the field.'

She tossed him a smile that seemed genuine, her face lighting as she gathered her reins. 'Race you to the other side.'

The other side of what? he wondered. Whatever it was, instinctively he knew he couldn't get to the other side fast enough. Normalcy lay on the other side, life as he knew it, life without Aurelia lay on the other side. The faster he got there the better. Red was the colour of danger. He kicked his horse and chased after Aurelia's red habit.

Chapter Six

*Sunday, December 1st,
the first Sunday in Advent*

The ruse began in earnest the next day, which was both apt and ironic, Julien thought as he handed Aurelia down from the carriage in the churchyard for Sunday services. It was, quite fittingly, the season for mummers plays with their heavily disguised players. And ironically it was also Hope Sunday, a time when expectation was celebrated, not only the expectation of a child, but as Reverend Thompson liked to remind his congregation, an expectation of the second coming which required watchfulness so that no one be caught unaware.

Julien felt such watchfulness was required of him now, concerning this second coming of Aurelia Ripley into his life. He needed all his wits to ensure the ruse was maintained in its fullness, that he didn't forget the true purpose of the feigned closeness between them: to protect himself from falling victim to a far more nefarious plot designed to trap him in a marriage neither of them wanted. By helping each other in the short-term, they were helping themselves in the long-term.

All he had to do was get through December and remember that none of this was real: not the easy way she slipped her arm through his as he led her up the church steps, not the way she glanced up at him with a smile from beneath the brim of her green-velvet winter bonnet. None of it was real even though it once had been. That was his biggest concern over the ruse. They were not pretending about something that had never been, but re-enacting something that once was. That had all the potential in the world to make the line between pretence and reality far too blurry if one was not vigilant, if one took his or her part too seriously. That was what Julien must be on guard against.

He smiled down at her in answer to her own smile because it was the expected response of a gentleman when escorting a beautiful woman and, ruse or not, Aurelia *was* a beautiful woman. Beautiful in looks, in carriage, and even in demeanour now that things were settled between them. There was a more relaxed quality to her that took the coldness, the edge from her good looks, that warmed her now that their pact was made, requiring a necessary setting aside of past hurts to mutually join together for the prevention of future hurts. Between them, they had their own rules for interacting, for playing this game within the game. They had grounds on which to understand each other and it had eased things for both of them.

Eased, not erased. There was a difference. Which was another reason the situation required his vigilance. As Seneca had noted, those who ignored history were doomed to repeat it at their own peril. Julien guided Aurelia down the centre aisle of the church to the Lennox pew, or pews as it were. The Lennox and Grisham family pews had become a combined effort since Tristan had married Elanora four years ago.

He was aware as they walked, of the not-so-circumspect glances thrown their way. The presence of a large party of ten was enough to garner curiosity under any circumstance in a small village, but when that large party included an earl plus a viscount who was considered the area's most *eligible parti* and who had arrived with an unknown beauty on his arm, such curiosity was ratcheted to its highest level.

At the pews there was a moment of greeting to introduce Tristan's family to the Earl's family and then the subsequent shuffling chaos of arranging seating. The Earl and Lady Holme ended up across the aisle with Julien's parents while he and Aurelia were seated with Tristan and family. Tristan sat on the aisle, Elanora beside him with their infant daughter in her arms, then Aurelia and, squeezed between Aurelia and him, his nephew, Alex. Julien slid a quick glance in Aurelia's direction to see what she made of the arrangements. Did she mind being flanked on one side by a baby and on the other by a squirrelly three-year-old? She'd once professed to wanting a family of her own. Had that been the truth?

Aurelia gave him a smile that seemed to stem from something more than play-acting, a smile that said she didn't mind the arrangement. Well, perhaps that was true at the moment. Maybe she didn't mind so much now with the baby asleep and Alex not fidgeting. He'd see how she took it later when the baby was awake and Alex was kicking his heels against the pew in boredom. She leaned towards him, over Alex's head. 'The church is lovely with all the greenery and the bows to match the cyclamen. Elanora was telling me how she grows the cyclamen for all the Advent arrangements in her green house.'

Elanora. Not Mrs Lennox. Julien noticed the discrepancy immediately. Aurelia was making friends fast, or perhaps the familiarity was Elanora's doing. Nevertheless, there was nothing Julien could do about it. He could hardly tell Elanora or anyone else not to befriend Aurelia and he couldn't tell anyone about the ruse. But surely Elanora didn't think Aurelia was a permanent fixture? She was here with her parents for business over Christmas, nothing more. Then again, he had to consider how the ruse was designed to look. He knew very well what Elanora would think, what she would hope for, loyal sister-in-law that she was.

Julien shifted in the pew, his thoughts suddenly uncomfortable as he recalled last Christmas and Elanora's declaration that this would be the year they found him a bride. If so, Elanora was running out of time, the year was nearly spent. Which made Aurelia's presence all that more dangerous to him, especially if Elanora didn't know all the details and she wouldn't know. Tristan didn't know. He'd been in the military when Julien had gone courting. Because of the ruse, Aurelia would look like low-hanging fruit to his eager sister-in-law. He would have to guard himself on that front, too. Perhaps even warn Aurelia.

Reverend Thompson took the pulpit and the church quieted. He welcomed their guests out of politeness and out of a need for self-preservation. If his congregation was too distracted by the newcomers, they wouldn't pay attention to the sermon. Then he got down to the business of worship with the prayer of Julien's adolescence.

'Today we light the candle of hope and we pray. Almighty God, give us grace that we may cast away the works of darkness and put upon us the armour of light...'

Thus it began, the comfort of Advent, the comfort of travelling this road again, this was what he'd come home for. Julien let the old words wash over him. This was what he wanted, what he needed, to be in this place with its swags of greenery and rosy bows, the cyclamen in their vases as they had been for so many years, Elanora carrying on her mother's tradition for the village. It was the perfect balm to a soul who spent the year amid the commotion and chaos of London just as it had been to come down the lane that first night greeted by the lights of Brentham Woods and Benjamin's bark.

Halfway through the service, baby Violet awoke and fussed. At the other end of the pew, Tristan took turns with Elanora settling the infant, and the sight of them working together in tandem was a quiet skewer of envy in Julien's side. How he hungered for that partnership. Beside him, Alex tugged at his sleeve, whispering loudly, 'Uncle Julie, are we done yet?'

'Nearly so,' Julien consoled, digging in his pocket for his stash of peppermints. He fobbed one to Alex with a conspiratorial grin, the little boy beaming back. 'Suck on this. We should be done by the time you've finished.' He felt Aurelia's gaze on him and he didn't dare look up to meet it. It's not real, he told himself. None of this is real. Although it might have been, once upon a time, if things had been different—if she'd been different. But she wasn't and he'd do well to remember it.

Such remembrance sustained him as the service ended and the horde of Lennoxes and guests filed out of the church through many stops and starts. Everyone wanted to greet the new guests, especially Aurelia, Julien noted. The Earl was too lofty for most to approach and his dour demeanour did not invite anyone to risk it. But Aurelia was all smiles, and smiles worked wonders for bringing people together, as did Elanora's patronage. Aurelia was surrounded on all sides with invitations to join the Christmas committees. Mrs Phelps wanted her to help with the pantomime at Heartsease and someone else wanted her to help with Christmas baskets. She said yes to both with what appeared to be genuine enthusiasm. Was it? Or was it just very good acting because she knew such things would please him? That it would add to the ruse?

How telling it was that he didn't know the difference, that he couldn't distinguish between the real Aurelia and the fake. It was a commentary on himself as much as it was on her. Seven years ago he'd thought he'd loved her enough to spend his life with her and yet he'd hardly known her at all. It was enough to make a man wonder if that ought to worry him.

* * *

This could have been her life. The thought rolled through Aurelia with the force of a mental tsunami as they sat to table at Heartsease: Sunday dinner with the Lennoxes. All of them, even the children, filled the long, polished table. Julien's mother, the elegant Caro Lennox, had been transformed into a comfortable grandmother, at ease with the infant on her lap while her daughter-in-law saw to the last details of the meal. Cameron Lennox, the obscenely wealthy patriarch, was more importantly installed as grandpa, entertaining Alex with a sliding thumb-and-finger trick while Tristan and Julien were engaged in a lively conversation about one of Tristan's new horses. There was no doubt of the affection the Lennoxes held for each other. The room was full of it.

All of this could have been hers if she'd said yes seven years ago. *This* was what she'd thrown away when she'd refused Julien: a warm family, a vibrant family life, an active community life, not unlike the one she tried so hard to cultivate at Moorfields. Inclusion. Affection. All of it had been waiting here for her and she'd turned it down. She'd been too afraid to take the leap, to leave all she knew. She'd not known this was where she could have landed. To be fair, she'd also not known her family would be facing bankruptcy either. Now, all she could have of it was through this ruse. She could have a facsimile only of what had once truly been on offer for her.

Julien took the seat beside her and gave her a smile, to which she smiled back, knowing that her father was watching her every move and would be quick to criticise if she wasn't warm enough to the Viscount. Julien had played his part beautifully so far. There was little for her father to complain about, there. Julien had been attentive at church, sharing the prayerbook with her and making introductions, his hand never leaving her arm or the small of her back as he guided her through the sea of eager strangers.

Despite knowing that his touch was all part of his role, part of their game, she'd felt more confident with him beside her. The townsfolk liked him. She knew it was for Julien's sake today that she'd been invited into the committees. The liking ran both ways. He liked them, too. Well, maybe not the banker, Mr Atwater, who seemed aloof as if there might be bad blood there—but the others.

He knew their wives, their children, their special projects, which was impressive for a man who spent most of his year in London running with a much more elevated crowd. He was Viscount Lavenham now. He called the Duke of Cowden his friend. His own consolidated trust competed with Cowden's in investment circles. He didn't need to entertain the notions of small townsfolk, but he did.

It was something her own father had never deigned to do. In the twenty years he'd been the Earl of Holme, a title he'd inherited from a son-less cousin and would pass on to another distant cousin, he'd never once mingled with the villagers. Perhaps that was why she tried so hard to make up for his coldness with all of her efforts at Moorfields—the baskets for the poor and the grammar school she hoped to establish. Or perhaps making up gaps just came second nature to her. She'd spent her whole life making up for things between her parents. It seemed a natural act to extend that behaviour to the village at Moorfields.

'Are you well?' Julien asked in low tones full of solicitous concern—all part of the role, she had to remind herself, although those tones had once been genuine, his concern real.

'Yes, I'm quite fine.' She gathered her thoughts, suddenly aware of having let those thoughts carry her from being present in this room. 'I was just thinking how different things are here.' That was putting it mildly.

Julien favoured her with a smile and nudge. 'Well, while you're contemplating those differences, maybe you could pass the potatoes.' He gave a nod in the direction of the dish in front of her. 'At Heartsease, we serve ourselves, all the dishes are on the table and we send them around,' he explained, a twinkle in his dark eyes, as if he expected that to be a surprise to her and he was watching her for a reaction.

Did he think the notion would displease her? If so, *she* would surprise *him*. Aurelia reached for the potatoes. 'Here you go. What a lovely idea this is.'

And it was. Aurelia couldn't recall enjoying a meal more. The absence of footmen and the subsequent interruption between courses had enormous social benefits. Conversation flowed in a chaotic, animated stream up and down the table. No one was limited to talking only with their partners on their right or left depending on the course.

Caro Lennox drew Aurelia's mother into the ongoing conversation, the two of them sharing an interest in plants with Elanora. The men tried to draw her father in with talk of the horses, but with less success. She could see her father's beady eyes assessing the whole scene with dislike. He might be the one in need of funds at this table, but he still thought he was above everyone here.

Aurelia wasn't the only one who noticed. Julien noticed, too. She saw it in the tightening of his jaw. That particular gesture hadn't changed in the intervening years. Julien would not take kindly to a man who snubbed his family.

A trickle of fear came to her. What if her father failed to get the loan through of no fault of her own? If *he* didn't improve *his* behaviour, Julien would deny him on principle, ruse or not. Her father would blame her. Elspeth would still be at risk. Even as the conversation swirled in her direction and bore her away in its current with talk of the committees and the Christmas panto, Aurelia knew she would have to try harder, do more, be more, to close the gap her father was creating.

Aurelia cut into the succulent pheasant and Caro Lennox beamed at her from across the table, asking questions about her own work at Moorfields, the irony coming to her again that all of this—the thing that she now needed—could have been hers years ago.

That irony followed her the rest of the day. It was there with her in the greenhouse where she and Elanora went after the meal to see the cyclamen. It was there when she relieved Elanora of fussy baby Violet so that Elanora could show her a new grafting process with both hands. How delightful it was to hold the infant, to feel the sweet baby weight of the child in her arms and to see the little face light with that special smile only an infant can make. She was used to holding the babies in Moorfields village and it had been a while since there'd been a little one. She gave Violet a finger to play with, feeling the baby's little hand wrap around hers.

The irony was still there when Julien found them two hours later.

'Are you still playing in the dirt, Elanora?' Julien stepped into the greenhouse, teasing his sister-in-law good naturedly, his dark eyes dancing, his hair mussed from being out of doors. He was the unguarded countryman once more. Once more, it did not last. His gaze and his teasing stopped when his eyes landed on her, jigging baby Violet on her hip. She lifted her free hand to her hair. Admittedly, she and Elanora were a little less tidy than when they'd come out here. Her hair had come loose in places, mostly from Violet's explorations, and at one point she'd unbuttoned the collar of her dress to remove her pin so that Violet didn't get at it.

Elanora's gaze travelled between the two of them. 'She's amazing with Violet. I got to work with both my hands today. What a treat.' Elanora wiped her hands on her apron. 'I can take her now.'

'No, you finish up. I've got her.' Julien came forward to take the baby, hefting her easily and lifting her high over his head to baby Violet's delight. 'I haven't had a chance to hold her all day yet and I miss my best girl.' He laughed up at the giggling infant.

Those moments transformed him. Here again was the

countryman she'd seen that first day at Brentham Woods when he'd been caught by surprise—the man who was at ease, who was free and open. The irony that plagued her at the table was on her once more.

This might have been us. This might have been our daughter, your daughter, if you'd not refused him. If you had trusted him.

If anyone should have children, it was Julien. She thought of all the orphanages he'd sponsored in London, the philanthropic committees he was part of, all dedicated in some way to child welfare. And today had illustrated to her that his efforts weren't all for show, simply to make an impression and meet the right people. She'd seen him slip a peppermint to Alex at church instead of scolding him for fidgeting. This afternoon, he'd spent time with his nephew while they'd been in the greenhouse. Julien and Tristan had taken Alex out for a riding lesson in the paddock. Children were important to Julien. Time spent with family was important.

'I did come on a mission to fetch you, Aurelia,' Julien said, settling Violet in the crook of his arm. 'It is time to go. Your father is eager to be off.' He smiled, but there was a meaningful look in his eyes that indicated a need for haste.

The great Earl of Holme was done rusticating for the day. He'd suffered to present himself at a village church to be fawned over, he'd dined at a table where he was required to serve himself, he'd been surrounded by children and noise and laughter, perhaps even undergone the indignities of talking with commoners while he stood in the mud of a paddock watching one of those children post around the ring on a leading line. What had been a beautiful day to Aurelia had been a beastly day to her father, a day so far beneath him he hadn't any word for it.

Julien handed baby Violet to Elanora and offered Aurelia his arm. She leaned close enough to whisper as they walked in the falling darkness, 'He's going to be ghastly on the ride back.'

To which Julien merely offered the dry reply, 'I know', as they exchanged a conspiratorial glance that made them both laugh and in that moment Aurelia thought the ruse might be suspended, that perhaps he might not hate her entirely, that there might be some kind of friendship at least wrung from this mess. But that was a dangerous thing to hope for. Hope had a habit of breeding more hope. What would she do with Julien Lennox's friendship even if he should offer it?

They made their farewells and climbed into the Lennox coach for the short ride to Brentham Woods, Julien electing to ride up next to the coachman to make more room inside, but he made sure, before he climbed on top, to hand her in and flash her a smile and she demurely accepted it, both of them playing their parts to perfection for all to see. Goodness, this was just act one and already turmoil was bubbling beneath her surface.

Today had been a glimpse into what could have been. She felt very much like poor Scrooge in the story that had come out a few years ago who was visited by the ghost of Christmas future. This could have been her future with the man who was riding up top now because the coach was cramped for six adults and he wouldn't hear of his father being out in the night air, the man who'd slipped his nephew a peppermint in church, the man who'd tossed his niece in the air to make her laugh, who thought the best way to spend a Sunday was church and dinner with his family—not at the gaming halls or the other vices offered to gentlemen of high society. And she'd thrown it all away. If only she could turn back time.

Chapter Seven

The clock had just chimed midnight when she invaded his peace in the library, slipping in like a ghost, swathed in white cotton flannel from head to toe. In the dark, he had the advantage. From the fireside, he could see her, but she could not see him. He set aside his book and made his own presence known from his chair in quiet tones not meant to startle. 'Can I help you find something?' No doubt, she'd not thought to encounter anyone at this hour. He certainly hadn't. He'd wanted to think. He'd come here with high hopes of being alone. Perhaps she'd come with the same.

Or perhaps not, the cynical businessman in him whispered.

Perhaps she wanted to find you here, alone. All the better to compromise you into a marriage you don't want, despite her protestations she doesn't want it either. You know women, always saying the opposite of what they mean.

A game within the game within the game. Now, even the ruse was beginning to look like a bad idea and not just because of this moment. The day had been potent, rife with echoes of old memories, of old hopes of a time when he'd once dreamed of just such Sundays with her beside him. His world had stopped when he'd come upon her in the greenhouse with Violet on her hip, a thousand images of what might have been rioting through his mind.

'I did not mean to disturb.' Her white-swathed form halted a few steps from the door.

Too late for that, Julien thought. The day had been an accumulation of disturbances. Out loud, he said, coolly, 'Not at all. I was just finishing up. I'll be on my way.' He could not stay here with her. It wasn't safe on any level.

She stepped forward, becoming more visible, becoming more than a gleam of white flannel. Her hair was down, braided in a long plait and hanging over one shoulder. She looked girlish and innocent. She ought not be allowed such a deception. Aurelia Ripley was not innocent. She was a flirt, a temptress, who led men on in London. *Be fair*, a small voice inside him cried. She was none of those things today. Violet adored her, she'd not minded the crowded pew, the ladies of the community had flocked to her.

'Don't leave on my account,' she offered. 'I hadn't expected company, but I will admit to not minding some. If it's you,' she added hesitantly, guilelessly.

'I do leave on your account,' Julien countered. 'It would not do for me, at least, to be caught here with you.' He arched a brow. 'Although perhaps it serves you and that's why you invite me to stay?'

Something in her body tensed, he could see it in the straightening of her shoulders, the tilting of her chin. There was a rigidness now to her posture that hadn't been there before. 'You don't believe me. You think there's a ruse within the ruse, that I've contrived a chance to draw near so that your guard is down and I can swoop right in.'

She gave a toss of her head. 'You didn't use to be so cynical, Julien. Now, you fear every woman is dying to marry you.' She cocked her head in mock contemplation. '*Is* that fear, I wonder, or just sheer arrogance?'

Ah, there was the woman he knew. Sharp tongued as she had been in the drawing room the first night. What had he expected? There was no need for the ruse to be in play at the moment. They were alone, with no one to see them. They might be as honest as they like with each other.

'If I am on guard, it is because I was once misled when my guard was dropped.' He matched her stare. This was not what he wanted, but perhaps it was the reminder he needed. The girl he'd courted and loved in London, the woman he'd seen today in the greenhouse, weren't real. The woman who'd refused him, the woman who sparred with him, was. That woman was heartless and self-serving. She was calculating and cool.

Aurelia broke first. 'I didn't mean to quarrel. I only wanted to get a book and, since you were here, I wanted to tell you what a good time I had today. Your family is warm and welcoming even to us, who don't deserve it. I wanted to apologise for my father. You missed out riding up on top, but he was awful on the way home. Your father was masterful and patient with him. This whole situation is hard on him.'

'Don't. Don't make his excuses when he should make apologies,' Julien cut in, his words sharp. 'And most definitely don't feel you have to play the part when there's no one to see.' His words wounded her, he could see hurt flash in her eyes. He tried to ignore the twinge in him that answered on her behalf. He was not in the habit of hurting people.

'I am not playing, Julien, not right now. Can you not countenance niceness from someone else? Are you the only one allowed to be kind?' It was not sharply said. If he'd wanted to bait her to another quarrel, he'd failed. This was said with softness, perhaps even with pity at his rampant cynicism.

'Since I stepped inside this room, you've accused me of wanting to compromise you, of reneging on our agreement and of lying. It's not a very flattering profile you have of me if you think I would do all those things.' She waved a hand. 'I understand, there is the issue of the past between us, but, Julien, I gave you my word that my intentions here and now are in our best interest. I *am* trying to save you from my father's machinations. If you can't trust in that, then you may be dooming yourself to the very thing we both wish to avoid.'

'It is hard to trust someone that I do not know.' Julien's gaze followed her warily as she took the spare chair by the fire. Clearly, she had no intentions of leaving now.

'I could say the same.' She gave him a smile and he found himself sitting back down. 'You are different here in the country. So different, I almost didn't recognise you at first. You're more relaxed. Happy, even. In London, you were always so careful, so correct, as if you expected someone to be watching you, looking for any mistake.'

She leaned forward. 'Country Julien intrigues me, I admit. He is still you, but there are depths to explore and there's access to those depths. City Julien was always so perfect, always so walled off. One would glimpse the existence of those depths, but not be allowed to explore them.'

Julien gave a cough. 'I'm not sure I like being so brutally assessed. I had no idea.' This was almost more intimate than being undressed in one's bedchamber. He wasn't sure he liked the intensity of that scrutiny.

'Does it truly surprise you?' She sat back in her chair, her hands folded across the flatness of her stomach beneath the folds of white flannel. 'I know it is something of a risk to bring the past up, Julien, but we were going to be married. At least at one point, I thought so. I spent a lot of that spring thinking about what it would be like to be married to you.'

She gave a shrug of her shoulder. 'I thought marriage would be akin to getting the keys to the kingdom. I thought if we were married, I would understand you, that I would be privy to who you were. Marriage would unlock you.' She gave a little smile. 'I never got to find out and now there are even more hidden rooms inside you.'

Rooms she would never see, Julien promised himself. He could not afford to let this minx hurt him again. Maybe she was playing with him tonight, maybe not. He did not doubt her words, only their purpose and what she sought to gain from this disclosure. 'I am glad you enjoyed today,' was all he said and then issued a warning of his own. 'My family is very important to me. I would not take any hurt done to them lightly. Elanora loves with all her heart. She will miss you when you're gone.'

Aurelia bowed her head. 'You think I was feigning

friendship with her. That was not the case. I like her. I will look forward to spending time with her over the next few weeks.'

'But you know what she'll think, what she'll hope for—that you will become her sister-in-law,' Julien cautioned.

'That is the ruse's fault, not mine, if people draw such conclusions. I cannot be responsible for that. I can only be responsible for saving our skins, Julien. And, yes, it might come at the expense of others' disappointment. But they don't have to live our lives.'

Julien offered a faint smile. 'I'm just asking that you be gentle with us.' To take care with the villagers he called his friends, with his family, and perhaps even with his own treacherous heart which even now was engaged in its own confused reaction to Aurelia Ripley, whom he'd sworn to despise to his dying day because she'd once betrayed him. He should not let himself be drawn in by any aspect of her, yet he feared that possibility existed.

She rose, smoothing the folds of her voluminous nightgown. 'You and I might be play-acting but not everything today was a ruse, Julien,' she said softly as she prepared to return to her room, where she would probably fall fast asleep, drat her.

He wouldn't. He doubted he'd sleep at all after that last remark. Instead, he'd spend the night sorting through which was which. Which things in the day had been real for her and which had been ruse? And why did it matter so much to him that he decide? What did he think that changed?

***

Julien was still sorting the next morning when he drove her in the gig to the ladies' meeting at the church. He mentally sorted and re-sorted as he met the architect at the station who would be drafting the remodelling plans for his estate. He lost track of how many times his thoughts strayed from the architect's report and had to be redirected. He spent more time thinking about Aurelia—what she had said last night. What was she doing right now?

What did she think of the society of Hemsford Village? Was she secretly thumbing her nose at them like her father? Or was she genuinely engaged in their work? And then there was the self-reflection that followed: why did he care? He only had to survive the month and she would disappear back to Yorkshire on the train, her freedom intact, her horse safe from her father's avarice.

*Until next time...*came the insidious reminder. Who would protect her the next time? Of course, he could ensure Holme had enough money to protect her for two more years, that was her magic deadline, wasn't it? Then she could ride off into the sunset on Elspeth, both of them safe. Why the hell did he care so much?

'Lord Lavenham, did you have a preference on the sliding doors between the drawing room and the dining room?' The question was asked with a certain hesitation that suggested the young architect, a Mr Floyd, whom Julien thought showed immense promise, had asked the question at least twice.

'Ah, yes, I think yes on the sliding doors connecting the two rooms,' Julien said with a confidence he didn't feel. These were questions a wife, a hostess, was better suited to answer. But he had neither and Elanora and his mother were busy at present with Christmas preparations: Elanora was chairing the panto committee and his mother had the annual Lennox Christmas ball to plan, both of which were anchors of the Hemsford Christmas celebrations. They were too busy to help with designs and young Mr Floyd could not dawdle in Hemsford endlessly. He had his own projects and family to get back to.

Julien checked his pocket watch. The ladies' meeting would be finishing shortly and he'd promised to be on hand to pick up Aurelia. He sighed. Thanks to his distractions, he and Mr Floyd were not done yet. 'Would you excuse me for a short while?' Julien solicited. 'I have an errand that I am afraid needs my immediate attention. Perhaps we could meet at the Red Rose Inn and continue our discussion there?' Hopefully, Aurelia wouldn't mind the delay.

At the church, he found himself playing the patient, doting suitor as he leaned against the door and waited for her to finish. The meeting was technically complete, but Aurelia was amid an avid conversation with the ladies over a feminine topic he didn't pretend to understand. She caught sight of him and tossed him a smile of acknowledgement that didn't go unnoticed by the others. Susannah Manning, the baker's daughter, leaned close and whispered something in her ear that made her laugh as the two of them shot him a considering look. He tipped his hat and smiled back.

Aurelia joined him shortly after that. 'Thank you for waiting, there was just so much to discuss.' Her eyes were lively like dancing jewels and her smile was easy as she let him help her into the green wool mantle that matched the green-and-gold tartan of her gown, a very smart, very fetching ensemble for winter and warmth. She tucked her arm through his and buried her fingers in the depths of a rabbit fur muff, still chattering about the meeting.

'I thought we might have lunch at the Red Rose Inn.' He was slowly working up to his confession. 'Although I do confess to an ulterior motive. I have unfinished business to conduct with my architect.'

'I don't mind at all. Perhaps, afterwards, we might stroll the High Street. I have a few purchases to make and you could advise me on where best to do that.'

He nodded with a chuckle. 'I see, it's a negotiation then. My business meeting for your shopping trip. It's a fair trade.'

Julien called for a private parlour for lunch and made the introductions, ordering the venison stew and a loaf of the bread baked down the street at Manning's for all of them along with a bottle of red wine and dried apple pie for dessert. If Aurelia was going to be bored, she might as well be fed. But by the time lunch arrived, it was clear Aurelia was anything but bored. She'd made a quick friend of Mr Floyd, who was telling her about all of his projects back in London and how he was working on a new plan to expand the docks. When it came time to roll out the plans for Julien's home, she chose to engage in the conversation instead of idly strolling the parlour, studying its mediocre landscapes.

'Julien, I cannot allow you in good conscience to put a window there instead of French doors,' she interjected at one point, tapping a finger on the plans. 'You will regret not having full access to the gardens from your office. Think how nice it will be for you to be able to get up from your desk after a long session of adding columns, and be able to step outside for a walk without needing to go through the house. A man like you who loves the country and the fresh air, will want the outdoor access.'

Floyd looked from him to Aurelia who favoured him, Julien noted, with a smile. 'I dare say Lady Aurelia is right, my lord.'

Julien sat back in his hardwood chair. 'A man like me, eh?' The thought warmed him ridiculously when he should not have allowed it to. But he couldn't help being caught up in the sense of play. He tipped the chair back on two legs. 'What else does Lady Aurelia feel I should have, in good conscience?'

'Well, if you insist, I do have some other suggestions,' she said with coy hesitancy, not wanting to appear too bold, no doubt, but being bold anyway.

Julien waved a hand. 'No, please, go on. I was just thinking to myself this morning that I hadn't the head for such things.' It was a reckless indulgence he was allowing himself, permitting her to make suggestions about his home, his refuge. These would be reminders of her that would be left behind. It was also a reckless indulgence of the ruse, of letting himself pretend that he could live in the moment without thinking about or being affected by all that had come before. Yet his usually calculated self was indulging heavily today.

They finished the meeting and Floyd rolled up his plans in a leather cannister. 'I'll be leaving on the three-thirty train, but I'll return next week with the decorator, Lord Lavenham.' He made a small bow. 'Perhaps Lady Aurelia will be of some use in that area as well. I do think a woman's touch is helpful, my lord.'

'Lord Lavenham.' Aurelia shot him a look after Floyd departed. 'Have you got used to it yet? The title?'

'Somewhat, but not here at home. Here, I am Julien Lennox for ever and that is fine. The title means very little. There's no land that goes with it, so it's entirely a courtesy from the Queen in recognition of my family's philanthropy.' He watched her carefully for a reaction. Had she been trying to suss out what had come with the title?

'I disagree—a title with land or without opens doors for you, allows you to broaden the scope of your work. It is no small thing, Julien.' She moved about the room, stacking their dirty lunch plates.

'I didn't think Lady Aurelia Ripley touched dirty dishes,' he commented, half-teasing, and moved to help her.

She tossed him a saucy smile. 'Or jigged wiggly infants on her hip? Or liked eating family-style at Sunday supper? Or volunteering for charity work of her own? You might be surprised at what Lady Aurelia Ripley does.'

She paused thoughtfully. 'Just like there is country Julien and city Julien, did you ever stop to think there might be country Aurelia?' She laughed and he knew his face had given him away—that, no, he hadn't. She brushed his arm lightly, a feather touch that sent a jolt of warmth up its length. 'A woman can be more than one thing, Julien, just like a man,' she lectured gently.

But Aurelia Ripley would never be anything 'just like a man'. She was femininity personified, her green-and-gold tartan skirts swaying gracefully as she piled the dishes on to a tray and shook out their napkins. Julien cleared his throat. 'The innkeeper can finish with this. We'll need to hurry if you want to shop.' He took her mantle from the peg and held it for her. He needed to get out of this room where everything had suddenly become so intimate. His reserves were slipping. The fresh air of High Street was much required.

'Don't worry about the shopping. I was going to suggest that we come tomorrow. I would like to dawdle over the stores, if you don't mind?' She turned her head, blue eyes looking up at him. Julien let his hands linger at her shoulders, settling the mantle longer than necessary. Yes, he definitely needed to get out of the room where they were alone. Outside, there would be other people and other distractions.

'I am sorry the meeting took so long,' he apologised.

She shook her head, her fingers working the frogs of her mantle. 'I'm not. It was great fun. A house, Julien, that is exciting. I hope that I was helpful as opposed to bossy.' She looked up at him, asking for an honest opinion with those blue eyes of hers.

'You were very helpful. I was in over my head on such decisions,' he assured her, then he sobered. 'But you needn't have played the ruse with Mr Floyd.'

'I wasn't playing this afternoon. Were you?' She

slipped her arm through his as they exited the private parlour and smiled politely at the innkeeper while Julien treated the response as a rhetorical question—one that didn't require an answer because both of them *knew* the answer. They hadn't been playing. But it bothered him deeply. They *hadn't* been playing this afternoon. They had, instead, fallen into the old ease they'd once known together and not even realised it, not even questioned it. Five days into her visit and she was barrelling past his defences whether she meant to or not.

That was the hard part, Julien thought, handing her up on to the bench seat of the gig. Did she understand what she was doing? Was this intentional or did she not realise the kind of havoc she could and was wreaking in him? They were supposed to pretend to like each other, nothing more. But this afternoon had gone far beyond that, laying a dangerous precedence for what could follow. He did not want to be taken in by her again, did not want to fall for her again only to learn it was its own ruse.

She tucked her hand into the pocket of his greatcoat as they drove home to Brentham Woods in the cold of the winter afternoon, her head turned up surveying the sky. 'Do you think it will snow?'

'Maybe. It's hard to say. We're close enough to the sea that snow is unusual.'

'What about ice skating? Is there a pond that freezes? I love to ice skate.'

'There's a likely pond out on the estate I purchased.' His traitorous mind was already considering the possibility of a winter picnic, although the ruse wouldn't require it. There'd be no one out there to see, to care.

She snuggled closer, tugging the lap robe about her legs. 'Then we should go. I want to see the place before Floyd comes back with the decorator.'

Great, Julien thought wryly. They would go to his estate and skate on thin ice and, if he wasn't careful, his heart would crack. Just like that the sorting started again—what was real? What was ruse? And the questions nagged persistently—who really was Aurelia Ripley and could he trust her?

Chapter Eight

She didn't trust herself with him. It was too easy to slip into old patterns, old familiarities from better times. Yesterday had been proof of it and today she'd have to do much better. Aurelia grabbed her reticule and gloves from the bed and gave herself a last look in the mirror before heading downstairs for a day of shopping in Hemsford. She ran a hand over the winter-sky-blue skirts of her ensemble. Her armour—such as it was—served as a reminder of her mission. She must be charming without being charmed herself. Otherwise she'd be setting herself up for disappointment and heartache.

She had hurt him in the past. He wanted nothing to do with her and she wanted her freedom. She needed to survive the next two years in order to claim it. Surviving didn't include falling for the impossible. Whatever chances she'd had of claiming Julien's love had been ruined seven years ago. Julien was not a man who forgot or forgave a betrayal. A successful businessman didn't get ahead by turning a blind eye to the wrongs done to him.

Aurelia settled a cream bonnet trimmed in matching blue ribbon on her head and tied the bow with a sense of preparedness. Perhaps yesterday had shown her exactly what she was up against. She would be more on guard against her own reactions now that she knew them: her tendency to smile at Julien, to laugh with him, to reach for his hand, to crave the warmth of his hand at her back even when the ruse didn't require it. Yesterday had been intoxicating. Not just the touches, but the conversation, the talk of his house.

The mention of it had done queer things to her stomach, not all of them good. He was making a home for himself and for the wife he'd share it with, the children who would eventually fill it. She'd not liked the thought of it, intuitively knowing that the wife would not be her, the children not theirs. It shouldn't matter. She'd given up those dreams and him a long time ago. She'd treated him shabbily.

Helping him now was part-atonement, part-penance. That was all it could be. In the long run, they'd both be happier that way. She tugged at her jacket. Good. Now that was settled, she would go shopping. With her father's money. That made her smile. It was about time her father's money went to do some good.

Julien was waiting for her at the bottom of the stairs, leaning against the newel post and looking dashing in his grey wool greatcoat. 'Are you ready for a morning of shopping?' He crooked his arm as she approached.

'A morning?' She laughed. 'A *day*. Have you forgotten how I shop?' She teased because, no doubt, there was someone nearby who would expect such repartee: his mother, her father, her mother. She teased to put on a show, she told herself, not because it came so easily between them.

* * *

Hemsford Village did not disappoint. For being a rural town, it boasted an array of shops and high-quality goods. The High Street was bustling with midweek shoppers and people who wanted to look at the shop windows which were decked out in Christmas themes to show off their wares.

'I do admit to being impressed with the village,' she commented as they stopped before the dressmaker's window to admire this year's Christmas creation—a long, warm cloak of winter white trimmed in rabbit fur with a wide, deep hood that paid tribute to styles of days of yore. 'A woman would feel like a medieval princess in such a cloak,' she said dreamily. 'I am surprised, though; it seems like a rather frivolous item for these parts.'

Julien cocked his head, giving it some thought. 'Perhaps, but isn't that part of the Christmas magic? Some whimsy? Some fantasy? I don't think people want to walk past windows sporting farming implements and workman's gloves or sensible aprons. It's the dream people want to see looking back at them.' With a light press of his hand at her back, he ushered her next door to the window at Manning's bakery. 'This window is a fantasy for children. A winter wonderland of white-iced cakes and dancing gingerbread people.'

Aurelia studied the happy, dancing gingerbread, but her thoughts were on Julien. 'Are you a dreamer, Julien?' She would have thought no. In his line of work the numbers never lied. They left little room for dreams to intrude, yet the Julien she'd known in London, who'd brought her little presents, had a hidden fanciful streak if one could get him to break out of his carefully constructed mould—and she had been successful on that account. It had been her personal mission back then to tempt him. She ought not tempt him now, but he'd tipped his hand at the dressmaker's window and she could not resist taking another peek.

'I have dreams of a world where children have homes, where they don't go hungry. Then I build those dreams.' His answer was less than she had hoped for, perhaps he knew that. Perhaps he'd realised his earlier error and was retrenching, careful not to make yesterday's mistakes.

'I meant dreams for yourself,' she clarified, cocking her head to take in his profile with the strong length of nose and the dark lashes.

He gave her a polite, cool smile and held the door for her. 'What I am dreaming of at present is a fresh-baked batch of gingerbread biscuits to sustain me through your shopping. Let me take you inside and show you their Twelfth Night Cakes. Manning's has some of the most stunning cakes I've seen. I dare say they rival those in London. You'll have to tell me what you think.'

What she thought was that Julien was better at playing the game than she was. They'd gone off course a little at the dressmaker's, but he'd quickly righted the ship, not allowing her to probe too deeply into anything that resembled overly personal conversation. Neither did he attempt to do any probing of his own. He kept their shopping conversation pleasant but impersonal. What did she think of the cakes? Did she like the gingerbread biscuits? Where would she like to go next? Could he take that box for her? Could he carry her basket? And in between polite questions, he gave her an interesting, informative overview of Hemsford.

'The railroad branch is changing things for us,' he told her as they passed the newly built station where the early afternoon train was disgorging its passengers. 'It's only an hour and a half from London by rail. It's become much more efficient since the London–Brighton railroad joined with a couple of other lines a few years back. Now, it's the London, Brighton and South Coast Railway and the train is direct to Hemsford. People can make a day trip of it if they wish. I've encouraged the Red Rose Inn to expand the amount of parlours they have available so that day trippers have a place to rest that affords them some privacy.'

'One of the ladies at the meeting yesterday mentioned you were on the Hemsford improvement committee. What other ideas do you have?' she asked, careful to make it sound like casual, polite, non-intrusive conversation instead of a look inside his brilliant mind as they strolled.

'I've encouraged folks to think about what Hemsford has to offer the outside world. We do Christmas like nowhere else I've been.' He was warming to the subject and his guard was coming down. They paused long enough for him to greet an acquaintance and make introductions, then he continued.

'We had advertisements printed in the London papers this year about visiting Hemsford for Christmas shopping, to come and see the quaint shops decorated for Christmas, to take a special Christmas tea at the Red Rose after shopping. A tea, by the way, which features

Manning's baked goods.' His dark eyes were starting to dance as he talked. 'Next week will be busier than this week.' He steered her towards the village green.

'We're setting up the Christmas fair which will start Saturday and run until Christmas Eve. We have vendors that come from all over the Continent: German craftsmen, Italian glassblowers, Swiss music box makers, French soap-makers, candy-makers. There are carollers in the evening and the whole place is lit up like Vauxhall perhaps in its heyday.'

'It sounds delightful. You must bring me,' she insisted with a smile. 'My mother would love it. She adores that kind of thing.'

'And you? Do *you* adore "that sort of thing"? Or would you tolerate it for the sake of the ruse?' They'd stopped walking to watch the carpenters building the market stalls and she was aware of his gaze on her, aware, too, that for a moment they'd stepped into a limbo between ruse and reality.

She met his gaze with a soft stare of her own. 'I would absolutely love an evening at a Christmas market, strolling beneath the fairy lights, looking at goods from far-away lands. There's something magical about it, I think. At least I guess. In my mind that's how I see it. I can't say that I've ever been allowed the opportunity to experience something like it. We seldom have such fairs up in our part of isolated Yorkshire. When we do, my father won't hear of me attending with the rabble.'

She sighed into the silence that followed. 'You must think me the worst sort of snob.' In London, during the Season, she attended only the best of events. 'I wouldn't blame you if you did. I've not given you leave to believe any differently.'

'I'll be sure to bring you. This year, we've expanded to include games,' Julien promised. But she noted that he had not answered her question. *Did* he think her a snob? It galled her that he might—no—that he probably did. The girl he'd known had been the pampered, protected daughter of the Earl of Holme. It was the only face she'd been allowed to show anyone in London. And he'd loved her even so, as she'd been back then, a young girl who had known so little of the world.

For a moment, she was tempted to set aside the ruse entirely, grab him by the lapels and make him look at her while she spoke the truth: that she wasn't a snob, that she was working hard to found a school for children at home, that in Yorkshire she far preferred riding her horse and hiking the hills than sitting prettily in silks and doing needlepoint, that when she played the piano, she preferred the loud, moody depths of Beethoven to the lightness of Mozart.

She was not a porcelain figurine who would break. Although, once, she had believed the latter. She'd not thought she'd survive if she was dropped from the life she knew. She knew better now when it was too late.

Julien pointed to one of the booths. 'There will be puppet shows for the children at that one. A man who makes the most exquisite marionettes comes from Italy and puts on shows he writes himself. But perhaps it will steal some of the magic if we see everything being constructed and know it's all just simple board and nails in the end.'

'The whole world's a stage, is that it?' she quoted with a laugh and then wished she hadn't. The line struck too close to home. They were performing their ruse on a stage of their making. He'd brought her shopping because the ruse demanded it. He'd made polite conversation with her because that too was demanded. But he'd been careful today not to let that conversation veer into the personal. Today's conversation had been entertaining, but neutral. It wouldn't do for someone to accidentally overhear them being testy with one another and have word get back to her father. They'd left no margin for complaint today. Anyone who had seen them would only remark that he'd been as solicitous today as he'd been yesterday, showing her about town.

His town. He loved Hemsford Village. His pride was evident in his words and in his efforts. He felt about Hemsford as she felt about the village attached to her father's estate. Something they had in common that would surprise him if he knew. He might build orphanages on a grand scale, but she had a servant's heart, too.

'Do you have more shopping?' Julien hefted the basket on his arm, filled to the rim with brown-paper-wrapped packages from her efforts.

'If we could make one more stop?' she asked. 'I wanted to get peppermints for the Christmas baskets. Where do you get yours for Alex?' She flashed a saucy smile.

'I get them at Wilson's Emporium, but if you'd be advised by me, I would wait.' He leaned close and she breathed in the scent of his soap and cologne, all winter spice—cloves, she thought—and the sharpness of citrus, that rare thing—a Christmas orange. 'There's a vendor from Germany that brings the most delicious peppermint sticks. I'm not sure what makes them different, but they are very good.' He gave the basket another hefting lift. 'Is everything in here for the Christmas baskets?'

'Yes, you didn't think all of this was just for me?' She laughed, but she didn't miss the considering look in his gaze as if he might be seeing her anew. 'I sit on a committee at home, too, for Christmas baskets,' she added. 'Don't be so surprised...' Then dared to say with a smile to soften the intention '...who knows what you might learn about me if you looked a little closer.'

'Is that wise, Aurelia?' he cautioned sternly, steering them towards the livery where the gig waited for them. 'This is not about looking closer. This about self-preservation for both of us.' She'd deserved that. She'd stepped too far over the lines and rules of their ruse.

'Of course, I do apologise. I just thought...' She didn't finish the sentence. What *had* she thought? That they might be friends? That he could get past her refusal? Perhaps it was easier for her to slip up because she'd not been the one refused. That didn't mean, of course, that she hadn't been hurt, too. But her wound had been self-inflicted. She frowned as the livery neared. 'Do we have to go back just yet? Perhaps we could stop in for tea at the Red Rose Inn. We could try out the Christmas tea you were telling me about.'

Julien shook his head. 'I have a meeting with your father this afternoon. I need to get back.' And she had work to do for the Christmas baskets. Handkerchiefs for the women weren't going to embroider themselves. The committee had decided to include something simple but pretty for the mothers in this year's baskets. Julien put her basket in the back of the gig and paused. 'Why don't you want to go back to Brentham Woods? Is something wrong there? Has anyone caused you trouble?'

She shook her head and helped herself up to the seat. 'No, everyone has been kind, even though I am sure we're an enormous imposition this time of year. I just like being…' She almost said *with you*. But she'd already been scolded for such familiarity and such honesty. She opted for the other truth. 'Away from him. Away from my father.'

Julien gave her a sharp look as he sat down beside her. 'Has something happened I should be aware of?' She had to be careful here.

'No. The sooner you give him the loan, the sooner you and I are in the clear.' She sighed and kept her gaze fixed on the road ahead. The sooner December was behind her, the sooner she could return to Moorfields and Elspeth and the safety of her life there, one step closer to her freedom. And the sooner she could put Julien behind her again. Which would be for the best. He was part of the past and he did not figure in the future she'd envisioned for herself.

Chapter Nine

Julien had not envisaged just how odious it was to deal with the Earl of Holme. Even without their contentious past, he would have despised the man. He'd never met a person more resistant to helping himself and yet more desirous of a handout.

Julien exchanged a look with his father that said covertly, *Are you sure you want to do this?*

To which his father replied with a barely perceptible shrug that said, *I think we must, for the ladies' sake.*

His father was not wrong. The more time Julien spent with the Earl of Holme, the more he disliked the idea of Lady Holme and Aurelia being at the man's financial mercy. He wouldn't want any woman reliant on this man who moved through the world with an elevated sense of his own consequence and not a practical thought in his head for how to care for those around him: not his tenants, not his daughter, not his wife.

Julien leaned forward, his hands folded on the surface of the large desk that separated him from the Earl of Holme and his father on the other side. He did his best business thinking in this room. 'We'll want to start by looking at the estates and restructuring how they're run in order to make them self-supporting, perhaps even profitable in the future. Right now, they are a drain on your resources, but that can all be fixed with management.' Something that had been in short supply from the looks of things. 'When was the last time you visited your other estates?'

'What does that have to do with anything?' Holme growled, his sagging jowls grimacing.

Julien fixed him with a hard stare. 'It has everything to do with it. We are here to help you mend your finances so that you do not find yourself in such straits again. We must repair what is broken about your management.' He paused for emphasis. 'We will not throw money into a bottomless pit of losses, Lord Holme. We must have assurances our investment is worth something. The assurance we would like is that this insolvency won't occur again. Without such an assurance…' Julien didn't need to finish the sentence. Holme knew what was implied. Without the assurance, theoretically there'd be no loan.

Holme huffed and gave in. Julien gave a crisp nod. 'Good, we are in accord. Let's start with your family seat.'

It took the rest of the afternoon to explain how to restructure the economy of the estate, how the crops would need to be rotated and how to manage the village. He did not think Holme would remember half of it, but it didn't matter. He had Holme's signature which gave him the power to enact the changes as a condition of the loan. In addition, he had a man in mind who would act as land steward for Moorfields and who would understand the plans Julien had spent hours drawing up. Plans that would help the estate recover. Plans that would protect Aurelia's home well past the two years she required.

The voice in his head nudged: *Careful. You're getting invested, too invested, and not just financially.*

His father showed Holme out of the office, making the appropriate affirmations about how much they'd accomplished this afternoon, and shut the door firmly behind the man. 'Well? What do you think?' his father asked, returning to his chair.

'He is ungrateful. He thinks help is his due, that he is owed success by dint of who he is.' Julien tossed his pen on the desk. 'We are securing his future and he has no idea how important that is.' Julien could not begin to fathom such a concept. The future was all he thought about. Investment banking was inherently future focused, his charity efforts were future focused. How did a man *not* think about the future?

'It's not that Holme doesn't think, it's that he only thinks about himself.' His father smiled and sighed. 'Other than Holme's reticence, I think the rest of the visit is going well. You and Aurelia seem to have sorted your differences. It was kind of you to take her into the village this morning.'

Kind was all Julien wished it had been. But it had been motivated by more than that. He'd wanted an excuse to spend time with her even after yesterday or especially because of yesterday. He could tell himself he'd taken her into the village because the ruse required it. But he'd taken her because he'd wanted to. When she'd come downstairs this morning in her winter-sky-blue ensemble, a cream, fur-trimmed mantle swinging from her shoulders, bright eyes shining, he'd nearly been lost, nearly forgotten every admonition he'd given himself.

'Do you still have feelings for her?' his father asked casually.

Julien looked at him sharply. 'No, why would you ask?' Dear Lord, what had his face inadvertently betrayed? If his father guessed at such a thing, who else might also guess? That was not tolerable, particularly when it wasn't true. He was not falling for Aurelia Ripley again.

His father shrugged and gestured to the papers on the desk. 'You've gone to a lot of work for someone you do not feel an out-of-the-ordinary attachment to. Perhaps one could say she's the reason you've worked so tirelessly on ensuring long-term security for the estate.'

'Wasn't it you who said we should think about the women?' Julien pointed out. 'I am merely doing for her what I would do for any other woman who has the misfortune to be a tied to a man who has mismanaged his finances.'

'Would it be so bad if it wasn't?' his father pressed. 'If you did have feelings for her? I do wonder if she still has feelings for you. To me, it seems as if she might. When I saw the two of you together at church, or when I watch you in the evenings playing cards, I can't help but think that this time things might be different? An eighteen-year-old girl doesn't know her mind the way a twenty-five-year-old woman does.'

Julien shook his head. 'Aurelia Ripley has always known her mind and she's always known her own power when it comes to men. She's good at curating an image and cultivating feelings. I do not think it would be wise, Father, to put too much stock in appearances.' If only such advice were as easy to take as it was to dispense.

Julien rose. 'I think I'll take Benjamin for a ramble before it gets dark.' Perhaps some time out of doors with his dog would help clear his head of the traitorous thoughts that were roaming around loose in there: that this time it *could* be different, that Aurelia had changed, that what he saw of her now was the real her. Most traitorous of all was the thought that *he* wanted those things to be true. He knew better. Loyalty and love didn't work like that. They were steadfast and true, unchanging, immovable against the tides of fate. Who knew that better than a dog? He whistled for Ben and Ben came. Benjamin wasn't man's best friend for nothing.

'Oho! You're not a pretty girl for nothing—the Viscount has made his offer of a loan. We started the paperwork this afternoon. Whatever you told him in the village has borne fruit.' Her father entered her room without knocking, his face florid with excitement, her mother close behind him. 'Things are going well. We're going to be solvent,' he crowed, turning to her mother. 'More than that, we might even be able to buy back your tiara, my dear, and some of the artwork.'

Aurelia saw her mother's face relax with real relief even as her father was already planning how to spend his newfound riches. What would Julien think of that? Surely that wasn't what Julien had planned for those funds. Guilt pinched her. This was what she'd talked Julien into. Tiaras and artwork were likely low on Julien's list of financial priorities.

'Of course, we must keep kowtowing to them for a while longer, pretend we're grateful and all that.' He waved a hand her direction. 'You must keep the Viscount dangling, keep him hopeful and charmed. We're not out of the woods yet.'

'We *are* grateful,' Aurelia cut in, feeling defensive on Julien's behalf. 'No one else was willing to lend you any money. Not even the moneylenders with exorbitant interest rates.' She gave her father a hard stare. 'What do they want in exchange for such a magnanimous loan? You do understand the loan must be paid back.'

'The terms are better than I hoped for. They want to restructure the estates so that the land is self-supporting and the estates pay for themselves without excessive taxation on renters. Fine, I say. If they want to play petty landlords from a distance, I am happy to let them muck about, especially if it doesn't cost me anything.'

That was not nothing, Aurelia thought. The import of the Lennoxes' terms was not lost on her as it was lost on her selfish father, but she kept the realisation quietly to herself. Julien was securing the estates into the future so that as long as her father lived, she and her mother would be financially safe. It was the most he could do— all he could do. He could not control that her father had no male heir of his own, only a distant cousin who would dispossess her and her mother of their home upon her father's death. But until then, they would be taken care of.

'I would like to push for a match between you and the Viscount, my dear, now that things are going so well.

It seems to me I could secure his backing more permanently if there was a wedding between us.'

That brought Aurelia to sharp attention. She ignored the rapid, worried beat of her heart. Julien would not thank her for that. Their ruse was supposed to preclude such an effort. 'There is no need. The estates are safe and I have done my part in charming him.'

That had not come without a cost to her. It had stirred old memories, old hurts and old guilt. Everything between them now was a lie, a show for others when once there'd been truth. That was her fault. She would rather have had truth with him instead of this ruse of politeness. He'd been strategic today in the village, a reminder that he did not trust her, that he was holding her to the rules of this particular engagement, that yesterday had been a step too far.

She'd promised him she wouldn't trap him, that she would protect him from her father's plan. Now she had to make good on that. She'd got her father the loan and now she needed to protect Julien from a marriage he didn't want. Besides, she didn't want a marriage either. She wanted her freedom to do as she pleased, to live knowing that the things and people she loved could not be used against her. Heavens, but she was weary of playing all sides. When would anyone be on her side?

'Don't push,' her mother counselled her father, helping him up. 'We have enough for now. There's no need and weren't you hoping that, once the finances cleared up, Aurelia might make a match in town this spring? Weren't you saying the other night that the Marquess of

Penumberton's son was home from the Continent and looking to wed?'

Placation. No real solution, just kicking the stone down the road, this was her mother's management strategy. It was a compromise: peace for now. She would deal with Penumberton's son and the Season in a few months. Her mother smiled over her shoulder as her parents left her room. 'Maybe nature will just take its course where the Viscount is concerned, my girl.'

Her first thought once they'd left was that she had to warn Julien. She sank down on the window seat and stared out at the parkland. Where would Julien be this time of day? Would he be in his office? Somewhere in the house? Or would he be out? She'd rather talk to him now than take the risk of talking to him before dinner when privacy would be minimal.

Movement drew her eye to the tree-line where the woods met Brentham. She sat up straighter as a man and a dog came into view. Julien and Benjamin. Julien's head was bare, his dark hair tousled, his boots muddy, and he looked entirely relaxed. Julien shouted a command to the dog and threw a stick. The dog bounded after it, ears flapping, and brought it back, earning a scratch and another throw.

Had he walked out to the meadow and checked the duck boxes? She wished he'd asked her to go, too. But why would he? He'd already done his duty this morning and the ruse did not require an invitation to go walking where no one could see. Yet the temptation to go to him whispered too loud to ignore. She grabbed her cloak, raced down the stairs and across the lawn before anyone could stop her.

Benjamin saw her first and sounded the alarm with a bark, but no menace. He came to her, licking her hand and begging for pats. 'Ben, come here,' Julien called in commanding tones and Benjamin reluctantly obeyed. 'He'll get mud on you if you're not careful.' Julien strode up and ruffled Benjamin's fur.

'I'm not worried, it's a durable cloak.' It was long and dark, not the fancy fur-lined mantle she'd worn into Hemsford. 'I saw you from the window,' she offered in explanation. Now that she was here with him, she was second-guessing her decision. She was invading his peace. Had she really come out for him or for her own selfish desire to be in his company again?

He glanced towards the house, perhaps wondering if anyone was watching. 'Did you need something?' He seemed mildly annoyed by the intrusion. Perhaps people only came to him when they needed something from him. People came to him to lay down their burdens, burdens which he would inevitably pick up. Now she was one of them.

'I don't think anyone is watching.' More was the pity. She had no reason to reach for his hand. 'But, yes, I do need something.' She stepped close to him, close enough to see his dark eyes harden with wariness. 'I need to thank you for what you're doing with my father, for what you've done for me. He told me how you've reworked the estate.'

She paused and said slowly, 'I know what it will mean for my mother, for me.' She brushed a hand down the sleeve of his greatcoat. 'You bought me my two years.' With his ingenuity and his money he'd built a wall that would protect her until she reached her majority.

'I would have done it for anyone in your situation. As for the estate, it's just good investing. I don't want my money going into a bottomless pit. I want the expenditure to mean something.'

Of course he'd deny it had anything to do with her. Of course his gaze would be impenetrable. Those were the rules. He needn't play at liking her when no one was around. 'It does mean a great deal not just to me, but to the village at Moorfields and all those who count on the estates for their livelihood.' She could see he liked that reference better, caring for the masses as opposed to one specific person.

'Is that all you needed? It could have waited until supper.' Julien was distant now, more distant than he'd been since her arrival a week ago. Even then, his anger had heat to it, but there was no heat to him now, just polite, neutral coolness. He removed her hand from his sleeve. 'Best not get careless, Aurelia. I wouldn't want anyone to get the wrong idea.' Particularly her. Or perhaps him. She heard the unspoken message quite clearly.

She tucked her hand back beneath her cloak, sorely missing her gloves in the cold. 'There is one more thing. My father feels that my charms have been met with good result. I have charmed you into the loan, in other words, and into generous terms where paying back the money isn't so literal. I thought that would be enough to keep you and me safe from any further contretemps on his part, but this afternoon…' She drew a breath long enough to study Julien's features. How angry would he be? 'He mentioned he thought a match between us would be beneficial and he suggested I ought to…' What was the right word? 'Manage it.'

Julien's face darkened to a thunderous hue. 'I am sorry, Julien,' she put in rapidly, reflexively reaching a hand out for his arm. 'I did not think he would look further than the money. I thought once he had the money it would be enough.'

His expression arrested. 'Do you think that's why I am angry? No, I am angry because the man would use his daughter to whore for him, to be bartered in marriage as if it were not the modern era.'

A trill of warm comfort swam through her at his defence. Never mind he would be the champion of any woman in such circumstances. For the moment, someone was on her side and that it should be Julien, touched her even as she knew it meant nothing. 'I thought you should know, Julien, so that you could take precautions.' For himself, for both of them. She had not meant to add to the burdens he carried, but she had.

He gave a curt nod. 'I will make sure he knows that I will pull the loan if he makes marriage a condition. He is in no position to bargain or dictate terms.'

She licked her lips and looked away for a moment. 'I don't think he will do it that way. I think he expects me to manage it entirely, so that it appears to be a natural evolution of our association.'

Julien turned from her and kicked at a pile of dead leaves. When he turned back, his eyes were like hard, dark-chocolate nougat. 'Does he do this often, Aurelia?

Send you to beg? Is this why you're unwed at twenty-five? It's not just the money, is it, that keeps you by his side. He can't imagine what to do if he played his ace for good?'

'If that were true, he'd not be pushing to see us wed.' She felt herself flush.

'But with my money permanently secured through marriage, he'd not need to send you out again. And your mother, what does she say to any of this? Does she do anything to stop it?'

She drew her cloak about her, suddenly cold. 'My mother does what she can. You've seen firsthand that my father is not an easy man to live with for either of us.'

He was silent for a while, his gaze unwavering as it bored into her, seeing too much, seeing the dysfunction of her life that lay behind the silks and satins and pretty smiles. It was embarrassing to admit to against the backdrop of his perfection: the home filled with the love, the family that adored one another, the life spent in service to others and not himself. She felt supremely dirty.

'Say something. I know it's awful,' she said quietly.

'What is awful is that it keeps happening. Will you permit me to put a stop to it? I can make it a condition of the loan.'

She shook her head vociferously. 'No, then he'll know I told you.' And that would be one more thing she'd spend the next two years paying for, one more thing that would put Elspeth and the things she loved at risk.

He nodded. 'Then I won't,' he said with firm assurance. 'I will think of something else, something more circumspect.'

'You must discuss it with me first,' she insisted. 'I do not want you entangled any more than necessary.'

He nodded. 'I'll walk you back to the house, and then starting tomorrow we'll give the ruse a brief rest. I have projects that can take me away from the house during the days. That will give avaricious minds some time to cool and reassess how grasping they need to be. I think it will have to do for now,' Julien said gently, offering his arm and calling to Benjamin who was interested in something at the base of a tree.

There was comfort in the strong arm beneath her hand. What a mess this had become. The ruse had invited her father's speculation instead of repelling it. More than that, the ruse had awakened her own remembrances of a time before things had gone sour, making the situation and her own role in it all the more painful.

Chapter Ten

She didn't see him again until Saturday, the day of the fair, unless one counted his appearance at the dinner table and in the drawing room after brandies to play cards or games or to read while the ladies sewed. One evening, she played the pianoforte, thinking to entice him to join her on the bench to turn pages, but he stayed firmly rooted at the backgammon board with his father.

In other words, there was no more time alone with him. No rides out to the duck boxes, no more drives in the gig to Hemsford where they had the privacy of the road between them and an undefined space of time where they were both in and out of the ruse. No more walks down the High Street, peering in shop windows and pretending he was escorting her for real and not because the ruse demanded it.

It made quite a long week even though she had plenty to keep her busy with handkerchiefs to embroider for the Christmas baskets and committee work to keep her occupied. When she wasn't sewing, she was organising baking for the baskets in the Lennox kitchen, which Caro Lennox had cheerfully turned over to her for the occasion. She even kneaded bread and rolled out sheets of dough for Christmas sugar biscuits that would be cut into enticing Christmas shapes like bells and stars. But while her body was busy with work, her mind found time to wander afield.

What was Julien doing? Where was he? Her ears found themselves craning for the sound of his boots in the hall. She imagined him coming to seek her in the kitchens, catching her with a smudge of flour on her cheek and wiping it away, his thumb lingering a little too long at the corner of her mouth…but those were fancies only, none of which came true. He did not seek her out once.

She went the rest of the week without seeing him. But she'd see him today for the Christmas fair. Aurelia rummaged through her wardrobe, looking for the long red-wool cloak she wanted to wear, trying to ignore the excitement that coursed through her at the prospect of seeing Julien today. Of course, she knew why he hadn't come to the kitchens. The ruse didn't demand it. Coming down to the kitchen where no one required a demonstration of their affections did not serve their masquerade. But also, they didn't want the ruse to be too convincing and start to work against them.

A little distance served them. If Julien appeared too eager, her father would take advantage. It would be better if Julien appeared to be charmed, but not besotted. Independent, not following her around like a puppy dog. Not that she could ever imagine Julien acting in such a manner. Not even when he'd been truly courting her had he played a lovesick swain. Julien was always level-headed, never unduly swept away. It was part of his charm and his mystique.

She remembered how the girls in the retiring rooms had chattered about him, about how wondrous it would be to wrap such a man around their fingers, to see that control completely undone. At the time, she'd felt very smug, thinking to herself that he was hers, that she alone had seen him set aside his gentlemanly façade and that she would be the one to see him undone once they wed. And she had seen him undone, just not in the way she'd wanted or expected.

There it was! She reached for the red-wool cloak just as her mother peeked into the room. 'Are you ready? I think everyone is downstairs.' Her mother studied her with approval. 'You're wearing the red over your grey ensemble today, that's perfect. Red brings out your hair and we want the Viscount to have his attentions fixed on you.'

Her mother came to her with a smile and straightened the narrow black belt at the waist of her grey walking costume with its black-velvet trim at the wrists and hem. 'The red will look nice and bright.' Her mother rummaged through the dressing table. 'Maybe some rouge today to go with it. Just a little on your lips. The cold will put the colour in your cheeks.' She dabbed a bit on her fingertip and patted the colour on to Aurelia's lips. 'There, perfect, my darling.' She stepped back with a smile. 'You are so lovely, my angel. When I look at you, I see so much of myself in younger days.'

But maybe not *too* much of herself, Aurelia thought, hiding her angst over the comment beneath a soft smile.

She liked to believe she was different than her mother, perhaps stronger than her mother. Her mother was a peacekeeper, but her mother's idea of peace required subjugation. Aurelia did not think she was willing to bend quite that much.

'You are in fine looks. Your father will be pleased. He's been worried the Viscount's attentions have been slipping after such a fast start.'

'The Viscount is a busy man. Many things vie for his attentions. I cannot expect to dominate all of them, all the time. I don't think he'd find such clinginess attractive.' She swung the cloak about her shoulders. 'Father should let me handle the Viscount and spend his time worrying about the estates.'

Her mother clucked her tongue. 'You have a saucy mouth, Aurelia. You should respect your father; it's been hard for him.'

'Hard? For him?' Aurelia scoffed as they left the room. 'He does as he pleases and no one says boo to him. When was the last time *you* disagreed with him? Stood up to him?'

'It's not a wife's place, Aurelia,' her mother whispered sternly. Nor was it a daughter's. A father should protect his child, not use her to advance his own needy causes, not wish that she'd died in place of his heir. Aurelia let the subject go as they descended the staircase. Today, she was going to the Christmas fair with Julien and, ruse or no ruse, she was going to have a good time.

The village fair did not disappoint. The festive excitement seemed to start on the outskirts of the village, with the signs driven into the ground on wooden stakes painted to look like peppermint sticks, assuring visitors they were on the right road to Hemsford. The closer their little cavalcade—she and Julien in the gig, Tristan's family in a coach and her parents and the Lennoxes in another coach—got to the village, the more crowded the road became. Neighbours called out to one another and there was laughter on the air mixed with jingle bell harnesses. Aurelia thought it was one of the best sounds she'd ever heard, second only to the peal of Moorfield's Christmas Eve bells.

'I bet Tristan can hardly keep Alex in his seat,' she said to Julien as he parked the gig outside the church. A few young boys had been pressed into service at the church to mind those who wish to park their gigs there for a few coins instead of making their way through the crowded streets to the livery.

Julien laughed, caught up in the good cheer of the day. 'If so, it serves him right. My brother was a handful at Christmas when he was younger. He loves Christmas, always has.' He leaned close as if to impart a secret. 'He loves it even more now that his favourite time of year is also his wedding anniversary. He proposed to Elanora on Christmas Eve and married her Christmas Day.'

'Oh.' She sighed, letting her gaze slide towards Tristan's coach, where Julien's brother had climbed out and was organising his brood. 'That's quite romantic.' She watched as Elanora stepped out of the coach last and kissed Tristan on the cheek, an unmistakable look of love and contentment in her eyes before she took her son's hand and gently steered him out of the way of a newly arrived carriage. Baby Violet was in her papa's arms, her curious eyes bright and looking all about her. What a picture they made, the four of them together.

The sight tugged on heartstrings she did not think could be tugged.

Did she still want that? How could she? After all, it was the antithesis of freedom, of what she was fighting for.

The ten of them formed into natural subgroups as they strolled the village green, now fully converted into a Christmas fair: Julien's parents walking with hers, she and Julien walking with Tristan's family. She enjoyed the chance to spend time with Elanora, to take her turn holding baby Violet, to see the fair through Alex's excited eyes which lit up at every curiosity. Most of all, she enjoyed the chance to be with Julien, to have his hand at her back, to have his attentions, to feel his gaze on her and the ruse be hanged. She knew he had a part to play today as did she, but she conveniently let herself forget it, let herself pretend that today was real.

'It hardly looks like the same place,' she told Julien as they strolled the aisles. 'It's so much more than plywood and nails.' Durable, dark-green canvas and festive red-and-green bunting held up with gold bows decorated the booths. Wreaths sporting holly berries and red gingham ribbons were hung at each stall. From there, vendors had contributed their own touches and decorations to their booths, adding to the festivity. Overhead, lanterns were strung across the aisles from booth to booth, waiting to be lit later at dusk.

The aroma of fried breads and baked biscuits filled

the air, tempting fair goers to a mid-morning tea or an early lunch. There were pasties, too, filled with hot, spicy meat that dripped when you bit into them, and paper cones of finger foods like roasted chestnuts a person could eat while they shopped. There was spun-sugar sweets, liquorice drops, peppermint sticks and chocolates of all varieties. There was a dancing space and a place for a band to play later. 'I feel like Alex,' she said, leaning against Julien's arm. 'I can scarce take it all in.'

Julien laughed. 'One would think you had never been to London and seen wonders far grander than a country fair.'

She smiled up at him. 'Nothing in London can match this. There's no marriage mart here, no posturing, just good clean fun.' For emphasis, she tugged him towards the booth selling milled soap of French lavender. She picked up a bar, closed her eyes and took a deep inhale. 'See, just good clean fun.' She reached for her reticule and signalled to the vendor. 'I'll take four bars of this, please.'

'Four?' Julien teased.

'Christmas gifts for our mothers and for Elanora, and one for me.' She fished for coins, but Julien's gentle hand stilled hers.

'Allow me, Aurelia,' he said quietly, but apparently not quietly enough. Beside them, Elanora and Tristan exchanged smiles full of knowing. 'Today is my treat. I want you to have a good time.'

'Julien, you don't need to,' she protested, suddenly confused. Was this part of the ruse because a gentleman *would* offer and he was playing a part for his brother and their families? Or was this...*real*...because it truly was his treat?

'I want to,' he said firmly, passing the vendor the coins and handing her the wrapped bars of soap to put in her basket. She might have enjoyed the moment more if she wasn't acutely aware of her parents looking on, her father's shrewd eyes assessing what every nuance meant...to him and how best to use it. A little of her joy went out of the day.

Perhaps Julien sensed it. His hand tightened at her waist and his smile widened, trying a little too hard for levity. 'I think your basket needs filling. We must shop some more. Elanora? Tristan? Would you care to join us?' It was a manoeuvre designed to separate them from her parents and Aurelia was glad for it.

What a delight it was to see the market though a child's eyes. They stopped at every toymaker's booth, while Alex gave serious consideration to a wooden ship with real linen sails and a colourful kite. There was a wooden Noah's Ark set complete with pairs of animals, hand-painted porcelain dolls from Venice and wooden marionettes in elaborate gay costumes.

They stopped to buy a cone of roasted chestnuts to share among them all and Julien teased her. 'I think you might be as mesmerised as Alex.' He eyed her now much fuller basket. 'And you've got the basket to prove it. Can you carry it for a while?' He passed it off to her and reached down for his nephew, swinging him up on to his shoulders. 'Are you ready for some games, Alex?' He winked at Aurelia while Alex cheered. 'You ladies have had your shopping, now the gentlemen must have their games.'

There were games for all ages: a ring-toss and a ball-in-the-basket toss for the children, darts, archery, knife throwing and a more aggressive knock-'em-down wooden bottle ball-throw for the adults. They clapped when Alex won a prize at the ring toss. They laughed when Julien and Tristan had a high-spirited match of dart throwing against Reverend Thompson and Mr Scofield from the bank which ended in a tie.

Aurelia found herself with a teary eye she had to turn around to wipe away when Julien presented baby Violet with the rag doll he won at the archery butts, the little girl gurgling with happiness as her uncle tucked the dolly into her arms. It was only because she'd never had a day like this, Aurelia told herself.

Reverend Thompson and Mr Scofield stayed with their group after darts and they drifted towards the game booth sponsored by the church's ladies auxiliary. Mrs Phelps was thrilled to see them as she waved them over to where three or four couples lingered in front of the mistletoe arch, laughing.

'It's a bit scandalous,' the Reverend said with a grin, 'but my wife assures me it's for a good cause. All of our takings today will go to the parish welfare fund. There's more and more folks on the rolls every year.' He exchanged a commiserating look with Julien, whom Aurelia was certain knew to a penny just how much was needed to support those who couldn't fully support themselves.

'What is it?' Aurelia tried to guess the scandalous undertaking. This had not been in her committee's purvey.

'We call it mistletoe madness,' Mrs Phelps boasted proudly. 'Gentlemen *or* ladies can pay to kiss whomever they want,' she ended with a giggle.

'I've got sixpence to kiss Miss Addy Brightman!' a young man slapped his money down at the booth, hoots and cries going up as the girl in question blushed coyly. This was followed by other couples committing their pennies for a kiss, but Mrs Phelps and Mrs Thompson, the Reverend's wife, kept glancing in her direction, clearly expecting something.

Tristan fished in his pocket and pulled out a coin. 'A guinea to kiss my lovely wife.' He made a grand show of it, sweeping Elanora into his arms beneath the mistletoe arch and kissing her full on the mouth. Then, to the crowd's delight, she kissed him back, murmuring, 'That's two kisses, Tristan. You owe the ladies auxiliary another guinea.'

Mrs Phelps crowed at their good fortune. Guineas went further than sixpence in the collection box. Caught up in the euphoria of the moment, Mrs Phelps boldly turned to Julien. 'Are you to be outdone by your brother?'

For a moment Julien seemed to hesitate, casting about for a suitable excuse. Mortification pulsed through Aurelia. What would people think if he didn't want to kiss her? It was only a ruse, but her pride couldn't handle the trampling. 'I'll match Captain Lennox's guinea,' she spoke up loudly. 'One guinea to kiss his brother.' The ladies in the crowd laughed and clapped their delight. Why not, Aurelia thought, extracting the coin from her funds. She was going to spend the money on Christmas baskets anyway. It was all going to the same cause.

Her eyes clashed with Julien's, sharp blue sapphires colliding against the hard onyx of his dark gaze. Then she was wrapping her arms about his neck, drawing him to her, her mouth taking his, all the while praying that he would help her put on a show, that he would kiss her back, even if it wasn't real.

Come on, Julien, dammit all, kiss me.

Then she felt it, the press of his hand in her hair, the opening of his mouth against hers, coaxing and sweet. She melted into him with relief. He might be angry with her later, but he was not going to leave her in this alone. She had acted rashly, but all that mattered was that Julien had come to her rescue. His rescue, though, had left her a bit breathless and maybe even him, too, although she didn't think he'd admit it.

Chapter Eleven

'Whatever possessed you to do that?' Julien's lips were still burning from the kiss, his body still humming with the echoes of it, his mind buzzing with all the things he'd say to her once he could get her alone and now, at last he had done that, although it had taken a Herculean effort. There'd been Tristan's family to see off after the mistletoe arch. The children were tired after a day at the fair. There'd been her parents and his to see off as well, her father claiming sore feet. Now, finally, he had Aurelia alone beneath the bare branches of the oak in the churchyard.

'Don't be angry about the kiss, Julien,' she cajoled, flashing him a little smile as Tristan's coach disappeared into the gathering dusk. He knew that smile from days past. It was a dangerous smile, for all its sweetness. 'It was nothing, just a sop to my pride.' It might have started that way, although it hadn't ended quite like that. Sops to pride didn't leave one breathless and wanting another. He'd seen the look in her eyes, and he'd felt the rise of his own hunger.

She gave a toss of her head, playing it light, trying to convince him and perhaps herself that the kiss meant nothing, that they hadn't unlocked Pandora's box. 'How would I ever face the Christmas basket committee again if they thought you didn't want to kiss me?'

'It was impetuous,' he countered, a scold in his voice. Someone had to take this breach of etiquette seriously. And yet he knew why she'd done it. *He* had hesitated and that would draw questions and speculations. It had embarrassed her, made her feel unwanted, something she was, perhaps, too used to feeling given what he'd seen of her parents. He was coming to learn that being wanted was the chink in her armour, the thing she craved and been denied—*seven Seasons with nothing to show*, the refrain came again.

'It was the only thing to do.' She gave a delicate shrug.

'It was illogical, using a kiss to cover up not kissing. It was backward, ironic logic at best.' Because she couldn't have anyone thinking he didn't want her, not even himself. But wanting her led to all sorts of problems, problems he couldn't solve by throwing money at them. *That* was the chink in *his* armour.

'Well, no more impetuous kisses, Aurelia. It's not what we agreed on.' He didn't think he'd survive any more. That one kiss had tempted him to remember too much, feel too much, want too much. The best he could do was secure her financial future until she could claim her inheritance and he'd done that for her by giving her father the ill-advised loan.

Her blue eyes glinted with mischief. 'What about planned kisses? Are those off limits, too?' She was teasing him now, making him laugh at himself and his strictness.

'We would never plan kisses, we know better. Kisses are private, hence, not part of what the ruse requires.' It was a reminder they both needed to hear. 'Now, we have the fair to ourselves.' Julien offered his arm, wanting to be away from the tree and conversations of kisses. 'What would you like to do?'

The mischief in her blue eyes remained undaunted. *As usual*, came the thought, but he quickly squelched it. He could not start thinking of her in terms where the past ran into the present. She was not his, perhaps had never been his. She had betrayed his love once. It had all been a game to her. 'I want to try the knock-'em-down ball-throw.'

'Really? I think it might be more challenging than you anticipate.' He tried to dissuade her as they walked. 'The wooden bottles are weighted with sand to make them harder to tip over.'

'Like you, Julien?' She smiled up at him, bold and careless. 'Sometimes I think *you* are weighted with sand and harder to tip over, too, although not impossible. I think I will try anyway.'

To tip him over or the bottles? Julien wondered, wishing his blood didn't heat at the prospect of her trying to win him over, which was not likely to happen because he couldn't allow it. 'I think the difference is that *I* am not a game,' he offered the warning in gruff tones. Neither was love itself a game.

They reached the bottle throw and she put down her coins, refusing to let him pay. 'You think it's folly,' she scolded. 'Julien Lennox doesn't make poor investments.' She hefted the first ball and eyed the pyramid of five bottles. 'I may have to play a couple of times to figure out the best strategy.'

She shot him a glance. 'Do I knock out the middle, take the top of the pyramid with it, and then gradually work away at the base one by one, or do I gamble it all on sweeping the base away and all else will follow?' she mused out loud, absently running her tongue across her teeth, and Julien had the unbidden thought that this might be how she strategised about men—eroding away their resistance to her charms as she was doing to him now whether it was purposeful or not. Did she come at a gentleman full force, or cut his legs out from under them? He'd experienced both and knew that few men could stand against either.

The bottles were proving more resilient than men, though. She managed to get two of the five bottles knocked off, but the other three remained steadfastly in place, perhaps giving a man hope, Julien thought. 'Stack them again,' she told the vendor, putting down a coin. She varied her throw, trying to work the pyramid from the bottom, but to no avail. She tried again, and again, this time throwing harder, the next time throwing at a single bottle. The fifth time, Julien intervened.

'Perhaps we should try another game,' he suggested delicately, only to be met with a burning blue stare.

'No, I want to win at this one. I want that prize,' she said stubbornly. She nodded towards a pile of cheap rag dolls garbed in colourful, eye-catching dresses with white aprons and braided yarn hair, much like the doll Julien had won earlier for Violet.

Julien leaned close to whisper privately, 'The doll

isn't worth as much as you're going to end up spending. I'll buy you one at the emporium, probably even a better quality one.' It was absolutely the wrong thing to say.

She gave a vehement shake of her head. 'I want to *win* it. I want to do it myself.' She put down another coin and Julien thought she was like her father in that regard, blindly stubborn to reality. She would not thank him for the insight, though, so he wisely kept the thought to himself.

He let her try again and fail again. By now, even the vendor was starting to feel sorry for her. The vendor flashed him a manly look that said, *Why won't you do something?* But what was he to do? The vendor thought he should step in and win for her. But they were too far gone for that bit of chivalry now. Stubbornness had set in and it would only make things worse if he managed to do in one attempt what she'd spent several trying to make happen. *That* would make her mad.

Julien stepped to her side once more. 'Will you allow me to give some advice?' he said quietly. 'See the three on the bottom? Aim for the one in the middle. Throw as hard as you can with everything you've got. If you throw hard enough, all of them will fall.'

'Are you sure?' She eyed him grimly like a general discussing battle plans. The simple game had taken on grand proportions.

Julien put down his coins with an emphatic slap on the counter. 'I am *that* sure.' It was also a neat strategy for being able to pay for the game. She had to be running out of coins along with her pride. He would save her both if he could and worry about his motives for caring later.

She tossed him a smile. 'Bottom centre, right.' And then she threw and missed, the ball bouncing short and rolling harmlessly away. She took a deep breath and concentrated, throwing her second ball which reached the target, but not with enough force to do damage. It took all of Julien's willpower not to offer more coaching advice full of the obvious: throw harder next time. She threw her third ball, hard and true, and the wood bottles clattered to the floor.

'I did it!' She threw up her hands in victory and gave a most decidedly unladylike whoop. 'I did it, Julien! Did you see it? I threw at the bottom centre, just like you said, and it worked.' Then she was in his arms, her arms about his neck, hugging him and laughing, and he was acutely aware of hugging her back, his arms about her waist, perhaps even lifting her toes from the ground and swinging her around, her laughter infectious as he gave a laugh of his own. They might have just won Waterloo for all the excitement coursing through them in the moment.

Later, perhaps, he'd think how ridiculous, how excessive the celebration was, but right now, it felt right to hold her, it felt good to laugh with her as if he hadn't a care in the world, as if he could trust how it felt to be with her. And for a moment he didn't question it.

'Which doll would you like, Miss?' the vendor asked after a while, breaking into their celebration.

'The one in red and green, the Christmas doll,' Aurelia chose, breathless in her excitement. She hugged the prize close, her eyes sparkling like gems in a crown. 'I've never won anything before,' she confided to Julien. 'I'll call her Christina, Chrissy for short.'

'And she'll live in the pocket of my greatcoat tonight.' Julien chuckled. 'I see where this is going.' Her basket had gone home with the carriages. She had no way to carry the doll.

'Yes, perhaps she'll need your pocket later,' she admitted. 'When we're dancing. I have nowhere to put her.'

'We're dancing, are we?' The euphoria of the gaming booth was still running strong in his blood. Suddenly, anything felt possible tonight. Julien would like to say that was the magic of fairs, but he knew better: it was the magic of her. He'd always felt that way with her. When they were together, anything was possible, until it hadn't been. Like the fair with its pasteboard and lights, it was an illusion only. But tonight, he was enjoying living in the illusion.

'Come stand right here.' Julien positioned them in a spot on the green where one could view the whole fair, she standing in front of him, her head barely reaching his chin. People were starting to gather on the perimeter, coming out of the shops on the High Street. 'It's dark now, the fair will turn on its lights,' he explained at her ear, breathing in the rose and amber scent of her—part-winter, part-spring, all parts comfort and woman. 'There will be carollers after the lights come on.'

She leaned against his chest, inviting his arms to wrap around her as many other couples were doing near them. It was an invitation he took as Squire Elliott, a bluff, heavyset country man, took the stage and made a folksy speech about the fair and about Hemsford Village's Christmas spirit. 'Next week,' Squire Elliott went on, 'Hemsford will have its first tree lighting. We'll be erecting a tall fir right here...' he gestured to a space on the square '...and lighting it in honour of Her Majesty's own Christmas Tree tradition, for all to see. There will be complementary cider and gingerbread provided by Manning's Bakery and the Red Rose Inn, for which we can thank, Viscount Lavenham.'

There was applause and Julien gave a brief wave of acknowledgement, but he wished the Squire had asked him before revealing that last piece of information. He didn't need everyone to know he'd funded the event. Recognition wasn't why he'd done it.

'Oh, we must come next week, too. I can hardly wait to see that.' Aurelia tilted her head to look up at him, her eyes shining. 'How good of you, Julien, to do something for the whole community.' Oh, God, that look was intoxicating. A man could drown in that adulation if he wasn't careful and Julien was not being careful, not with the memory of the mistletoe arch on his lips, the feel of her in his arms, the exhilaration of her joy coursing through his veins. 'Tell me we'll come,' she insisted.

We'll come.

What a dangerous elixir those words were. As if they were a real couple. 'Of course I'll bring you,' he promised recklessly, already imagining himself on the dais with her beside him in her red cloak looking like Christmas itself, her gold hair gleaming, her smile beaming at him. He laughed at himself. He'd not known he was so vain. Or that he was so hungry for companionship, for something that was real.

This is not real, do not make that mistake.

But the warning of his mind was soft. The scold

hardly registered against the joy of the moment, of watching the fair light up, of hearing Aurelia's gasp of delight at the coloured lights, of listening to the carollers singing familiar songs from the little stage. This was what he'd come home for, for Christmas, for hope, for renewal. One could not throw money at joy.

It was hard to say who felt joy the most in the evening that followed. Him or her? After the carollers, the music began and she took him by the hand, dragging him to the dance floor for country dance after country dance until they were exhausted. They shared a tankard of cider, her cloak and his greatcoat long since discarded with Chrissy safely tucked inside, their bodies warm from the dancing despite the December cold.

People came by and shook his hand as they drank, telling him how much they loved the new additions to the fair this year and how much they were looking forward to the tree lighting next week. 'We won't have a tree of our own, of course, our place is too small,' Manning, the baker, said, his arm about his wife. 'But we can all share in the town tree. That will be something.'

'That's the point.' Julien shook Manning's hand with a smile. 'The Queen's tradition can be for all of us, not just a select few.'

Manning smiled. 'And good for business, no doubt. More people will come to Hemsford to see the tree. I've laid in extra flour for baking. We can't keep the gingerbread biscuits on the shelves.'

'I am glad to hear it,' Julien said honestly. 'Sell enough gingerbread, Manning, and you might be able to expand to a shop in London soon. I'd love to get your cakes and biscuits into the right hands.' He clapped the man on the shoulder. 'Let me know if you want to talk business after Christmas before I go back to town. I'd like to help you get started.'

This was the sort of the investment he preferred to make, helping a man realise his dream, instead of propping up greedy men like Holme. But Holme would have his uses, too. Manning had to have access to men like Holme to sell his product, or more specifically, people like Holme's wife. He would be the bridge to that connection.

They finished the tankard and Julien looked about. The crowd was thinning. 'What else would you like to do tonight?' he asked Aurelia. There might be time for another game or another dance, although the music had slowed and the couples were dancing close. He wasn't sure his nerves could handle it.

She gave him a slow smile. 'I want to go home. Before they turn off the lights. I don't want to be here when it goes dark.'

His thoughts exactly. He helped her into her cloak and they walked back through the street to the church and the gig, arm and arm, her head resting against his shoulder. They were in no hurry. He helped the boy on duty hitch the horse, who'd been allowed to graze and wander about in a roped-off area during the day, and they set out into the starry night, Aurelia's Christmas doll sitting on her lap.

Chapter Twelve

'Why does that doll mean so much?' Julien chuckled. He asked in part from curiosity, in part to distract himself from the nearness of her and the heightened vulnerability of his senses which seemed to be attuned to everything from the jingle of the horse harness to the rose-amber scent of her soap, to the warmth of her body tucked beside him on the bench. A body he'd spent too much of the day thinking about, too much of the day resisting after that kiss at the mistletoe arch had left him alive and aching in a way he'd not felt for years and not with any other. Only her.

'Because I won her. She's mine. I *did* this,' Aurelia declared with a winsome smile that did nothing to soothe the ache she raised in him. She looped her arm through his and leaned against him with an easiness that was oblivious to his own discomfort. 'I've never had a day like today, Julien. Not just the fair—I know I told you before that I'd never been allowed to go to one. It was more than that. I got to be part of a group, part of a family. I loved seeing everything through Alex's eyes.'

He had, too, and a part of himself he'd prefer to ignore warmed to the realisation that this was something they shared. It had made all of his hard work putting the fair together, all the meetings, everything the fair board had endured for months, worth it to see the smile on Alex's face, to see the smiles on all the childrens' faces as they'd walked the aisles.

'I'd not realised you liked children so much.' It was one of the discoveries he'd made during this visit, something he'd not fully understood when he'd known her in London. In those days, she'd been at charity events, it was how he'd met her, but it had seemed then that her interest was more in the event itself than who the event benefited.

Perhaps he'd misjudged her, although it would be easier if he hadn't. It didn't necessarily suit him to discover similarities, to reassess who he thought Aurelia Ripley was.

Remember, once you thought you would marry her, knowing less about her than you do now.

Yes, but that was before he'd seen her true colours, felt the sting of her betrayal. He didn't want to reconsider now.

She sighed. He could feel the rise and fall of her body against his arm. 'Children are precious. I don't know why the world seems to treat them as nuisances instead of luxuries.' She played with the doll in her lap.

'At home, at Moorfields, I've been trying to establish a school. Right now we just meet wherever there's space. We have no dedicated place, just a few slates and benches. In the summer, we meet beneath trees and, in the winter, we meet sometimes in the church.' She gave a shrug perhaps to minimise her efforts. 'It's nothing grand, not like your projects. The children come when they can.'

She'd started a school. How amazing. Yet it was one more thing he'd not known or guessed about her. For the sake of his own sanity, he ought to ignore the remark and let it pass. He didn't need one more thing to draw him to her, force him to reconsider his previous assessments. But in good conscience, he could not dismiss the disclosure.

What she was doing was important and she was doing it on her own. He didn't think for a moment her father supported the work. She needed, *deserved*, encouragement. It was becoming clear her family provided her very little of that. 'You're wrong, Aurelia. It's a start. That's the most important thing of all, to simply begin. It was how I started. I didn't begin by building a whole orphanage.'

She cocked her head, looking up at him with those blue eyes a man would willingly drown in. 'How did you start, Julien? I confess to never having wondered. I suppose I thought of you as having sprung full grown into the world like Athena from Zeus's head.'

That gave him pause as she reached for his gloved hand and held it, her touch sending a jolt of awareness through him despite the leather between them.

'I think that's a mistake we can all make,' Julien said quietly. Hadn't he made the same mistake about her? When he'd first known her, before the betrayal, she'd been a debutante, lovely, perfect, a polished diamond. In those early days he'd been overwhelmed by her. He'd not thought about the obvious—that diamonds are formed over time.

It had taken this visit to start to see that. Aurelia Ripley had layers that he was just beginning to peel back. Although that peeling came at his own risk. Between the halcyon days of what he'd once thought of as their courtship and now, there was the not insignificant issue of her betrayal. When the question had been put to her, she'd not wanted him as much as he'd wanted her.

'Tell me, Julien. What was the first thing you did in regard to your philanthropy?' she murmured, and it struck him that here, beneath the Sussex stars, with seven years of hurt between them and no hope of a future, this might be the first truly personal conversation they'd ever had.

'I got on to boards. I applied the same principle I applied to my investing. A man never invests alone, the risk is too great. It should always be a joint venture so that the risk is shared, distributed across many. I could not build an orphanage on my own, but I could align myself with men whom, together, we could build an orphanage,' he explained. He talked for a while about those early projects before looking down at her. 'Are you a good listener or have I put you to sleep?'

She brought her head up. 'I'm a good listener, thank you very much.' She laughed before adding, 'You could never put me to sleep. You're interesting. But I suppose that's not what I was really asking. What I want to know is why did you take an interest in children in the first place? Not every man does. There are lots of charities you could have chosen if it was simply to make a name for yourself.'

Julien gave a self-deprecating laugh. 'I got myself into

some trouble. I was out late one night in town, walking between Mayfair and Piccadilly and I was pickpocketed. It was a novice mistake of mine to be out alone but I thought I didn't have far to go and I'd wanted to walk. Tristan was away in the army, so I was on my own. A girl approached me, she was maybe nine and she was crying, or so I thought. While I was busy helping her, her accomplice picked my pocket. I ran them down once I realised what happened and I did catch them. But I hadn't the heart to turn them in. That wasn't going to fix anything. It was only going to be revenge and that didn't sit well with me.

'Why should nine-year-olds be on the streets? Why should they already be committed to a life of crime with no hope for escape? These questions meant more to me. I bought them a meal at a tavern and I took them back to the town house. I gave them jobs in the kitchen and running errands. They're still with me. John is a footman now. Ellie is a cook's assistant and makes the best bread in Mayfair. But that didn't solve the problem. I couldn't hire every pickpocket in London. The system had to change.'

'And so you've begun to change it.' She gave a contented sigh at the happy ending.

'One step at a time, like your school in Moorfields. Keep at it, Aurelia. It will make a difference.' He would see to it. Perhaps there was a way he could induce her father to offer support as part of the estate restructuring.

They'd reached the drive at Brentham Woods and she squeezed his hand. 'Stop the gig,' she instructed softly. 'I'm not ready for the night to be over.' She shifted on the bench seat and turned to face him. Julien felt his pulse quicken in anticipation, excitement. What did the minx have planned now? Such a reaction alarmed him. He knew too well how intoxicating she was, how her mere presence could work on a man without even trying.

Did she mean to do it, to charm him? Or was this part of the ruse? Or perhaps she was simply being herself? After all, there was no one to see, no need to play the game at the moment. 'I had an extraordinary day with an extraordinary man and it had very little to do with the agreement we made. It may have started that way...'

But it had not ended that way. His heart knew what she might have said had she continued. Had it all been about the ruse, they might have come home earlier with the others. Nothing in the ruse had required him to remain with her, to dance with her, to stand by while she threw balls to win a cheap rag doll that meant the earth to her, to swing her about and celebrate that victory with her. None of it had been required, but all of it had been desired.

Her gloved hand stroked his jaw and he caught her wrist, caution exerting its last defence. 'Aurelia, we said no more kisses.'

'We said no more *impetuous* kisses. We decided nothing about planned kisses and I've been planning this one for quite some time today.' She leaned in and feathered his lips with hers. His body rocketed to attention as she whispered against his mouth, 'Truth be told, Julien, I think you have been, too.' And damn it if she wasn't right.

He let her be right, let his choice be ruled by his body,

let his mouth take the kiss from her, deepening it as his hand sank into the thick coil of hair at her nape where the winter bonnet exposed it. He tasted the sweet cider and the spice of ginger on her tongue, a lovely, apt metaphor for the woman in his arms, who tempted him to taste and to take, and to travel a path his common sense forbade him.

'Aurelia, this is madness.' The hoarseness of his voice surprised him, undermined him. Who would believe him if his body didn't believe him? If it betrayed him at every turn?

She sat back, her eyes filled with disappointment. 'Is a little wildness not allowed? Not even for old time's sake? You kissed me once in the Graftons' garden in the rose bower. We rather more than kissed there, actually. Do you remember?'

It was a dangerous memory. He'd been sure of her then or he would not have allowed them to pursue the heat between them, just as he was *not* sure of her now. On the grounds of that unsurety, he needed to resist this heat for both of them. This interlude did not suit their ruse. Memory of the Graftons' garden was no less dangerous now, his body craving her touch as she'd touched him then, his hands aching to stroke her as he had then. 'You are burning me alive, Aurelia.' The admission was a scold, a warning.

She was not put off. 'The universe burns, Julien. The sun burns, the stars burn, why shouldn't we burn?'

'Perhaps it's best then that we burn alone,' he said gruffly, abruptly picking up the reins. He clucked to the horse and just like that, the magic of the evening was behind them, the perfect day over.

* * *

She was playing with fire and it was she who was going to get burned. Aurelia settled on the window seat of her chamber, her white nightgown billowing about her, and looked out into the night, out on to the drive, stretching down the road she and Julien had driven just an hour ago. Her doll sat waiting for her on the bed with its turned-down covers inviting her to sleep, but Aurelia thought sleep would elude her for a while.

She ought to have been exhausted from a long day spent out of doors full of activity. She ought to go to sleep with a head full of happy remembrances: mind pictures of little Alex's laughter, the thrill of the fair games, the delicious foods, the fun of strolling the booths and purchasing gifts. Instead, what dominated her thoughts were not those mental pictures, but other pictures: images of Julien, tall and commanding in his greatcoat, striding through the fairgrounds, stopping to talk with the townsfolk, to shake hands and listen; Julien's dark eyes lighting up as he talked about expanding the bakery with Jonas Manning; Julien helping his nephew win a prize at the ring toss.

Those images stoked sensations, too, like how it *felt* to stroll booths beside this man who'd organised the fair, who'd found a way to combine Hemsford's love of Christmas with the new railroad branch line to bring economic opportunity to his village.

But he'd not been a slave to his own importance, as a lesser man might. Instead, he had made her experience his concern, shopping with her, handing out coins for her purchases without complaint—very unlike her father who begrudged her every penny. Even after the families had departed for home, Julien had made sure she enjoyed the fair, even after she'd set him up at the mistletoe arch.

She sighed and fingered her braid, watching a star. The night had been magical, almost as if they'd been able to step out of time, able to step away from the past and its mistakes when darkness had fallen. These were the remembrances she treasured most from the day. When the ruse hadn't mattered, she'd leaned against the strength of his chest, and his arms had wrapped about her as the lights came on and the carollers sang.

Then they'd danced. She wrapped her arms about herself in a hug. That had been the most magical by far, his hand in hers, his hand at her waist, his smile, his eyes unguarded as they laughed, enjoying the music, the night and each other, their bodies remembering the ease with which they used to dance together, used to touch.

'It made me reckless.' She looked across the room to the doll. 'It made me want more.' She stifled a yawn and made her way to the bed—perhaps sleep would come after all now that she'd let her mind relive the day. She flopped back on the pillows. 'I shouldn't have pushed him. It's just that he's so handsome and so kind, always thinking of others,' she told the doll. 'I've never known a man like him before.'

In truth, she'd not known him half as well seven years ago as she felt she knew him now. That story he'd told her on the way home about the pickpockets had moved her, but it had also informed her. Here was a man who turned difficulties into opportunities. He offered a hand up instead of a hand out. He inspired her.

'I've done it now, Chrissy.' Aurelia pulled up the covers and turned down the light. 'Just when I'm on the brink of winning my freedom, I've gone and fallen for the one man I can't have, the one man who doesn't want me.'

Except that he had wanted her. He burned for her—his own words. Both kisses had supported that. She'd heard the ragged desire in his voice tonight even as he'd warned her, denied her. She knew when Julien Lennox was on the verge of breaking. He'd been there tonight and so had she. The only difference was that he had been able to resist the pull between them and, in the last moments of clarity before sleep claimed her, she knew the heartbreaking answer as to why.

Chapter Thirteen

That night she dreamed of him. Of them in the Graftons' rose arbour, of her memory where hands and mouths and feelings need not be constrained, where he whispered his desire at her ear, laughing at his own romantic nonsense while she clung to his broad shoulders, urging him on…

'You are driving me wild, Aurelia.'

There was an edgy rasp to his voice that exhilarated her, that made her want to push the boundaries of their control.

'No, I think it's you *who are driving* me *senseless.'*

She laughed up at him, leaning back on the bench hidden in the bower and drawing him down with her, the pastel-pink skirts of her gown falling back in invitation.

Julien gave a growl, pressing a kiss against the column of her throat as he followed her down, his body coming over her on the bench, covering her with the delicious breadth of his shoulders, surrounding her with the heat and strength of him, the hard proof of his desire pressing against her through the layers of skirts and petticoats. She reached for him, tracing that long length through his evening trousers.

'Did you doubt me?' Julien laughed. 'The proof is in your hand.'

She looked up at him, locking gazes as she gave an exploratory stroke. 'It's amazing.'

She'd never touched a man like this, never seen a man without so much as his jacket off. But with Julien, she wanted so much more than what protocol and manners allowed.

'Am I too bold?' she whispered up at him, half question, half coy flirtation, watching his chocolate eyes go onyx-dark.

'Never too bold. Only honest. You admit your passion, not like these other girls who simper and feign shock.'

He kissed her, long and lingering, his mouth moving down her body to her neck, to the bare expanse of skin shown off by the delicate pink of her decolletage, his hands pushing her skirts further up until she could feel the cool evening air on her thighs, his mouth moving to the silk-stockinged length of her calves, kissing one and then the other, working his way upwards, her breath catching as she realised his destination.

He kissed her inner thigh and paused, hot, dark eyes looking up at her from his intimate crouch, his hair tousled from their efforts. She would hold that image of him in her mind for ever.

'You must tell me if now I am the one who is too bold.'

Even in the throes of desire, his concern was for her.

She gave a wicked smile. 'Be as bold as you like. After all, you're speaking to my father tomorrow.' She gave her hips an upward undulation to encourage him. 'Don't you dare stop now.'

And he didn't, bringing his tongue to bear at her damp seam, at her wet core, his hands gripping hard at her thighs, her own hands tangled in his hair, desperate for an anchor against the sea of sensations he roused in her until those sensations collided in one resounding cataclysm of euphoria that, for a few seconds, splintered through her like lightning through a tree, shocking, electric and powerful.

He was panting, too, as if the giving of such pleasure had its own satisfaction for him as well. For a long while they laid against each other, draped on the bench, her skirts askew and trailing, and there was a peace such as she'd never known, a peace so serene, she didn't want to leave the bower.

She wanted to lie here for ever with the weight of her lover's head against her body, her hands in his hair. If he wasn't her lover in truth, he soon would be. As soon as she could manage it. She would argue for a short engagement and a special licence.

'I wonder why some women fear the marriage bed,' she murmured, stroking his hair into order. 'I can hardly wait.'

Julien looked up at her, eyes dreamy with contentment, and in those eyes she saw her future. She was the luckiest woman alive to claim this man as her husband.

'Because they are not in love...not like we are.'

It was the last time he would ever looked at her like that...

Aurelia woke slowly, hot and aching as if the dream had been a fantasy come to life. Her body felt the echoes of it, as did her mind, perhaps both wanting to cling to the images, the sensations. To wake meant to give those images and sensations up, to face the reality she'd fallen asleep to last night—that she wanted him like that still, but he would never want her enough, not like that again, and it was her fault.

It wasn't until the maid came in that she noticed how bright out it was. 'My lady, you're awake, that's good. We'll have to hurry. You slept a bit late and there's church to get to.' The maid set down the ewer with warm water for washing and briskly set about gathering what she'd need for dressing. 'Do you have a dress in mind, Milady?'

Church. The second Sunday in advent. Peace Sunday. Was that apropos or simply just ironic given her current circumstance?

'The pink wool will do with the short white mantle of fox fur and Great-Aunt's pearls.' The same great-aunt who'd left her the small trust. Pearls and independence. Perhaps today she needed a reminder of that.

If the pearls were a tangible reminder to herself of what her real goal was—to live independent of a man's support, to make her own choices, to no longer have to work in tandem with her father, to be used by him for his own gains, then perhaps the soft pink wool would serve as a reminder to Julien of another pink gown, of another time when he'd felt differently about her. If she couldn't have peace, he couldn't either. The ghost between them wasn't hers alone. They would have to find a way to exorcise it together.

* * *

'This Sunday we light the second candle, the candle of peace,' Reverend Thompson intoned solemnly as an altar boy lit the first and then the second of the four advent candles. 'I urge everyone to consider the promise of Christ's peace for themselves, and for their community against the tumult of the world.' If only it were that easy. She slid an unobtrusive glance at Julien sitting beside her. Was he thinking of peace as well? His face was inscrutable.

There were no secret glances, none of yesterday's warmth. His eyes had lingered on her when she'd come downstairs—perhaps her pink dress had evoked old memories for him as well. He'd not looked her way since, although he'd gallantly seen the ruse through, escorting her to the carriage and to the pew. But there'd been no words. All of his words and smiles had been for others at church, people who congratulated Julien on the first successful days of the fair, people who were excited for the tree lighting next Saturday.

There were women who'd talked to her as well. What a difference a week had made. She'd come to church last week as a stranger, but this week she felt a part of the group, as if this was the beginning of warm friendships. It was irrational, of course, she'd be leaving at the end of the month. When Christmas was over, this would be over. But still, she'd not had such easy friendships before, thanks to Caro Lennox's and Elanora's efforts.

Most women at Moorfields were intimidated by her being a lady. That had been one of her biggest obstacles in starting her school and recruiting students. But here, it had been surprisingly different. Her father's influence had been mitigated, replaced instead by the warm friendliness of the Lennoxes. For a place she'd been dreading, she was now not nearly so eager to leave. *And the man you'd been dreading seeing?* Well, that was complicated and it took the rest of Reverend Thompson's sermon to figure that out.

He raised old feelings, old passions, old wants that threatened to supersede new wants, and the constant reminder that she managed to numb at Moorfields that such fantasies were out of reach. Unless…unless she tossed caution aside and threw herself on Julien's mercy. It was why she'd worn the dress, after all. She was dressed for a reckoning.

That dress was killing him. She was so damned beautiful in pink, especially that shade, like a rosebud, full of innocence and promise. It was easy to forget such things were a lie when she turned that golden head and those blue eyes his way. A winter fairy she'd been in her short white cape in the frost this morning. His heart, traitor that it was, had constricted with unfortunate longing at the sight of her.

Had she worn it on purpose, remembering how much he liked that shade on her? Or because of the memories it might evoke? She'd mentioned the Grafton arbour last night. Was this her idea of torture? Or revenge for him having stopped their kiss? What did she think such a reminder proved for either of them except that he still roused to her?

It had taken a cold ride up top with the coachman

to get his senses back in order. He'd barely managed to recover himself from last night's episode before this new assault had been launched. Tristan had not helped matters, sending him knowing glances and smiles all through church that said he knew exactly what was up. Worst of all, that he approved. But Tristan had been away, he didn't know all that lay between him and Aurelia. Perhaps his brother would think differently.

He'd survived church, now he just had to survive the ride home. Family supper would be at Brentham Woods today, but it would be supper—not dinner. Tristan and family would drive over later in the evening. It meant he could escape this afternoon. He would take Benjamin and ride out to check his duck boxes. It would give him time alone to get his thoughts in order, to remember what was real and what was play. The two had become mixed in recent days.

He was nearly free. He'd made short work of changing into breeches and boots when he got home and he had his foot in the stirrup, about to swing up on his big bay, when she cut off his escape.

'Trying the old avoidance tactic again, are we?' Aurelia's dark silhouette stood in the stable doorway, dressed for riding in a dark-blue habit, a crop in her hand.

'I need to check the duck boxes,' he answered coolly, nudging his horse forward, making it clear that she was not invited and she was expected to get out of the way.

'And I need to talk to you. We'll ride out together. I'll be tacked up in no time.' She gestured for a groom.

'I mean to go alone, Aurelia,' he said firmly.

'I mean to go with you. If you leave now, I'll simply

follow and run you down.' She gave the crop a whack against her skirts for emphasis. She would do it, too—hound him to the ends of the earth. She was already hounding him in his sleep.

The groom returned with her mare, a saddle over one arm. No, not *her* mare, Julien berated himself. He couldn't think like that, it gave her permanence, a sense of place. Her place was far away in Yorkshire where she couldn't trouble him.

'Thank you, Joseph.' She favoured the head groom with a smile that Julien envied and helped speed the tacking up by slipping on the bridle. She managed the buckles with deft fingers, flashing him a cooler smile than the one she'd given Joseph. 'We don't want to keep the Viscount waiting.' Julien rolled his eyes. Somehow he'd ended up giving her permission to tag along which defeated the entire purpose. Well, he didn't have to happy about it.

Once she was saddled up, Julien kicked his horse into a light trot, making her work for the chance to come alongside him on the trail. He slanted her a look when they were away from the stables. 'What is it that you so desperately need to talk with me about?'

She shot him a look that equalled his in coolness and he felt that they were back where they were a week ago before they'd made their pact: rivals. There was no reason why that should disappoint him. But it did. 'I know why you stopped our kiss last night,' she said with a haughty air as if she were in possession of an important piece of knowledge, some grand secret of the universe.

'What might that be?' He raised a brow to indicate he

held only a mild interest in what she thought, although that was hardly the truth. He cared too much for his own peace of mind to ignore what she thought.

'You are carrying a grudge. Which compels me to ask the only question that matters. Will you ever forgive me for London, Julien?'

He huffed, his breath coming out in puffs. She did not know what she asked. 'You say it as if I should forgive you for reneging on an invitation to the theatre or a forgotten dance on a dance card.' He slid her a sideways look. What was she playing at? What new game was afoot? To forgive her was to lay down his last and best piece of armour against her.

'You were the one who refused me. You threw me away for rather superficial reasons given what we'd shared.' Intimacies he would not have initiated with an innocent he didn't intend to marry for one, their hearts—at least his—for another. 'Perhaps there's another question to be asked. *You* rejected *me*. Why do you care if I forgive you or not?'

She slowed her horse. 'Because you're the only man I've ever loved and I can't stand being in a world where you despise me.'

Julien scoffed. He would not be taken in by such twaddle. Those were easy words to say now when there was apparently something she wanted—something more than what he'd already managed to give her. 'You call that love? You had a funny way of showing it.'

'Well, maybe you would, too, if you were raised in my house. We can't all be Lennoxes living the perfect life. Some of us have to fight and scrape for everything we have.'

'You expect me to believe that Lady Aurelia Ripley lives a deprived life?' Julien gave her a stern look that said he didn't find her charge humorous in the least.

'Yes, I do. You've seen my family. Would you have wanted to be raised in that home? What sort of lessons do you think a child would learn there?' Her chin lifted with determination. 'Perhaps if you knew the whole story you would believe it.'

Julien halted his horse at the edge of the meadow where the duck boxes were. He swung down and picketed the horse. They would go the rest of the way on foot. 'All right, you win. We have time as I conduct my observations. Make me believe it.' And with that, he surrendered to the inevitable. Aurelia Ripley was going to have her say.

Chapter Fourteen

To her credit, she delayed until they were seated on a log some distance from the duck boxes and he'd had a chance to pull out his field glasses. Or maybe not. Perhaps she wasn't waiting. Perhaps something else held her tongue: he'd called her bluff and now she had nothing to say. Julien surveyed the field, noting a few brown heads of wood ducks poking up from the boxes. He reached for his field book and jotted a few notes about the numbers. Still, she remained silent and stoic beside him on the log.

He raised the field glasses again and said drily, 'For a woman who insisted on talking, you've suddenly become quiet.'

She slid him one of her smug looks. 'I am waiting for you to recognise your error.'

'*My* error?' He chuckled at her audacity. 'You manoeuvred into coming with me and then begged for a chance to talk.'

'*Begged* might be too strong of a word,' she countered. 'I asked you a question—why won't you forgive me? I came because we should talk about what really happened seven years ago and why. You see, it's not that I need to talk, but that we need to talk and listen.' She reached for his hand, forcing him to put down the field glasses and face her. 'Don't you think we deserve a second chance?'

He said nothing. This was exactly the conversation he'd hoped to avoid, the very reason why he'd given her a wide berth in London these past years. If they spent enough time together, they'd have to talk about it, eventually. Talking about it meant reliving it. Apparently ten days of enforced proximity was the required amount of time that would cause the rather toxic topic to surface. 'Don't freeze me, Julien,' she admonished at his silence.

'I'm not freezing you, Aurelia. It's just that I don't see how talking about it does any good.' He set her hand aside and raised his field glasses again. It had been a bad idea to let her come. He should have anticipated *this* was what she wanted to discuss. 'The past is finished and gone.' He borrowed from one of Reverend Thompson's favourite lines, ironically for prayers of atonement.

'Everything has become fresh and new?' she concluded for him. She'd heard the line, too. 'But it hasn't, has it? You carry the past, our past, around with you all the time.'

'*Finished* doesn't require it being forgotten.' He set aside the field glasses and jotted another note, pressing too hard on the page. His pencil broke. He nearly swore beneath his breath, but caught himself just in time.

'It's all right, Julien.' She laughed at his restraint. 'You can curse in my presence.' She reached for the field glasses. 'Where did you get these?' She held them up, experimenting with them. 'They're like opera glasses, only bigger and sturdier.' She wrinkled her nose. 'Everything's blurry.'

'I had them sent from Vienna.' He watched her fumble with them for a moment before giving in to the urge to help. 'Here, hold them to your eyes like this.' He rose and knelt behind her as he offered instruction, his hands guiding hers into position. That was a mistake. Even with the barriers of gloves and outerwear, he loved touching her. 'Then, adjust them like this. The bridge is flexible.' He made the motion. 'Is that better?'

'Yes, much better. I can see the ducks and their heads peeping up from the boxes.' There was a natural enthusiasm to her voice, the thrill of success, perhaps. 'Oh, what wonderful things these field glasses are.' She stretched out a hand and laughed. 'It feels like I could touch the ducks and yet we must be several hundred feet away.'

'Any closer and we'd scare them. But the glasses make it possible to do elaborate observations.' He guided her hands to move the field glasses around the meadow, his voice low and quiet at her ear out of necessity for their surroundings, but also because he liked the intimacy, the privacy of it, too much. 'Do you see it, at the other end of the meadow, the deer?'

He heard her breath catch as she breathed, 'Yes, he's magnificent.' Then in the next moment, she turned into him, her face alive with worry, one hand clutching his coat. 'Julien, you won't hunt him will you? You won't kill him? You said you didn't hunt ducks for sport.' There was hope in her eyes that that moratorium extended to deer.

Her worry startled him, so intent and genuine it was. Out of a reflex to comfort, he covered her hand with his. 'No, of course not, not unless the deer population has run amok in Brentham Woods.' He gave a chuckle. Part of good land stewardship was living in harmony with all who shared the land: farmers, gentlemen and the animals. 'I do ride out occasionally and take tallies of the animals so we can keep track of the herds. But to be honest, when there is a surplus of deer, hunting does fill the village larders with a needed meat source and ensure that people eat through the winter.'

'It's just that he's so majestic.' She smiled and blushed, perhaps belatedly embarrassed by her outburst. He should have released her, should have gone back to sitting on his section of the log. He should not have said the first thing that came to his mind. But he did.

'Of course. You have a good heart, Aurelia, a soft heart.' It was a truth that had always been on display. In London, she'd accompanied her mother to charity meetings although he'd not understood the motives for that as he did now. It was certainly a truth that had been in evidence during her visit here—her efforts in joining the ladies' committees to ensure everyone had a Christmas and in the kindness she showed young Alex and Violet. But it was also a truth that made him vulnerable, that suggested he noticed, that he thought about such things.

Something shifted in her eyes before she cast them downwards, modest at his praise. 'I do, Julien, which is why your forgiveness matters to me.' She lifted her gaze again. 'I hate that I hurt you. I hate that you have avoided me ever since. I hate that when you look at me all the love you once professed for me has entirely disappeared. For someone who doesn't like to hate, that's a lot of hate. I do despise what I became when I hurt you.'

Her earnestness was reflected in her blue eyes, in the tightness of her grip where she held his hand. It was a potent combination that challenged the logic of his mind and the armour, with which he'd protected himself for years. He would not, could not, let those protections be washed away by the sea of her blue eyes in a matter of minutes.

Yet a large part of him wouldn't mind if that happened. Things would be so much easier if the little realities that had seeped through the boundaries of the ruse could be pursued, could be allowed to take root, could be believed. The most important one of all being that he could trust his feelings for her and that he could trust her feelings for him. Once it had been beautiful between them. Did the possibility exist that it could be beautiful again? Did he dare test it?

She gripped his hand more tightly. For his attention or for her courage? Confession was never easy. 'I was scared, Julien. Too scared to do what loving you required. I was weak while you were strong. I could not stand up for myself or stand up *to* my father.' Her eyes darkened with sadness and regret. 'So, I chose hurting you instead. I chose failing you, failing us. I was the lowest of cowards.'

He was silent for a long while. What did he say to that? He supposed it depended on what he thought of it. Did he think it was true? She was looking for absolution. She'd made that plain from the start. She wanted him to forgive her. But she also wanted something more. 'You are seeking empathy. Understanding,' he warned. Forgiveness *and* acceptance. It was a tall ask and yet he might want or need the same.

'Can you give me that? Do I need to beg, Julien? To ask you to put yourself in the position of an eighteen-year-old girl who'd never been beyond Moorfields until that year? A girl who'd been groomed by her parents to make an advantageous match upon pain of familial disappointment? Everything had been so carefully calculated—the early arrival that November in London to "practise" upon society at Christmas fairs and charity balls.'

He'd met her at the Duchess of Cowden's November charity ball. She'd been fresh and exuberant, laughing, full of life. Uncomplicated. Or so he'd thought. 'Then, to take the winter among the full-time politicians who never leave the city so that I'd make no mistake come spring.' She furrowed her brow, pleading with him for understanding. 'The pressure was immense. I was to be one of the Season's Diamonds, to make an extraordinary match.'

Bankers' sons with aspirations were not extraordinary matches for daughters of earls. 'I had known you only seven months when you proposed.'

Julien gave a dismissive snort. 'People marry after having known one another for less time. The Season itself is only twelve weeks. Seven months is a lifetime by comparison. You say you want understanding, but I want some, too. I laid my heart at your feet. We had an understanding based on what I thought were real, deep and enduring feelings. You loved me when it was easy but not when it was hard, not when it required sacrifice. That showed your true colours.'

Flames fired in her eyes. 'You were asking me to

choose between a man I'd known seven months and my family.' She let go of his hand and stepped back from him. 'Listen to how that sounds, Julien. Would you have given up your family for me?' She made a wild, wide gesture with her arm. 'Of course, you'd never have to make such a decision. Your family is perfect. But I did have to make that decision. I had nothing but my family. I'd not received my great-aunt's trust, nothing to support me if I lost them.'

'You had me,' Julien interrupted, his own old anger heating him.

'I didn't know about all of this, about Brentham Woods, about your family, about Hemsford.'

'That's why it's called a leap of faith, Aurelia,' he snapped with equal intensity. 'When two people love each other they step into the unknown together with trust that they will see each other through.' He paused before adding, 'Of course, I didn't have the title then. That seemed to matter a great deal, although you didn't bother to mention it in seven months of courting.'

'It mattered to my father, not to me,' she corrected. 'He said no daughter of his would marry a commoner.'

'Yes, I know. He told me that as well,' Julien said acerbically. 'I told him it wasn't his decision to make, that it was yours. I was that sure of you. I've never been so wrong in my life.'

'Is that what hurts? That I refused you or that you were wrong? The great Julien Lennox, who never made a financial misstep, who never guessed wrong on the Exchange, was wrong about a woman.'

Good heavens, the woman didn't fight fair. 'Yes, I felt

like a fool. But what hurt the most was that you didn't trust me,' Julien said quietly. 'It's what still hurts when I look at you, when I think about our ruse and how it makes me feel. I can't trust those feelings because now *I* can't trust *you*.'

He stuffed the field glasses into their leather case. It was time to head back. Tristan and family would be arriving shortly. 'We've aired our feelings. I hope you got what you came for,' he said shortly, turning his back to her as he headed to the horses picketed in the little copse.

'I damn well didn't get what I wanted!' she called after him, her voice loud with anger and rife with frustration. She was beside him in five strides, running to catch up to him, grabbing his arm and yanking him to a standstill. 'I came for you, Julien. I came out here for *you*, to fight for *you*!' Her arms were about his neck, and her mouth pressed to his, forceful, full of hunger and his own hunger answered, roughly, completely.

This, *this* was what she craved, to be devoured by him, to break him out of his defences and protections, to feel him against her, alive and throbbing with real and overwhelming emotion: hunger, anger, want and need, and the truth that despite what he thought he knew of her, despite the hurt in the past, he still hoped. For what he still hoped didn't matter in the moment. It mattered only that hope flickered there. That she still had a chance to right the wrongs.

A sob caught in her throat, tears wet her cheeks, chilly in the late-afternoon cold. His thumbs were at her cheeks, stroking away the wetness and she let the words spill out, searching his dark eyes. 'My father demanded I refuse you. I told him I wouldn't, that I wanted to marry you.' She'd mounted a rebellion, but it hadn't lasted long. 'But I had nothing to defend my position with, no leverage, no threat that would cause him to waver, and he had everything. He said I'd never see my mother again. He wouldn't allow his wife to associate with commoners.'

She felt her lip tremble as the horror of the threats came back to her. 'He said he'd disown me, that I'd be dead to him, that he'd shoot Elspeth since she might as well be dead, too, if her rider was dead. Julien, I was afraid to stand up to him because others would suffer. I had to choose who suffered.'

Julien's eyes went impossibly dark. 'It wasn't really a choice. To choose between two impossible situations?' His voice was a low growl, the anger coursing through him was alive and pulsing, but it was not anger directed at her. 'And the bastard wields those cards often and still.' Julien let out a harsh breath and she felt a type of comfort in the shield of his anger. For once, someone was on her side, for once, she had a champion.

'Tell me you at least understand why I did it? No one was going to die for me. I could not have lived with that. I could not have loved you, or committed to a marriage without being burdened by inescapable guilt knowing what the cost of that love had been.' This had been the rock of logic upon which she'd made her decision. She could not have lived with herself knowing others had suffered for her happiness. The dead could not be brought back to life.

Julien lifted her hand to his lips, kissing her gloved knuckles with slow tenderness between careful words. 'Sacrifice. Selflessness. These are not the acts of a coward. You were wrong about that earlier.' His dark brows furrowed. 'All these years, I've been hurting, but you have been hurting as well. I blamed you for my hurt. I condemned your motives for refusing me. I was committed to seeing you in the worst possible light because you stood in your father's shadow and everyone knows apples don't fall far from the tree. Now I am the one seeking forgiveness.'

She shook her head. 'You mustn't be hard on yourself. How could you have known? There was evidence a-plenty to support your position.'

'You were brave.'

'My bravery hurt you.'

'I let my hurt be more important than your need. All this time I have left you to fight that monster alone.'

This was more than she'd expected. She'd not come out here seeking his penitence, only his understanding. For once, she was overwhelmed, out of words. What was there to say and yet there was so much perhaps *to* say. Perhaps he was overwhelmed, too. It was a long while before they moved, before they spoke, impervious to all else around them except each other.

'Julien,' she whispered at last, a flake fluttering from the darkening sky. 'It's snowing.' He turned his dark eyes skywards, a smile curving on his lips. 'Quick, Julien, make a snowflake wish.' She closed her eyes and sent a wish heavenwards. 'What did you wish for?' she asked when she opened them.

Julien tucked her arm through his as they sought the horses, his voice full of regret. 'I wished that years ago you'd come to me and we could have solved the problem together instead of letting someone else's threats throw it all away for us.' He gave a rueful smile. 'What did you wish for?'

'I wished things could be different between us now, that we might have a second chance.'

They reached the horses and he helped her mount, fussing overlong with the stirrup of her side-saddle. 'Do you think wishes come true, Aurelia?'

She cocked her head and looked down at him with a smile. ''Tis the season for it.'

As they rode the trail home to Brentham Woods, side by side, sneaking careful glances at each other, she thought that perhaps today the candle of peace did burn a little brighter within her, after all, right alongside the candle of hope. Never mind that having peace was not the same as having a solution or knowing what came next. For the moment, peace and hope were enough. All else could follow.

Chapter Fifteen

'I do not know what comes next. I can solve the man's money problems, but I can't solve *him*. Short of duelling, at least. The man's an evil bastard.' Anger hummed in Julien anew as he recounted his afternoon to Tristan.

They were alone at last, after a long Sunday supper that seemed to go on for ages, after playing with Alex and after hours of watching Aurelia with his family. He had minded none of these, begrudged his family not one minute of his time, but each moment with her, each glance in her direction had indeed added to the complexity of his problem—his *new* problem—Aurelia's wish: a second chance. He wanted desperately to sort through his thoughts with his brother, his best friend.

'I can't say I am surprised. You've been distracted all night.' Tristan swirled the brandy in the snifter, a little smile teasing at his mouth. 'I would say my brother has fallen in love at last, but I don't think that's quite the truth, despite what you led me to believe when I was courting Elanora and seeking your advice. You told me you'd never been in love. But I think that's not true. You've fallen before and for her.'

For a moment the revelation stunned Julien. How had

Tristan known? Then he rolled his eyes and laughed. 'Father told you? That man is a gossip.'

Tristan sat back in his chair, stretching his legs out and resting his heels before the fire. 'Why didn't you tell me yourself?'

'It was in the past, it was embarrassing. She refused me outright, made me believe everything we'd shared was a game, a sham to her while I'd been wearing my heart on my sleeve. It's nothing a man brags about. At the time, I didn't think it was love in retrospect, just infatuated, misguided feelings, considering how it ended. But now I know differently and it's more confusing than ever.'

'Do you, though? Know differently? You believe her?' Tristan asked, the query catching Julien by surprise.

'Why, yes,' Julien said slowly, not understanding the import of that until the words were required of him that he had indeed decided to believe her, that he had accepted what she'd shared at the duck boxes as truth. He shifted in his seat to watch Tristan's face. 'Don't you? I thought you liked her.' All those nudging glances Tristan had been throwing at him at church today certainly suggested as much.

'I do like her, at least I like the person I met here. She's delightful with the children, she gets on with Elanora splendidly. She's fit right in with the town ladies and joined their committees, thrown herself into Christmas work whole-heartedly. She's pretty.' Tristan paused his litany of Aurelia's traits long enough to take a swallow. 'There wasn't a young man in church today who could take his eyes off that pink dress and golden curls.

Does it bother you how seamlessly she fits in? How easy it is to imagine her as a future sister-in-law or permanent member of the Sunday supper table?' Tristan sighed. 'I do like her, but I like you more. I don't want you hurt again. When we're in the throes of love we can't think. When that was me, you thought for me. You helped clear the way. Now, I will do the same for you.'

Tristan's scepticism surprised him. Tristan was always positive, always looked for the best in everyone and in every situation. He shot his brother a long look, his brother's questions taking the sharp, euphoric edge off his own elation. 'Why do you think she'd lie this time? What would she gain?' In his mind there was no reason for it. In fact, it was an about-face on the freedom she'd contracted the ruse with him to protect.

Tristan gave a shrug. 'She's here because she is her father's tool, as she has always been.' Julien's fist clenched at his brother's choice of words. Tristan gave a friendly laugh. 'I can see you don't like my framing, but that's my job. To help you see beyond what you want to see.'

'What do I want to see, Tristan?' Julien sighed, feeling suddenly weary from the mental gymnastics he'd been doing all day, his mind turning endless cartwheels as he tried to sort through the revelations and realities.

'You want her love to be real. You want to trust her. You want to claim the life you once imagined you'd have with her. It's not so very hard to know.' Tristan set his glass aside and leaned forward.

'You want a family, a home of your own. You're hungry for it. I see it in your eyes when you play with Alex, when you hold Violet. They are wonderful things to want,

Brother. They have changed my life, cured my wanderlust. But only because of the woman I have beside me. The happiness you want will not follow if you cannot trust her or if she insists on remaining tied to her family. If she's to be believed, they're the root of her problems. Marriage won't solve that. But it may intensify it.'

Julien nodded. He'd thought of that. Before, he'd not known the depths of the Earl's treachery, or his avarice, only that he was a man with a certain conceit as many aristocrats were. But now, Holme was even less appealing as a father-in-law.

He could imagine scenarios where Aurelia was caught between the two of them just as she had been before. As before, there would be no good choice for her, or even *a* choice at all. As his wife, she would be obliged to choose him. 'No, marriage exacerbates certain problems, not solves them.' He gave a brief smile. 'But I am not sure we're there yet. Marriage seems a bit of a jump from merely exploring the possibilities of a second chance.'

Tristan gave him a sharp look. 'What else is there but marriage? What is the point of a second chance if not to get back to where you once left things, which was on the way to the altar?'

'I'm just saying we don't have to run there. We can walk. Perhaps last time we were too quick.' Indeed, he felt he'd learned more about her in the last ten days than he had in the months he courted her in London.

Assuming the face she'd showed him here at Brentham Woods was real.

Tristan finished his drink and rose. 'I promised Father I'd check the foot on that new gelding he's brought in before we left and it's getting late. The children will be tired.' He grinned. 'Nothing like a cranky toddler in an enclosed coach.' But Julien knew his brother wouldn't trade it for the world and he envied him, even the crying child.

Julien raised his glass in salute. 'Thank you for the advice and the caution, I do appreciate it. Would you mind if I said goodbye here? I want to sit a while longer with my thoughts.'

'I'll make your excuses, Brother.' Tristan smiled and clapped him on the shoulder in understanding. 'Enjoy your reprieve.'

Her father had been pleased with yesterday's outing, understanding it in a far different light than how Aurelia had intended it. But since it had resulted in a reprieve from his nightly visits and harangues as to why the Viscount had not proposed, she'd not bothered to argue his assumptions. She'd enjoyed the quiet of her room, the time for reflection and the time to savour the day, the dinner.

She smiled to herself as she dressed for going into town for the Monday committee meeting. She was coming to enjoy those Sunday dinners. She'd held Violet on her lap, giving Elanora a chance to eat with both hands, and she'd not missed the subtle looks that had passed between her mother and Julien's, the stories in those glances, those hopes. Perhaps both mothers' hopes were honest and heartfelt, matching the hopes she carried in her own heart. She was certain Caro Lennox's were. It was harder to tell with her own mother, who walked such a thin line between her daughter and her husband that her own wants had long since been lost.

Hopes was a generous word for it. Daydreams more like it. Aurelia chided herself for such foolishness as she rifled through her wardrobe, looking for her green winter bonnet. It would be better to focus her thoughts on today's committee meeting. They were going to finalise the Christmas baskets. She had her stack of embroidered handkerchiefs packed and ready to go. Elanora was discussing the pantomime today as well. It was going to be a busy meeting. She was looking forward to it.

Perhaps she'd coax a lunch at the Red Rose Inn from Julien afterwards if he wasn't too busy with arrangements for the tree lighting at the end of the week. She was already planning what she'd wear: the green-velvet ensemble. She'd thought to save it for Christmas Eve, but she'd just have to wear it twice. It seemed perfect for the upcoming occasion.

More daydreams. She couldn't think any further than the moment because she had no answers. What did happen after Christmas? What did a second chance look like? Lead to? Kisses and another farewell? More than kisses? Perhaps that was for her to decide, to show Julien she trusted him, that she was ready for this relationship this time, that she would choose him. For what? For now? For ever? Those considerations came with complications.

Would he want her for ever? Did she dare claim him for ever, knowing that her family was her greatest liability? Did she dare to claim his love should it be offered and shackle him not just to her, but by association to her father? But surely the loan arrangement already associated him with her father. However, that was a legal agreement which could be completed or terminated. Marriage not so much.

She settled her green bonnet on her head as her mother entered without knocking and in her usual state of half-excitement and half-anxiety, always on the brink of anticipating something going wrong. 'Are you ready? The Viscount has just pulled up with the gig.' Her mother adjusted the bow of her bonnet. 'There, I think it's more fetching off to the side. You look like a picture of the season in your green and gold.' She was wearing the Christmas tartan again.

'The Viscount is taken with you,' she said softly. 'He couldn't keep his eyes off you at supper last night. His thoughts were clear watching you with his niece.' She leaned near. 'Your father thought it a stroke of genius to offer to take the babe. For me, I thought it was kind. And I am sure, for the Viscount, it was a peek into the future. He has a title now, he must be thinking about the succession, an heir. He's thirty-eight. It's high time he settled down.'

Never mind, Aurelia thought, he could have settled down at thirty-one if she could have managed it. That particular idea was tinged with sadness. What a waste of time. Seven years suddenly seemed an eternity.

'Do you think we might have a Christmas Eve proposal?' her mother asked softly, but Aurelia knew she wasn't asking for herself.

'Father has sent you to spy,' she scolded. 'He knows I won't give him an answer, although my answer would be the same as it was before. I did not come here to snare a proposal from Julien Lennox. I said only that I would charm him to help Father get the loan.'

Her mother fussed with the folds of her mantle, although it didn't need adjusting. 'But this seems quite apart from that, as if you and the Viscount have found your footing with each other again. You once held him in high esteem and he once wanted to marry you. Is it so hard to believe he might entertain those thoughts again?'

'We've changed. We're different people now. Perhaps we no longer suit as we once might have.' Or suit even better, came the errant, rather unhelpful thought. Knowing Julien had changed her, empowered her to take on her own work in the years that had passed. As a result, they had far more in common now than they'd had in the beginning. There was something more to build their marriage on than passion.

'Still, should things evolve and he proposes, his suit would not go amiss this time.' Her mother smiled and stepped back, having delivered what Aurelia had no doubt was her father's latest dictate, not her mother's own thoughts on the matter.

She stared at her mother, looking deep into her eyes, searching for some sign that *she* was still in there somewhere, that she wasn't entirely lost. She loved her mother and pitied her, that this was what her life had come to: a messenger between her headstrong, self-centred husband and her stubborn daughter. If her mother was lost, perhaps that was Aurelia's fault, too.

Aurelia took her mother's hand. 'If I were to marry, Mother, would you come live with us?' Perhaps if she could get her away. Not a divorce, of course, her father would never allow it and the legalities were too time consuming and costly. But she could fabricate excuses to need her mother, especially if she lived far from Moorfields. She'd need help setting up house. With luck, she'd need help navigating a first pregnancy and then help with the new baby. Her mother would like being an active, involved grandmother. Out here in the country there would be no one to see or judge like in London. Her father might even discover he liked the arrangement.

The offer seemed to shock her mother. 'Well, I don't know. Newlyweds need time on their own,' she prevaricated.

Aurelia squeezed her mother's hand. 'Just think about it. I don't even have a proposal yet.' Perhaps there was no sense in getting any hopes up over hypotheticals. Did she want to marry? It would mean the end of the freedom she'd spent the last five years imagining for herself. That was not a dream set idly aside, yet it paled in comparison to the dream of Julien, of life in Hemsford Village.

Downstairs, Julien was waiting patiently. When they tooled the gig down the drive and out on to the road leading to the village, she gave him a swift peck on the cheek.

'What was that for?' he asked, startled.

'That's because we don't have to pretend any more.' She gave a smug smile as the enormity of that settled on her. They didn't have to pretend to like each other, because they did. Perhaps they'd never stopped the liking. Perhaps it had just been buried beneath the weight of the roles the world made them play. 'And because I want to persuade you to take me to lunch at the Red Rose after the ladies' meeting.' She'd not realised how light she felt, the weight that had been lifted after yesterday. Did he feel the same? Or had their conversation added to his heaviness?

He made an exaggerated show of considering it and she thought perhaps the former was true. 'Here's my counter. Yes, to lunch. No to the Red Rose Inn. I have a better idea. I'll ask Peter at the Red Rose to pack a picnic hamper and we'll eat out at my estate, the one the architect discussed last week. He'll be here tomorrow and I haven't made one single decision that he asked for.'

She offered her own mock consideration. 'And ice skating?' It had snowed last night. Although the snow hadn't stuck to the ground, it was still cold. Cold enough to sustain a frozen pond.

'We can ice skate, if the ice is thick enough,' he acceded.

'Then I accept.' She paused. 'But I think it best we keep it to ourselves. I haven't told my father about the estate. If he were to know you were setting up house, or that you were consulting me... Well, you know how it would look to him.'

'Just between us, then.' Julien gave a thin smile she couldn't quite decipher, although she could guess. She answered him by snuggling close on the bench seat. For real. A Rubicon of sorts had been crossed. The ruse was over. Reality had begun. She'd got her wish. The rest was up to them to make the most of it however they could for as long as they could.

Chapter Sixteen

Julien's new home was beautiful, or at least it would be once the work was done. There was ivy to clear from the walls and the outer façade could use a good wash to do away with the moss and weather. But even in the grey light of winter, the potential of the house was evident to Aurelia. 'It's enormous and so stately. Whatever will you do with a house this size?' Aurelia looked about, trying to take it all in from the drive. As she dismounted, a young groom ran up to take the horses. She tossed Julien a smile. 'You already have staff on hand? I'm impressed.'

'I think it's necessary given the amount of workers that will be out here shortly. I will be spending more time here as that work progresses, and I imagine Mr Floyd will need a few overnight stays to oversee his work as well on occasion.'

Aurelia nodded. That was likely all true, but she saw beyond that. He simply failed to mention it also gave a few more people work before Christmas, which was also true *and* kind-hearted of him.

'One of the things I liked about this house was that it was built using local resources, not just local labour.' Julien gestured to the Georgian façade and the rounded vestibule that stood over the front entrance. 'The sandstone was all quarried at West Hoathly and inside you'll see that the wood is local timber as well. The house itself isn't terribly old as houses go,' he explained, ushering her under the roof of the vestibule as the drops of hard rain began to fall, part-rain, part-sleet. That would put paid to the idea of ice-skating later.

'It was built after the wars by one of Robert Adam's protégés. The owner was an eccentric who wanted to embrace the Sussex lifestyle, which is a nice way of saying he wanted to observe smuggling, race thoroughbreds and hobnob with the Duke of Richmond at Goodwood. When it turned out the smuggling trade died out after the war and the Duke of Richmond wasn't interested in his horses, the man moved back to London, deciding town life was more his style.

"That was ten years ago. Since then, the previous owner has let the property at varying times, enjoying the rental income it provides. But I finally convinced him to sell this autumn.' The last was said with undisguised pride. As well it should be. Homes like this were rare finds outside of family inheritances.

Julien held the carved oak door for her to step inside to the marbled hall with its soaring ceiling and sweeping staircase off to the right side. 'Sussex marble?' she queried, more to tease him than anything else. The marble at Moorfields had been imported from Italy as had the marble at Holme House in London.

'Yes, Sussex marble from Petworth.' Julien's answer surprised her. 'And English oak for the banister.' Which his new housekeeper apparently kept polished and glistening religiously.

'It's beautiful, Julien,' she said, her words picking up an echo.

'And empty. That's where you come in. I have rooms that need filling. The place did come with some furnishings,' he told her, leading the way to the public drawing room on the ground floor. 'Although the owner took much of it back to London with him. Mother has kindly loaned me spare dish sets and things like that until I have the place settled to my satisfaction.' He opened the drawing room's double doors and Aurelia could only stare at what was inside, well aware that Julien's gaze was on her, watching for a response. What did one say to *this*?

Julien spoke first, perhaps to give her permission to say the obvious. 'As you might be surmising, the things left behind are useful but not to my taste.' That was a gracious way of putting it.

'Not to *anyone's* taste that I know of,' Aurelia responded without thinking and then covered her mouth. 'That was mean. I should not have said that out loud.'

'It's truthful. It's hideous, isn't it?' Julien sighed,

'Well, thank goodness the owner didn't leave too much behind then,' she said, and they laughed together. It felt good to laugh with him, *not* because it reminded her of old times, but because it was the beginning of new times. This was who they were now, in the present: two people enjoying each other's company.

They walked the perimeter of the room, Julien taking notes as she dictated. 'I think the problem with the room is that every piece is talking at once; the turquoise-tangerine sofa, the bright orange tall-backed chairs, the patterned vases on the mantel, the multi-coloured stripe and floral wallpaper—all of them want to be noticed when all we really need is one bright item to build the room around if you wanted to keep a few pieces.'

Julien shook his head. 'I don't want to keep any of it, at least not for this room. I am not sure bright, exciting colours are an accurate extension of me. You said earlier that you thought the exterior of the home was stately. That's the message I would like to send with the interior public rooms as well.'

'Warm creams then, or cool blues and greys,' she suggested, studying him anew. 'Creams might be more versatile in that they can be both masculine and feminine in tone and I think they're more economical because they can adapt. Should you wish to change the furniture or carpets, many things complement cream wallpaper.' She was already imagining the walls covered in cream on cream, with peach-and-cream or blue-and-cream Thomas Whitty rugs on the floor, the spacious room accommodating three different clusters of seating, a pianoforte on one wall for musical evenings, Sussex landscapes on the walls evoking scenes of the seasons and Julien's love of the region.

'You've a good eye,' Julien complimented, listening intently to her ideas. 'When you talk, I can see the room come alive. Here's where Floyd wants to put the sliding doors between the drawing room and the dining room.'

They went from room to room, Aurelia designing with her words, Julien writing furiously as the house came to life between them. She saw the office where

Floyd had suggested the French doors. 'The doors are a good choice.' She smiled over her shoulder at Julien.

'There isn't much to do to this room.' She looked around, taking in an oak desk of a suitable size for a businessman like Julien who would want to work from home and the empty built-in oak bookcases. 'You'll have to fill those, of course,' she teased. 'Perhaps I would add a new carpet, something in deep greens to complement the outdoors beyond.'

She trailed her fingertips over the surface of the desk. 'I can see you here, Julien, working. Planning.' She gave a sigh. Perhaps this would be the space she'd imagine him in when all this was over and she was gone. 'You can look out over your gardens. You'll have a lovely view. I envy you a room like this. How wonderful it must be to have a private place that is yours alone.'

'Surely you must have a similar place at Moorfields.' Julien came to her, slipping his fingers between hers. Did he know how much she loved it when he was the initiating contact? Did he guess she took it as a sign of togetherness, of the walls between them coming down? Did he mean it that way?

She shook her head. 'I have my chamber, but my parents make a habit of disturbing me regularly there without warning if there's something they need. In a big house like Moorfields there's always a servant nearby. Being unobtrusive, of course. But between unobtrusive servants and intrusive parents one is seldom alone.' She smiled. 'It was one of the first things I noticed at Brentham Woods. Your mother has her own space where she keeps her own books, apart from the library. She has a space for her own things, a place where she conducts her own work. It gives her a voice. I like the idea so much I think I might try to set a space up similar to it for my mother.' Perhaps having her own space would translate into having her own thoughts, to rediscovering herself.

Julien gave a little smile, his dark eyes soft. 'You care for your mother very much.'

'She is all I have, really, but that doesn't mean it's not complicated. She is always standing between my father and I, trying to make peace, which means I can't always count on her to take my side.' In fact, almost never. She was always begging for a compromise on Aurelia's part. 'It's not like your family, Julien. When I see you and your brother together, I wonder what it would have been like to have a sibling, to have a best friend like you have in Tristan.'

'It must have been hard growing up alone.' Julien raised her hand to his lips, kissing her finger tips. Perhaps it was the nearness of him, the heat of his body, the softness of his eyes, the hope that they might have a second chance, that encouraged her. She whispered her secret without thought.

'I had a brother once.' She had shared space with him for nine months in the womb—nine months with their little souls suspended together between heaven and earth. Julien's gaze fixed on her and she knew she'd surprised him.

Of all the things she could have told him here in the quiet of the office, he'd not expected that. He'd done his research thoroughly on Holme as part of the loan process and that had never featured in his paperwork. 'I'd never heard, I never knew,' he offered solemnly, his mind rife with questions, but his heart was attuned to the sadness, the thoughtfulness in her eyes.

'No one knows outside of Moorfields,' she said quietly. 'We were twins. He died shortly after birth. He was born second. He was smaller, not as strong. He couldn't get enough air.' It was a factual recitation of events she'd no doubt been told over the years by her parents, perhaps in answer to a young girl's question about her own origin story, or perhaps in answer to the question 'when am I getting a baby brother or sister?' Alex had asked Tristan and Elanora that question not long before Violet had come into being. Julien remembered laughing about it when Tristan told him Alex had given him his 'marching orders,' he'd best get busy on a sibling. But this was not a funny story. Who would tell a child such a tragic tale?

The answer came too swift. Someone who wanted leverage, pitiful as it was, over a child. Julien would not put it past the Earl. Of course, the story could be told delicately, but he did not think that would have been case with Holme. 'I am torn about the wisdom of telling a child such a thing,' Julien confessed.

Anger mixed with the sadness in her eyes and she looked down, focused on her hand where it worried the carved edge of the desk. 'My father felt I should know it was my fault. My fault his heir died. My fault that my mother could not have more children. One must understand their place, one must understand all that has been sacrificed for them so that one can give obedience in equal measure to that sacrifice.' Despite the anger, her voice trembled. 'I have tried, I really have, to pay that debt, to close that gap, to make up for it.'

He had never seen her so vulnerable. Julien's own anger surged in response, his desire to protect, to care for those who were in need erupting. He wrapped her in his arms and held her close as if his body could be a shield against years of hurt and guilt, against the emotion he knew she was feeling.

'It's not your fault. It could never have been your fault, not your debt to pay,' he whispered against the softness of her hair. Surely her mother had told her that at the least. But if she had, it had carried no weight, overridden by a father who felt the universe had played a cruel trick on him, giving him a son and then taking the son away.

She was crying softly against his coat, her head buried in his shoulder, arms wrapped about him, her hands clutching his back. He saw much now that he hadn't seen before, understood more. Dear Lord, what it must have been like growing up in Holme's home, carrying the knowledge that you had lived while your sibling had died and knowing that your father blamed you personally for something that had been a matter of luck and fate.

What it must be like still to know that the debt for the sin could never be erased and having payment constantly exacted often and arbitrarily. Julien could imagine how those conversations went. He could hear in his head Holme's loud, angry voice threatening his daughter all those years ago.

Refuse Lennox or I will forbid you your mother and I will kill your horse as you killed my son, so that you will know what it is like to go on without the thing you want most.

Of course she'd turned down his proposal under those conditions. Of course she'd dared not run away, although she might have wanted to. Marriage to him would be a physical escape, but with a price too high and a mental anguish she'd never outrun. Such a marriage would have been doomed before it ever began. Her father had known that. He'd known from the beginning he'd win either way. His real victories were about exerting control, about manipulating people, starting with his wife and his daughter and rippling out from there. The man was a bastard of the highest order.

'Your father must be stopped,' Julien whispered. 'He can't go around terrorising people, intimidating them like that.' With something as simple as words. Julien might control the man's money for now, but he couldn't control what came out of the man's mouth, at least not directly.

She lifted her head and laughed up at him, her tears drying on her cheeks. 'Oh, Julien, you're always looking to save the world.'

'Right now, I'd settle for just saving you.' He meant it. The sight of her tears and the reason for them undid him, it did things to his heart, to his head, that made it hard to think, hard to breathe. He wanted to fix this for her. Nothing else mattered.

She gave a tiny shake of her head. 'I don't want to be pitied, Julien.'

He kissed the top of her head. 'I wouldn't call it pity, Aurelia,' he said quietly, although he dare not name what he would call it out loud. 'I *can* feed you though,' he cajoled, trying to change the tenor of the moment. 'We've done good work, redecorating the rooms. I think we deserve some sustenance.' With that, he took her hand in his and led her out of the room to the kitchen where the groom had left the hamper on the worktable. 'Do you mind eating here?' he asked, unpacking the luncheon.

'Not at all.' To prove it, she moved about the space, pulling out dishes and utensils, setting places for them at one end of the worktable. 'I've been down baking in your mother's kitchen. Did you know? Nothing to rival Manning's, of course, but breads and biscuits that will keep for the Christmas baskets.'

Julien chuckled. 'I'd heard a rumour. Smelled a rumour, more like it.' He sat and watched her finish. The sight of her puttering around the kitchen pleased him, settled him, not that a viscount's wife would spend much time working in a kitchen. Maybe his would. He allowed himself the luxury of that thought. He'd allowed himself the luxury of several similar thoughts today.

Walking through the rooms of his house, listening to her bring them to life, had been a potent elixir to swallow and one he hadn't choked on. It was easy to picture her here, hosting evenings in the cream-on-cream papered drawing room, entertaining from the piano she'd place against the inner wall. She fit effortlessly into the spaces she'd brought to life today and effortlessly into the pictures in his mind as if she was meant to be there, as if perhaps she'd never left, but had simply lingered on the edges.

'Doesn't that worry you, that she fits in so well with

your life? As if she's curated herself to be exactly what you need, what you want?' Tristan's concern nudged itself into the peace of his thoughts.

No. It didn't worry him, not after today. She could absolutely not be in league with her father after what she'd revealed to him in the office. For the first time, he fully understood what she'd been up against, even after yesterday's disclosures at the duck boxes. For the first time, he understood the dark, driving depths of her life. And yet, her own innate kindness and concern for others had miraculously survived the emotional brutality of life with the Earl of Holme.

'There, I think we're ready.' She set down two mugs to complete their place settings and favoured him with a smile. 'Why don't you slice the bread and tell me what in the world are you going to do with all of this space? We haven't even gone upstairs yet.' There was a reason for that, Julien thought. If it had been easy to see Aurelia as his hostess downstairs, it would be all too easy to see her as another type of partner upstairs: his lover, his wife, the mother of their children, the person with whom his dream of family came true. But it was too much too soon for him to fully embrace the possibility of that. Did they dare run ahead that fast for fear they might trip? Again. He did not think he could bear it if that was the case.

Julien cut into the loaf of dark country bread, putting thick slices on their plates, and then carved into the quarter of ham sent by the Red Rose Inn for sandwiches. 'I want this home to be a gathering place for the best minds of Sussex and London, perhaps later for all of

Britain. We're living in an extraordinary time with extraordinary technology: mills, factories, railroads. Life and its tempo is changing and opportunities abound to make that life better for so many if we're willing to be innovative and open.'

He poured cider for them from a stone jug. 'I'd love to have the Duke of Cowden's Prometheus Club join efforts with the Lennox Consolidated Trust on a few investments that could create jobs here at home. I'd like to invite them out, to spend a week riding, hiking, fishing, eating good food, drinking good wine and talking business in congenial, relaxed circumstances.'

They ate and he talked about his idea of creating a retreat, spurred on by the intent in her eyes and the interest in her questions as if she were already a partner in this vision. He talked until the stone jar was empty and there were only crumbs on their plates.

'Shall we go upstairs and see the other rooms?' Aurelia asked as they cleaned up the dishes and wrapped the ham. She made to put the ham in the hamper, but Julien shook his head. He didn't quite trust himself to go upstairs, nor did he trust his feelings. Today had been… overwhelming and he had something to take care of back at Brentham Woods after he consulted Tristan and his father. The Earl of Holme must be dealt with.

'The rain has let up.' Julien nodded to the window. 'We better make haste while the weather permits.' She was notably disappointed. 'But let's leave the ham and the rest of the bread so it will be here for us tomorrow.'

'Tomorrow?' She brightened at that.

'Yes, we'll do the upstairs rooms and then we'll be

back with Mr Floyd the day after.' Julien smiled at her eager response. 'And, of course, we'll need to look at the stables, too, so perhaps the day after that as well. If you have time.'

She laughed and came to him, wrapping her arms about his neck, his body revelling in the easy intimacy even as it put his mind on alert, warning him to be careful, to acknowledge that his own feelings were running high. 'I might be able to squeeze you in between helping with pantomime costumes and Christmas baskets, and helping Elanora with the flowers for Sunday,' she teased.

'I am glad you like it here.' Here being Hemsford, Brentham Woods, his new house. All of it.

'I do like it here, Julien.' She gave a coy whisper, her lashes downcast, sweeping against her cheek before her gaze looked up at him. 'Because you're here. Because these are the spaces you've made, the spaces you've marked with your visions.' She wet her lips. 'Do you think you might kiss me before we go?'

'You would tempt a saint.' Julien gave a wry grin at her suggestion. 'I would like nothing more than to kiss you…' His mind was rife with images of what a future could be if…there were so many ifs. *If* Tristan was wrong, *if* her father could be silenced, *if* all she'd told him was true. 'But I think that if I did, I would not want to stop, Aurelia.' It was a confession and a warning. But it had to be acknowledged. He wanted her and he wanted to believe that she wanted him, too, the way they'd once wanted each other—honestly and completely, with no holds barred.

She nodded solemnly, fixing him with a blue-eyed stare that seemed to him more intimate in that moment than any kiss. 'And I would not want you to.'

Chapter Seventeen

'If I started kissing you, I would not want to stop.'

The words were an aphrodisiac, an absolution to Aurelia in the days that followed. Surely it meant that he'd forgiven her, that he understood what she'd been up against. Surely, it also meant that they were free to move ahead as they saw fit with this second chance they'd carved out for themselves.

He'd not said the words, but Julien Lennox loved her still, wanted her still and she wanted him. For the first time since coming south on her father's ill-conceived venture, she could allow herself some hope that perhaps the future she'd once imagined might honestly be within reach.

'I wouldn't want you to stop.'

She'd meant it with every fibre of her being. She wanted to be with Julien. Perhaps she'd always wanted it. Perhaps her dreams of freedom and independence were simply replacements for what she thought she could no longer have. But now the real temptation lay in thinking she could have both Julien and her freedom. There would be freedom with him, freedom to continue her work and even be encouraged to do it.

With Julien there would be that rare combination of freedom within partnership. What she felt with him, she'd felt with no other and there'd been plenty of others. There'd been seven Seasons of dancing and courting and no one had raised in her the level of emotion that Julien had. She'd burned for no one, had not craved another's kisses, although there'd been a few stolen pecks in lantern-lit gardens as an experiment. She had not hungered for another's touch.

There'd been gentlemen who had made her laugh, who had danced divinely, who had showered her with gifts and attention commensurate to her fortune until that fortune had ceased. Perhaps it was for the best she'd not been emotionally invested in those gentlemen. They'd dwindled exponentially with her family's financial situation.

Marriages were financial and dynastic alliances. Once, she might have settled for such a match, having been raised to expect not much more. But meeting Julien had shown her the possibility of more, that marriage might be based on love as well as practicalities. In short, he'd ruined her for other men, for other marriages. In that ruination, he'd unwittingly sowed the seeds of a new dream—one of freedom and aloneness. If she could not have love, could not have Julien, she would have no one. Now that she knew what was possible, she would not settle. But now, Julien was back, their past resolved, their future uncertain but possible.

Was it, though? Reality nudged, horning in on her joy. There would be a cost if she meant to keep Julien for ever. Could she truly do that to him? Tie him to her family? Or was it best to think of her happiness in the short term. To have Julien for a wondrous Christmas and find the courage to let him go again, to keep him safe as he'd tried so very hard to keep her safe. Perhaps it was best to focus on claiming happiness for the moment.

If this was to be a pursuit of short-term happiness, she was determined to make the best of it. Aurelia rose in the mornings full of energy and purpose. There was so much to do. The Christmas preparations were coming together as the calendar days sped by, Christmas rapidly nearing. And there was so much to look forward to: the tree lighting at the end of this week, the Christmas cantata at the church, the Lennox Christmas ball, the Grisham–Lennox panto at Heartsease, then Christmas Eve and Christmas Day, St Stephen's or Boxing Day, all the twelve days' fun, and Twelfth Night with cakes from Manning's.

She didn't let herself think beyond that. That was weeks away. Who could say what happened then? It was hard to imagine leaving this place that had become like home to her in such a short time. That was the power of relationships, of caring and love. People made the place, people were what caused one to feel they belonged.

Even her beloved Moorfields seemed far away as if it belonged to a different life, despite her efforts to make a difference there, despite her school and the relationships she was so painstakingly cultivating one day at a time. These days she didn't mind being in Hemsford for Christmas. She was looking forward to it actually. Because of Julien. Because she would not let him stop the next time he kissed her.

It had become an implicit understanding between them, underlying their interactions. He had confessed his want and she had thrown down the gauntlet with a confession of her own, daring him to act on that want. His desire would be welcome. She would not turn it away, she would instead feed it with her own.

That tension quivered between them aspic-like when they were together, silently asking the question of 'when?'. It was there when he drove her into Hemsford to work on Christmas preparations, when he picked her up after the ladies' meetings and took her out to the estate where they found reasons to spend every afternoon, walking the halls, mentally decorating and rearranging the rooms, or sitting in the kitchen and eating long lunches, skating on the pond, and always the big four-poster bed of English oak in the master's suite, tempting and taunting them with the question, *When?* And always the answer was: *Not yet.*

Days passed, marked with activity. The tree lighting came and went in all its brilliance, she standing beside Julien on the dais in the town centre dressed in her green velvet. Gaudete Sunday passed, the third Sunday, the Sunday of joy and anticipation which was rather too apropos for her. *She* was full of joy and anticipation and it seemed he was, too, but still, Julien resisted acting, which meant she had to settle for his touches, but none of his kisses.

He went a frustrating step further, announcing that Monday when he dropped her at the ladies' meeting— the last one before the pantomime at Heartsease—that he'd be taking the morning train to London to handle some business, business that he would not specify other than to say there was a chance he might be away overnight.

'If he can't get in to see the archbishop.' Mrs Phelps gave a sly smile while the other ladies nodded.

'Or if Rundell's is out of rings,' Mrs Manning added coyly. Aurelia smiled and laughed with her new friends. She knew they meant well. To them it was clear: she and Julien would marry. To them it was a whirlwind Christmas romance between two well-suited people. They couldn't possibly know the angst behind the scenes, the uncertainty that still simmered beneath the surface of her happiness, the hope that lingered there, too, and the obstacles that remained.

Silent questions plagued her as the ladies sewed the final sequins on the costumes for the pantomime. Was Mrs Phelps right? *Did* Julien mean to propose? Is that why he'd gone to London? To get a special licence and a ring? Was that why he'd resisted the urge to act on their private contract? Was he waiting until he proposed or until they were wed, traditionalist and stickler for propriety that he was? That one night in the Graftons' garden had occurred only because he believed they would wed. Perhaps he believed that again. As did she. But did she dare say yes, knowing what she'd saddle him with—a father who would not hesitate to use him for money. But perhaps Julien had a plan for that?

'*Your father must be handled,*' he'd said the day she'd told him the horrible story about her brother and she had cried against his shoulder. Still, her conscience pricked. Hadn't he done enough for her? He'd given the loan in large part because it protected her dream of freedom and this was how she was going to repay him: by taking away his.

She stabbed her finger with a needle and drew blood in her distraction. She quickly stuck her finger in her mouth and sucked on it. 'Here, let me wrap it or you'll be staining the costumes.' Elanora was beside her with a bit of gauze, winding the bandage about her finger, her voice quiet and soothing. 'Don't let the ladies get to you.' She smiled reassuringly.

'How did you know?' Aurelia glanced at her new friend.

'You just had that look about you.' Elanora gave a knowing shrug. 'I remember the angst that comes with the lead up to a proposal once you sense it might be on the wind. I both wanted and feared Tristan's proposal. Come outside and get some fresh air?'

The outdoor air was welcome and, to her credit, Elanora didn't press her with questions, just sat next to her in the little courtyard at the side of the church. From there, they could watch the Christmas fair in progress, full of week-day visitors.

'I remember growing up, the fair was only three or four booths. It's expanded gradually over the years, but the last four years, it's become extraordinary, thanks to Julien,' Elanora said quietly. 'He's a man with vision. He can take something that is nothing and see its potential. When Tristan was in the military, Julien was just starting out with his investments and Tristan would send whatever funds he could spare home to help Julien build his stake. When Tristan sold his commission and came home for good, Julien had amassed a portfolio worth slightly over ten thousand pounds for him out of Tristan's pocket change, essentially.'

She gave a little laugh. 'It made me wish my family had taken his offer when he'd volunteered to do the same for us. But it was too risky and we couldn't afford to lose any more. We had some other investments turn out poorly. We should have trusted Julien to see us to the other side. I nearly lost Heartsease because we didn't. I would have lost it, in fact, if Tristan hadn't come home when he did.' Aurelia wondered if that disclosure was meant as a parable for her, that she ought to trust Julien's instinct?

Elanora was quiet for a moment, suddenly unsure of what she should say. 'Forgive me for me prying, but I know there is history between you and Julien.' She gave a little laugh. 'Perhaps it's Tristan you should forgive. He's the one who told me and it may be bad form for me to bring it up, but Julien is my brother-in-law, the best of men. I want to see him happy. When my father passed away and then when my brother passed away, Julien and his family were there to help me. I was stubborn. I wanted to do things on my own. I was embarrassed by my family's situation. I'd been left in horrible financial straits. I should have swallowed my pride. Julien would have handled everything. I don't know many men who would have done it for someone they were not obliged to help.'

'I know,' Aurelia said softly. 'That's what worries me. My family hurt him once. I don't want to set him up for that again.'

Elanora looked confused. 'You would refuse him?'

Aurelia shook her head. She knew what she wanted to say to him should he ask again. But did she dare? 'I would spare him the hurt of me saying yes. I do not want to tie him to my family through me. He would come to regret it and me.' She sighed—even disliking her father as she did, she was reluctant to speak poorly of him to Elanora, to shame him and the family with exposition of their finances.

Instead she said, 'You've met my family. My father can be a difficult, prideful man. When people marry, they don't just marry each other. They marry each other's families. I would definitely be getting the better end of that bargain.'

Elanora studied her with thoughtful eyes. 'Julien is very capable. All the Lennox men are. My advice would be to let him make that decision. No doubt he's already decided if he can live with your father or not.' Elanora squeezed her hand. 'As for me, I would be very glad to have you as a sister-in-law and I would miss you very much if that's not how Christmas ends. Don't be hasty. Let Julien and love handle whatever obstacles you imagine.'

It was good advice even if Aurelia felt that leaving things to luck and love hadn't necessarily served her well in the past. It was time to take matters into her own hands, although she'd have to wait until the next day to do it.

Aurelia was waiting for him at the station when the late morning train pulled into Hemsford, loaded with festive day-trippers eager for the fair. She was on the platform, dressed in her green velvet, her green winter bonnet on her head. Aside from the pink dress, this was definitely his favourite outfit. She was beautiful in it, quite possibly because she represented Christmas and all it stood for when she wore it.

He would remember always the way she'd looked the night of the tree lighting, standing to the side of the dais, looking up at him, her eyes aglow with undisguised affection, dressed in her green velvet, like Christmas come to life, the embodiment of peace, joy and love. She looked like that today, her gaze searching the windows of the train cars for a glimpse of him. Did he imagine that? Did he fancy she sought him because *he'd* missed her so desperately while he was gone?

Everything he'd seen in London had reminded him of her. He'd found himself turning to tell her something, to say, *Did you see that?* or to laugh with her, only to discover she wasn't there and to realise over and over again that he wanted her to be there. For everything. For the little things like shopping along Bond Street or the Hemsford High Street, and the big things like turning his new house into the retreat he imagined and the family home he craved.

If the trip up to London had shown him one thing, it was that there was no use denying it. For better or for worse, he was in love with her. He patted his coat pocket in reassurance. He was determined this time that would go differently. She waved, giving an excited hop as she spied him through the window. He smiled and waved back, finding that he could hardly wait to get off the train.

She met him with a smile, her arms flung about his neck, holding him close. He breathed in the sweet scent of her. 'This is the best surprise. I didn't think you'd be here.' He held her too long for propriety's sake.

'We need to go out to the house and I thought it would be quicker if we went straight from here. If you don't mind?' Her eyes sparkled. 'Mr Floyd and the decorator have sent swatches. They arrived yesterday after you left. But we have to make decisions as soon as possible. I have a hamper packed so we can spend the day before anyone knows that you're back. You can tell me about London on the way.'

Something was definitely up. Julien was convinced of it as they drove past the turn to Brentham Woods and on out to the house. Her eyes were bright, her colour high and he'd never found her more alluring. At the house, he was sure of it. He stepped inside the hall to discover the place decorated for Christmas. 'What is this?' He turned about, taking it in: the boughs draping the oak banister, the swag of greenery over the drawing room door.

'I thought we should see how the house looked for Christmas, since it's your favourite time of year. I did it myself yesterday after the ladies' meeting. Elanora helped.' She tugged his hand, dragging him to the drawing-room door. 'Do you like it?'

'I love it.' His voice was husky, betraying the emotion the scene evoked for him, a ghost of Christmas future if he could have his way. The only thing missing was three or four children pelting down the green-boughed staircase on Christmas morning.

Her arms were about his neck again, her face tilted up to his. 'You owe me something,' she flirted, her eyes flicking upwards to the green boughs. 'Mistletoe. I think that means you need to kiss me, Julien.'

He smiled, willing to play along. He loved this about her, her sense of fun, her spontaneity. 'I've been wanting to do that since I stepped off the train,' he murmured taking her lips in a lingering kiss that said, 'I'm home.' He gave her a lazy grin, confused when she became stern.

'You stopped. You promised you wouldn't,' she scolded, her eyes turning a desire-darkened sapphire-blue. 'I expect a gentleman to keep his word.'

His body, already roused, hardened at the implication of her words. 'Aurelia,' he warned, 'this is not play.' His want, his need was very real.

'I'm not playing, Julien. I've had enough of games between us.' She took his hand. 'Come upstairs. I've decorated up there, too.'

'Aurelia Ripley, are you seducing me?'

'Actually, I'm inviting *you* to seduce *me*. Is it working?'

In answer, he swung her up into his arms and carried her upstairs. If it worked any better, they wouldn't even make it that far.

Chapter Eighteen

Her heart was pounding as he carried her to the bed festooned with greenery wrapped around the four posters, a mistletoe ball hanging from the frame. This was what she wanted, this moment with Julien, when it could be just the two of them, all obstacles and interferences set aside. But now that the moment was here, her stomach was a flurry of butterflies.

He set her down, his hands at her waist, his mouth at her lips, his kisses confident and soothing even as they heated her blood, his words reassuring. 'May I play the lady's maid?' He gave her a smile, his fingers working the taffeta bow of her green bonnet and tossing it gently aside.

'You'll have to tell me what you want, Julien.' She was suddenly nervous.

He kissed her softly. 'You know what I want, you have touched me, our bodies are not entirely strangers to one another. Trust your instincts, but, yes, I will be there with you every step of the way.' He cupped her jaw, his palm warm against her cheek. 'Are you sure you want this?'

'Yes.' She moved into him then, kissing him full on the mouth in demonstration of her want. It must be now *before* they talked about the future that couldn't be, especially if he'd gone to London for a special licence, especially if her father chose to make trouble and tried to leverage their marriage to his benefit. And if none of those things were to happen, if Mrs Phelps's intuition was wrong, then she most definitely wanted this with Julien before she had to leave, before she went back to pursuing her dream of personal, lonely freedom. In either case, she would be losing him. 'You have played my maid, now I shall play your valet.'

The kiss had warmed her, stirred her to more action and less thought. The idea of undressing Julien, of revealing him to her eyes, was a heady one that outweighed the nerves of being undressed herself. Her hands worked the knot of his cravat, unwinding the length of cloth from his neck and setting it aside before undoing the polished tortoiseshell buttons of his waistcoat, the buttons of his shirt... 'Goodness...' She gave a breathy, teasing sigh 'You're like an onion with all these layers.'

Julien gave a husky laugh. 'I hope I smell better than an onion, though.'

She reached up on tiptoes to the pulse at his neck and took a deep breath in. 'Most definitely. You smell like citrus and sandalwood, like oranges on Christmas morning.' She smiled, pleased to see his eyes darken with desire at the description. 'Perhaps I am unwrapping you like a Christmas present, instead.'

He drew her close for a kiss. 'I like being a present far better than being an onion,' he murmured against her mouth, sending his shirt to join the pile of clothes accumulating on the floor. 'Now, perhaps it's time I did some unwrapping of my own.' His dark eyes glinted with mischief and want.

'But I'm not done with you,' she protested, a hand sliding between them, the hardness of him against the flat of her hand, a heady reminder of just how she affected him. She was not in this alone. Beneath his gentlemanly exterior, Julien was all hot male.

'You need to catch up,' he whispered against her throat, his hands working the frogs of her fitted green jacket. 'And I don't want to hear about how many layers a man has when I have to contend with all of this female frippery,' he growled playfully. He made delicious but short work of her jacket, of the bodice beneath and the tapes of her skirts, petticoats and all, leaving her in quite 'reduced circumstances' by comparison, his gaze hot on her as he took in his work.

He shook his head. 'No, not done yet. The chemise absolutely must go—shall I do it or shall you?' His tone was low, seductively wicked. This one last piece and she'd be entirely nude and yet she didn't feel exposed in the least. She felt powerful.

'I'll do it.' She matched his tone, her eyes never leaving his, her gaze enrapt by what it saw in his—desire, want, hunger, all for her, all because of her, and it was empowering. She *wanted* to stand before this man naked, wanted the sight of her to please him, wanted his gaze on her and her alone.

She reached for the hem of her chemise and drew it over her head, acutely aware as she'd never been before, of how the movement affected her body, how her breasts were pushed forward by the motion, how she could hear the sharp inhalation of his breath. She tossed the garment aside. 'Do I please you, Julien?' she whispered, surprised by the throaty huskiness of her own voice.

'You know you do.' There was a primal rumble to the words and it emboldened her.

She reached a hand to her hair and began to remove the pins from it, one by slow one, letting each tress tumble down, a silken, wavy length of golden curl. 'And this? Does this please you?'

'I think *please* is too tame a word.' He growled appreciatively as she shook down the last of her tresses. 'Minx. I can't decide if you're Rapunzel from the fairy tales, or Venus rising from the sea.'

'Venus.' She gave a wanton smile. 'I've seen that painting, too. The one by Botticelli.' She licked her lips, her hand dropping to the juncture of her thighs. She was going to be very wicked. 'I used to think she covered herself here out of modesty.'

'But now?' Julien's dark eyes glittered, following her hand down, his voice a dangerous rasp.

'Now, I think she feels the birth of her own arousal, the birth of love, the awakening of her desire.' She stepped towards him, her hand against the smooth plane of his chest, her voice sultry. 'When Venus touches herself she feels the dampness of want between her legs as I feel it now, as I have felt before with you.' She cast her gaze upwards to his face, finding his eyes aglow, his jaw set hard against the onslaught of her touch.

Her hand drifted downwards to take him in her palm, to wrap her fingers about his trousered length as she whispered against his mouth, 'Venus doesn't acknowledge her desire only to herself, she *proclaims* it to the world. Venus says, "No matter that men tell me I should rise above passion, that I should forgo it because passion is sin and nudity is sin, I am woman. I am not afraid of what I feel, of what I think, or of claiming what I want from a man in bed or out.'"

She breathed the seductive revolution, the very thoughts spoken out loud exciting her as much as the man before her. 'Thus, I claim you, Julien Lennox. It is time for those trousers to go.' And she set to work on the fastenings of his trousers, because neither of them was free until they were both free.

His member sprang free and pulsing into her hand the moment his trousers fell away. Julien could not recall a time in his life when words had nearly made him spend on the spot. But he was definitely in danger of doing that now. Aurelia was not just a seductress, but a revolutionary, a woman who had awakened to her own power, her own want, and it was a whole new level of intoxication to be with her. The time for gentleness was gone, replaced by a hungry desire that drove them both.

They fell to the bed together, his member grasped tightly, decadently, in her hand, their mouths seeking each other in a chaotic hunt for satisfaction that only spurred them to further want.

She was perfection in his arms, her hand stroking his phallus as his mouth sought her breast, laving it with the same attentions she lavished on him, his body trembling with pleasure, with anticipation of the completion to come, the joining. But trembling, too, with the responsibility of that joining. He wanted her, he wanted the pleasure of the joining, but he also wanted pleasure *for* her, he wanted her initiation into passion's ranks to be a source of joy and selfishly he wanted the prideful knowledge of knowing he had done this for her.

She gasped and moved against him, her body urging them forward in their passion. He needed no further encouragement; he was more than ready. Then, he was over her, her beautiful face laughing up at him, her eyes dark, her hips pressed to his, her legs open, instinctually inviting. And he accepted, his phallus nosing at her entrance, adding its own slickness to hers, sliding inwards and forward, his body attuned to hers, to each gasp, each arch of her hips as she shifted to accommodate him, to take him and the very thought of it filled him with a primal thrill. He gave a strong, final push, feeling the triumph of arrival, and her eyes went wide, her breath catching with the realisation that he was fully sheathed, fully within.

Her arms were about his neck, pulling him down, her voice a whisper at his ear. 'Oh, Julien, we are one now,' she breathed and Julien chuckled.

'This is not it, there is more.' And he began to move, slowly at first to accustom her, to teach her the rhythm, although she needed little instruction, picking up his tempo with wide-eyed delight in the intimate dance. She wrapped her legs about him, her hands clutching him, nails digging into his back as their pace increased and intensity soared, their bodies caught up in the pleasure together.

He felt sweat bead on his brow as he struggled to

keep himself in check, his body wanting to run rampant in the surf of pleasure cresting towards him. His body was gathering, tightening, racing to meet the waves, his thrusts became faster in repetition, closer together as his need surged. Her hips rose up and pressed hard into his, signalling the rising of her own need, the nearing of her own completion. His hair fell forward into his face, wet with his sweat, his exertions.

His gaze locked on hers, the sight of her exhilarating to him, her hair spilling across his pillow, her entire being swept away in the moment, caught up in the discovery of pleasure. She gave a gasp of disbelief, of wonder, and then they were there together, letting the final wave of pleasure wash over them as they held each other tight.

Good Lord, lovemaking had never rivalled this intensity for him. It had both completed him and left him undone. It was a long while before he let her go, let her shift to lying beside him, her head tucked into the hollow of his shoulder, her body aligned against his side, her fingertip drawing a lazy masterpiece on his torso, her breathing gentle, her own words a soft aphrodisiac even spent as he was. 'Dear God, Julien, that was the best thing I've ever done.' Immediately he felt his body stir beneath the approbation of her praise. His arm tightened about her, possessive. Please God that she never do it again with anyone else.

It was both an unnerving and yet realistic place to have arrived at after the tumultuous pleasure of their love making. Of course she would do this with no other. Of course no other man would behold the naked splendour of her. She was his and he was hers. Yet, that held an enormity of its own. She ran her thumb over the tiny peak of his nipple. 'Am I not supposed to say such things? Is it not ladylike?'

He bent his head to look down at her. 'You may say whatever you like to me, about whatever you like. I am glad it pleased you. First times are not always as pleasant as subsequent times.'

She raised her head with a saucy smile. 'First times. I like that. It implies more times to follow.' She sat up. 'Are you hungry? I am ravenous.'

He groaned, wishing he'd had the foresight to bring food upstairs, but how? He'd been too busy carrying her, too swamped with desire, as he recalled, to have thought much about lunch hampers. He was going to pay for that now. 'Are you going to make me go downstairs and fetch lunch?' He'd never felt less like leaving bed.

She grinned. 'No, the hamper is under the bed. I thought it might come in handy.' She leaned over the side and pulled out the basket.

'I adore you.' He laughed as she hauled the basket to the bed. He shot her a wicked look as she wrapped herself in a sheet and laid out the food on the bed. 'You were pretty sure of yourself, Minx, if you were stashing food beneath the bed.'

She made him a ham sandwich and passed it to him. Their bed picnic was underway. 'I've heard of breakfast in bed, but never lunch.' He took a bite, thinking how delectable she looked, her hair falling loose over her shoulder. 'I like you this way, better than your white nightgown. Voluminous is hardly an apt description of that particular garment,' he teased.

She cocked her head, studying him, her bold gaze making him quite aware that he sat there with only a sheet across his lap for modesty, his torso on full display, and that the sheet didn't quite disguise the rising fascination his member had with lunch. 'I like you this way, too, Julien. Naked and relaxed. Country living agrees with you.' She reached into the basket again and pulled out a bottle. 'There's champagne, if you would open it. And glasses.'

He took the bottle from her and popped the cork, laughing when the foam spilled on to the sheets. 'It's easy to like the country when it comes with bed picnics in the middle of the afternoon.' If he had his way, such picnics might become a regular fixture of his days. He poured them each a glass. 'Cheers.' He clinked his glass against hers, privately toasting to a future of lunches in bed, feeling that his life had finally come full circle. They would need to have that discussion before they left this place, but not yet.

They polished off the ham and bread, and made love again, she laughingly compared his phallus to the bottle of champagne and its foamy eruption and he revelled in it, in her. Their lovemaking took on a playful quality that delighted him. She was bold and coy by turn, leading him a merry chase, one moment the temptress with her daring, the next moment the innocent eager for his instruction.

'Can I be on top some time?' she asked drowsily as the long shadows of afternoon reminded them of the shortness of winter days. He didn't want to get out of bed, didn't want to go back to Brentham Woods. He'd not meant to have this discussion in bed, but rather downstairs, or on a walk through the woods, but he was running out of time for that unless he wanted to delay it and he did not. His honour demanded it.

'You can be on top next time.' He closed his eyes with a sigh, already imagining next time and enjoying the assurance of knowing there *would* be a next time.

'Tomorrow, then?' she said playfully, levering up on one arm to face him.

'If you're not too sore.' He opened one eye, counselling caution. 'Lovemaking can be hard exercise. It uses muscles we don't always engage.' In her case, muscles that had never been used. He reluctantly tossed back the covers and got out of bed in a fluid movement, padding naked to the wash basin, feeling her eyes on him, his body celebrating the attention and the knowledge that the woman he loved was pleased by him. 'See anything you like?' he drawled, wetting a rag for her.

'Why don't you turn around and I'll tell you,' she teased. 'I didn't get to look at you when you undressed. We were in too much of a hurry and you're my first naked man, artwork aside.'

He turned, aware that his member was eager to please her scrutiny, rallying its recently exhausted self to half-mast for the sake of her approval. Her eyes settled on the core of him as he padded back to the bed. 'It's amazing to think something that size fits, well, where it fits,' she said at last. 'You seem rather large, rather thick, Julien. Are all men designed like you?' she asked boldly, taking the rag from him, her eyes coy and innocent while her enquiry was anything but.

'What sort of question is that?' He laughed, gathering his clothes from the floor and turning his back to give her some privacy.

'An honest one, a curious one. Did I embarrass you?' He could hear the sheets rustling behind him.

'I don't go around looking at other men's parts, so I'm not sure I have an honest answer for you. Perhaps I am a bit larger than the usual.' He turned in partial dress, his shirt open and loose, his trousers undone. She'd given him an opening and there was no time like the present— he was, in fact, running out of time. 'You will have to take my word for it though, Aurelia. I don't intend for you to have a chance to compare.'

She stilled, her gaze serious, looking like an angel, her golden hair over her shoulder, the sheet drawn up over her breasts. Julien sat on the edge of the bed. 'You cannot be surprised, Aurelia. I am hardly the sort to take a virgin to bed without the expectation of marriage between us.' He'd made assumptions today; the most important one was that he'd not withdrawn from her body. He'd assumed there was no need. In his world, marriage followed lovemaking *and* he'd assumed they both understood that, agreed to that.

As if to prove his intention, he reached for his greatcoat and withdrew a folded paper from its pocket. He took her hand and simply pressed the paper into it. He did not list the arguments for accepting him, he did not lay out his wealth and worldly goods to be tallied in his favour. Just his affections. This was to be a love match, not an alliance.

It wasn't about money, about position or a title, although he had all three. It was just about them, about two hearts who had found one another amid the chaos and distractions of living. 'Will you marry me, Aurelia?' It was the simplest of proposals and he hoped it would be followed by the simplest and most immediate of answers: yes.

That was not the case.

She lifted her gaze from the paper in her hand, but her gaze gave nothing away, at least not the joy he thought he'd see in them. Julien felt his heart in his throat, the old fear coming to him again that somehow he'd misjudged the situation, that he would be refused. But he was certain there was no rationale for such fear, just the nerves of an anxious bridegroom. 'Julien, what is this?' She held up the paper and he breathed a little easier. He'd only managed to stun her.

'Unfold it and see,' he urged. Most men proposed with jewellery, but in his opinion jewellery did not carry the power of a binding contract. After all they'd been through, he wanted her to know in a very palpable way that he meant to marry her. And he'd wanted an honest answer from her, one that was not influenced by a dazzling diamond ring, although he had that, too, in his pocket for later.

She undid the paper and spread it on her lap, staring at the words as if they didn't make any sense. 'Read it out loud,' he said quietly. His own nerves were straining at their tether. Patience was taking all he had. He'd rather hoped patience wouldn't be necessary, that she'd simply answer the question.

'"The Archbishop of Canterbury has granted exceptional permission for Lady Aurelia May Ripley..."' She looked up, 'You remembered my second name.'

'Of course I did. Keep reading,' he prompted.

'"And Lord Julien Ebenezer Lennox, Viscount Lavenham, to wed at a time and location of their choosing."' Her voice trembled at the last. When she looked up at him, her eyes were glassy. 'Julien, this isn't just a licence to wed, it's a special licence.'

The first tear fell and Julien reached out a thumb to wipe it away, concerned by her reaction. 'Yes, I went all the way to the Doctors' Commons in London yesterday for it. Aurelia, why are you crying? This was not meant to make you sad.'

She smiled through her tears. 'I'm crying because my heart is full. I'm crying because you love me.'

'Of course I love you.' He pulled her to him, relief pulsing through him. She hadn't said yes yet, but she would.

Chapter Nineteen

He *loved* her. Her heart wanted to explode with the knowledge of it. Her eyes wept with the joy of it. 'No one has ever loved me before,' she breathed the awful truth against the comfort of his chest, the safety of his arms. Her parents did not love her. Her mother perhaps had affection for her, but affection didn't also attain the status of love. She'd known the absence of love for years, but not love itself. Now, here was Julien offering her that rare and precious thing.

Julien *loved* her. It was evident in his forgiveness, in his willingness to extend her a second chance at the happiness they'd once thought to have together. Perhaps it hadn't been freedom she'd been seeking all along but *this*. Love. The way it made her feel was extraordinary. He wanted to marry her! She wanted to revel in that, celebrate it with him. Perhaps she could allow it for the moment. But she couldn't claim it, not for ever. It was never meant to be for ever, only for now, and she wanted to hold on to this perfect moment as long as she could.

'You can decide the date.' Julien was rocking her gently. 'We can wed as soon as you like or as late if you'd rather plan something. If it were up to me, it would be sooner rather than later. Will you let me announce our engagement tonight at supper?'

For an instant she let her mind imagine the scene. His family would be present. He would send word to Heartsease and invite Tristan's family for the occasion. She would be beside him, his hand in hers. She would wear the pink dress and her great-aunt's pearls. He would kiss her in front of his family. There would be candles and champagne. Hugs and tears and joy. But she was not destined to travel that path. Her father had ruined it.

She lifted her head—fear, dread, even anger warred in the pit of her stomach, turning the glorious moment dark. He was not allowing her to put off the inevitable. Instead, he was pushing her towards it, forcing her hand. The anger she felt was for him. Why had he asked her today? Why couldn't he have waited so that they could have enjoyed more stolen afternoons like this one without having to make a decision? Without having to talk about the future? The dread was for Julien, too, and for herself. Dread over what she'd have to do to make things right, to protect him. But the fear was for her father.

'Julien,' she said slowly, 'have you spoken to my father?' Dear Lord, she hoped not. But Julien was a stickler for traditions. He'd asked her father's permission the first time. She didn't want her father to know Julien had proposed. Of course, this time, her father would say yes without hesitation. He'd already be trying to use his new son-in-law's money to his advantage. Perhaps he'd even attached financial strings to the granting of his permission.

'No, this is between us.'

Julien's dark eyes held hers and she was reminded of his words years ago. *'There is just us now.'*

'Marriage is between two people, Aurelia. That is all. This is our decision alone.'

She still disagreed with him, even more now than she had the first time he'd made the argument seven years ago. 'A marriage does not exist in isolation, Julien. You know your family will be part of our lives. It stands to reason that my family will be, too, like it or not. Our decision to marry will have consequences.' She scooted away from him. She'd be stronger if he wasn't touching her. She would need all of her courage once he realised where this was going.

'What are you afraid of, Aurelia?' Julien was studying her intently, the special licence lying forgotten on the bed. 'Is this about your father? He has no sway here, not any more. The past is finished and gone, my love. No one will hurt you again as long as I have any ability to prevent it.'

It would be easy to believe that in Julien's love she would be safe. It was what she *wanted* to believe. She allowed herself to bask in that belief for one last moment before she steeled herself for the task before her: protecting Julien by letting him go. And for that, she'd have to convince him she didn't love him enough to marry him. It would break her heart and it would break his. But it was better to break those hearts now than to watch them break gradually, worn away over the years as her father came between them and turned Julien against her with his constant demands.

Julien was silent for a long while. He wetted his lips.

'You haven't said yes yet, Aurelia. Is your father the reason you withhold your consent from me?' There was a terseness to his tone that boded ill.

'You know it is. He'll be there, always, in the background, managing, manipulating, threatening.' The irony was not lost on her that once she'd refused Julien because her father had asked her to. Now, her father would be elated if she said yes. Once, she'd lacked the courage to say yes and now she needed the courage to say no.

'I can manage your father, Aurelia. I am managing him now,' he reminded her sternly and for a moment her argumentation faltered.

What had Elanora said? *'Let Julien handle things.'*

'But despite my assurances, you hesitate. I have to say I did not expect hesitation after this afternoon. I expected you to readily accept, if I'm being entirely honest. I was sure of you, Aurelia.' She'd upset him, taken a beautiful moment and turned it into a defensive one.

'I want to say yes,' she told him solemnly, wanting to mitigate the hurt while still ensuring that she could protect him. 'Inside, I feel all those things—joy, elation, wonder that this man beside me wants to spend his life with me. I am overwhelmed with what that life might be, here in this house. You are everything I ever dreamed of, Julien, and more.' She looked down at her hands. 'When I think of wanting to marry you seven years ago, I can hardly imagine my audacity. I barely knew you. I wonder if that is a tribute to love or the naivety of youth?'

She dared a look up at him, at his handsome face with his dark eyes. 'Now, I feel I know you better than I ever did, seeing you here in your home, with your family, in your community. What I am wondering, Julien, is not if I *want* to say yes, but if I *can* say yes.' Oh, how she wanted to say yes, with him sitting beside her, his shirt open, showing off the smooth, sculpture of his torso, his muscular thighs shown off in tight fitting breeches that had yet to be fastened. There was something erotic about a man in half-dress which hinted at the possibilities of his body, of the pleasure he might be capable offering. There was no 'might' about it. In this case, she was very clear on the pleasure Julien could offer. Her body echoed with it even as she was on the brink of losing him.

'If you *can*? I've told you, your father is being handled.' There was a growl to his voice, his anger was surfacing. Good. Let it come. She would need all their anger to get through this.

'I don't think you understand what life with my father is like. I've tried to tell you. I've shared my story with you,' she said. 'It's one thing to control him on paper. A loan is a legal document. But real life isn't like that. Everything has to be negotiated with him. One is always walking around on tiptoe for fear of springing a trap or being ambushed or having some misstep held against them.'

Julien nodded. 'Aurelia, I love you and I will handle your father, that is all that matters. Will you marry me or not?'

He was going to make her say the words. She could feel her heart break as she summoned the courage. 'I will not drag you into the dysfunction that is my family, Julien. He wants you to marry me, Julien. I've told you as much. I've warned you. That he wants to see us wed ought to scare the living daylights out of you.' Her voice rose with her anger. Why did *she* always have to do the hard things?

Dear God, she was refusing him. Again. Julien rose from the bed, shocked to his core by her response and the reason for it. Anger began to surge. He let it. It was better than the alternative. He wasn't ready to hurt. He was ready to fight. He crossed his arms over his chest. 'You're being stubborn, Aurelia. You are saying no because he wants you to say yes.'

'I *am* being realistic. How can we ever think to find happiness with him looming over our shoulders? Or us looking over our shoulders, waiting for the next crisis?'

'*Will* you be looking? I won't be. Because first, the loan ties his hands. I have appointed stewards to do his job for him and to do it well. Any misstep on his part, any threat towards you, and I will leverage the loan against him and call for immediate repayment. Secondly, I will not be manipulated. He will find out very quickly that he cannot outmanoeuvre me.'

'If anyone is being stubborn it's you. And naive, if I might add.' She rose from the bed and began to dress. 'You refuse to see reality. I will always be your weakest link. He will get to you through me if we're married. I have lived in his shadow long enough to know better than you.'

Julien levelled a glare her direction, his mind whirring, his insides churning. This wasn't only about her father. 'You don't trust me. That's what this is about. You didn't trust me back then and you don't trust me now.

You simply won't leap.' And, oh, God, did the knowledge of that hurt him. Once more, when it came to doing the hard thing, she simply wouldn't do it, wouldn't commit to him. She might love him—*might. C*ome to think of it, had she ever *said* the words? Even so, a man had to wonder if her love was not equal to his.

He swallowed. Hard. It occurred to him that perhaps her father was a shield for a bigger question. 'Do you *want* me to convince you? Is there anything at all that I can say to change your mind? Any proof you will choose to accept?' Because he could not change a mind that didn't want to be changed and the conclusion that led to was positively damning. She didn't want to fight for them, for him.

He began to button his shirt. She had only her shoes to put on and he felt the sand running out of his hourglass. 'You don't trust me. You don't or won't put confidence in me to manage your father. You pretended towards feelings.'

'My feelings are not pretence, Julien. I have told you that on multiple occasions. Should I name them for you?' Her blue eyes flashed.

'Did you ever mean to act on those feelings? What was your end game?' He was feeling used. She'd invited him to play a game with her, a ruse to mitigate her father, but all along for her there'd been a game within a game. She'd been playing with him.

She gave a snort and gestured towards the bed, one shoe dangling from her hand. 'I did act on those feelings, this very afternoon, in fact.'

'To what purpose? Was I just a conquest? An affair?'

In his anger he slammed his hand against the oak poster. 'Were you using me for sex? You condemn your father for manipulation, but you are better at it than he was. A man never sees you coming. You had me believing you cared for me then and you cared for me now. Right up until that pretty speech just a few minutes ago about wanting to say yes, but knowing you couldn't. Perhaps you missed your calling. You should have trod the boards.'

'You're being mean, Julien.' Her eyes were hard, so unlike the misty, glassy gaze she'd turned on him such a short time ago when he'd shown her that special licence. How did such extremes happen to them? One moment on the brink of celebrating and the next on the brink of despair? 'You're hurting and I am sorry for it, sorrier than you'll know.'

She brushed past him and he reached for her arm. He couldn't let her go without knowing. 'Did you ever intend to marry me, this time?'

Their eyes locked. He searched hers for a truth that made sense to him, a truth that he could understand. She shook her head. 'If you're asking if my feelings for you are real, the answer is yes, but, no, I never intended to marry you, although what you offer is potent. I'm sorry, Julien. It's better this way. You want me to trust you, but now I am asking you to trust me.'

His grip on her arm loosened and she gave a dry laugh. 'Trust is so much easier to ask for than to give, isn't it?'

'This isn't trust, Aurelia. This is an impasse. You want it your way and I want it mine.' And they were both too stubborn to relent. 'I am asking you to take a leap of faith into marriage with me and you are asking me to walk away from…' From what? Real love? *Was* this real love? It didn't feel like it at the moment.

'From trouble, Julien. I can only make you unhappy. Thank you for these past weeks and for everything you've done. This must be the end between us. I think it would be best if my father never knew about this.'

Best for her, Julien thought as he let her go. She would not benefit at all if her father knew what she'd turned down. But he nodded anyway. He would do this one last thing for her. He waited until he heard the front door shut before letting loose his rage in a howl that shook the windows and the depths of his soul. Why hadn't he seen it sooner? That the bridge between them was unmendable? What could ever be possible between two people who couldn't trust one another? Aside from love, trust was an essential foundation of any long-term relationship.

She'd broken his trust not once, but twice. Once because she'd been coerced to it, and once because she chose to. That latter hurt the most, not because it was the most recent, but because she had control over it and had chosen to do it anyway. She could have chosen him and she hadn't. How would he ever find his way back from this?

Chapter Twenty

'I thought I might find you here.' Tristan's voice roused him a few hours later from his chair by the fire in the office. 'Your new space is cosy. Were you planning on spending the night?' Tristan moved about the office, turning up the lamps and setting down a hamper of food. 'Mother was worried when you didn't make it for supper.'

'I wasn't hungry.' Julien tracked his brother's movements with a narrowed gaze, resentful of the intrusion. 'If I wanted company, I would have come back.' He let his tone make it clear that he wanted to be left alone. He was in no mood for companionship. His world had fallen apart and he was entitled to at least a few hours of wallowing in the despair and the anger that swamped him. 'If I promise to eat something, will you leave?'

Tristan responded by sitting down in the chair across from him and getting comfortable. 'No, I will not be leaving without you. Whether you eat or not is up to you. Do you want to tell me what happened, or should I guess?'

Julien glared at him.

'All right then, I'll start.' Tristan crossed one leg over a knee, ignoring the stare. 'You and Aurelia came out here for an afternoon, perhaps for a tryst and it turned into a lovers' quarrel. Now, it's your turn. *You* tell *me* the details of that quarrel and we'll solve the problem together.' His brother was trying to cajole him into reason.

'Tristan, really, I don't need this.' Julien pushed a hand through his hair. 'I don't need you to help solve *my* problem. Besides, it can't *be* solved. I love her and she does *not* love me, not enough.' Not enough to make a life together. Saying the words aloud opened the wounds afresh. The hurt began again.

'It's not only an issue of love, Tristan. It's also an issue of trust. She doesn't trust me enough to take a leap of faith.' The anger of the afternoon began to stir again—anger at her for not trusting him to make things right, to ensure her father was controlled, and anger at his own inability to make her see reason, to see that he was right.

Tristan nodded, silent and encouraging as the words, the hurt and the anger spilled from him. Now that he'd started to talk, he couldn't seem to stop. 'I was so sure of her. This time was going to be different.' Julien let the feelings come. He talked of the night at the Christmas fair, of how it felt to sit beside her at church, to have her beside him at the tree lighting.

'I was so sure of her, of *us*, I went to London for a special licence and a ring. I was so sure that I made love to her upstairs here in my home, the place where I want to raise my family, and then I proposed.' His fist clenched, anger and hurt rocketing through him. 'I never dreamed she'd turn me down. I thought we'd already implicitly agreed.' The recriminations came again. What had he missed? How had he allowed himself to be duped one more time?

'I can't go back to Brentham Woods, Tristan. She'll be there.' Heaven knew what it would do to him to see her right now and know that he'd lost her.

'Then we won't go back,' Tristan said quietly. 'We'll stay the night here.'

'She's here, too.' Julien could hear his voice shake with emotion, with *every* emotion. His body was a riot of them: anger, rage, disappointment, failure, stupidity. He could deal with those, eventually over time. They could be rationalised, dissected and understood. Anger would sustain him as it had before. The hurt was harder to cope with, its pain more immediate.

'I brought her here. We planned every inch of it,' he told Tristan as he grappled with his self-control, something he had little experience with. He was always in control, always knew what to do. This was new and unpleasant territory and she had brought him to it. 'She touched every room here. When I walk into them, I hear her voice in my head talking about cream-on-cream wallpaper and Thomas Whitty rugs.' More than that, he saw the future he'd imagined. A future that was possible because he'd chosen to believe in her.

Julien paused. 'I forgave her, Tristan, for not accepting me the first time because she was too young, too alone to stand on her own, too threatened with the loss of those dearest to her to rebel. I forgave her because that was the only way we could go forward. I forgave her because that was the way to change things. But it wasn't enough.'

Tristan pressed a roasted beef sandwich into his hand. 'I am sorry, Brother, so very sorry.'

Julien held Tristan's gaze. 'So am I. In the end, she

still didn't choose me. She was never going to choose me, not for the long run. I didn't see the truth because I wanted the truth to be different. Maybe she can't love. It would be understandable after being raised in that home.' Even now, when hurt and anger were riding him hard, some part of him was willing to make excuses for her or at least try to explain away her actions in her defence or to mitigate his own hurt.

Julien scrubbed a hand over his face, feeling the night's growth of stubble on his chin. 'I hope there's no child,' he said quietly. Damn, why hadn't he been more careful? But he knew why. Because he'd been imagining three or four children on the staircase Christmas morning, a life where his wife could be trusted, where she loved him and they were a team, unencumbered by outside agendas. It would serve him right, though, if she was pregnant, if he spent his life shackled to his folly, like Prometheus, having his liver eaten out every day only to grow back every night. Only for him, it would be his heart.

Tristan tendered an opinion at last, carefully wading into the fray of his feelings. 'Leaps of faith can be tricky things, though, no matter how cautious we are.'

'It was just so good with her, all of it—the laughing, the loving. What I wonder is how could all that have been a lie?' This was the one question that had plagued him, the one thing that didn't ring true about her arguments. How did one feign those things so thoroughly? So consistently without meaning them?

'Are you sure you're reading the situation correctly?' Tristan spoke the other question. 'Her father is strategic and manipulative. You know that's true. Do you think she still fears his power more than she trusts your love? Fearing him is a habit and habits are hard to break. Love, real love, is new to her, a foreign thing.'

Julien nodded, remembering. 'She cried today when I showed her the special licence. She said it was the first time anyone had loved her.' He glanced at Tristan. 'She was reluctant to accept the proposal, she worried about her father using the marriage to his advantage.' That had been her first level of rejection. There'd been other levels, too.

By the end they'd said harsh things to one another in the heat of the moment. But fire often revealed hidden truths. Those words had been harsh perhaps, but that didn't make them lies. Maybe it was best those things had been aired before things had gone further. Maybe it was simply impossible for them to be together. But that didn't make losing her hurt any less.

'I simply don't know how I'll move on without her,' he told Tristan. 'I don't know that I can do it again. But I must if I am to have a family.' He shook his head. It was like his world truly had stopped and would never start again. 'I can't imagine any of that without her.'

'Then don't imagine it.' Tristan stretched out his legs and yawned, settling deep into his chair. 'You've never given up on anything in your life. Don't start now. It's late, you need to rest.'

'You're a good brother, Tristan, to sit up with me. I'm costing you time away from Elanora and the children,' Julien said, only to be answered with a snore. Well, maybe Tristan had the right idea. At least if he slept, he wouldn't hurt so much, wouldn't think so much. He slouched down in his chair, letting the fire warm him. How was it that a man who successfully invested pounds by the thousands had managed to lose the woman he loved not once, but twice?

A pounding on his door woke him and Tristan rather joltingly the following morning. Their father strode in, brisk and efficient, his greatcoat and boots spattered with December mud. His demeanour suggested he'd ridden hard for good reason. 'Good, you're both here, I thought you might be.' He looked from one grown son to another. 'You need to get up and help us search. Lady Aurelia is gone. She wasn't in her room when her mother looked in on her this morning.'

Julien's first reaction was fear—for Aurelia. She was in a strange place where she didn't know the land, she could get easily be lost. He was out of his chair, ignoring the crick in his neck and the stiffness in his shoulder for having slept sitting in a slouch. Then he remembered. She'd betrayed him. Again.

That wouldn't do.

That same part of him which had made it possible for her to keep her freedom by securing her father's estate regardless of their past spoke in his mind.

She's out there alone, somewhere, maybe lost, maybe hurt in the heart of winter.

Tristan was asking questions. 'Did she take a horse? Did she take anything from her room?'

'No horse. Nothing from her room. Only whatever she was wearing. Her mother says her green carriage ensemble is gone and her winter cloak.' The green-velvet ensemble she'd worn to the tree lighting, Julien thought, the ensemble which made her look like Christmas. Julien's heart began to ache.

'And whatever fits into her pockets. Jewellery?' Julien asked, tamping down on the pain that followed thoughts of her.

'I don't know, I don't think anyone looked for smaller items. Lady Holme is beside herself,' their father said with a meaningful look.

'Well, it's about time. She didn't seem too concerned about her daughter when everything fell apart last night,' Julien growled. He had little sympathy there.

'Julien, we can't ever really know what goes on in someone else's home,' his father chided. 'I know you don't care for the Earl.'

'He's a bastard.' Julien didn't mince words. 'No one cares for him.'

'All that aside, we should also consider why would she run?' Tristan interrupted with a queer look that made Julien stop and think. Tristan put a stalling hand to his shoulder. 'Do you think her father found out about the proposal and her refusal? The proposal would have elated him, but her refusal would not have.'

No, it wouldn't have. Her father would be furious. 'She would not have told him. He couldn't have known,' Julien said.

'If she was as half as upset as you were yesterday, I doubt she could have hidden it. Or perhaps she told her mother and her mother told her father,' Tristan postulated.

If her father knew, Julien could imagine how that

would have played out: threats. Threats against Elspeth, against her mother. His gut twisted. There was more than one history repeating itself.

'What if her father *didn't* know? We should consider that as well.' Tristan voiced the question quietly. 'Perhaps she ran pre-emptively *before* he could learn of it.'

Julien held Tristan's gaze, a long look passing between the brothers. Hope warred with despair, tying an uncomfortable knot in his stomach as Tristan said the words he could not. 'If she ran pre-emptively, she ran in order to protect someone. To protect you.'

'Dear God.' The realisation left Julien struggling to breathe. She'd intimated as much yesterday that she was refusing him on the grounds that she wanted to save him. He'd not listened then, not with the right ears. He'd heard only refusal, only excuses from a woman who didn't trust him enough to make things right, a woman who didn't love him as much as he loved her. But this morning, it looked different. She'd run to protect him.

And people protect the ones they love.

He recalled the afternoon they'd ridden out to the duck boxes the first time and she'd put the ruse to him. She'd told him then, the first time her father had threatened Elspeth she'd vowed to take the horse and run, disappear, where no one could find her.

Three things ripped through Julien at once. First, he knew where she'd gone. Second, he knew where she'd be. Third, he knew he'd been wrong yesterday. She'd left for him, his brave, selfless girl, always seeking to protect those she loved instead of fighting for herself. Julien groped in a pocket for his watch. Damn. It was later than he thought. 'I have to go after her. I know where she went.' He was already striding through the hall, grabbing his greatcoat from a peg. He patted the pockets to make sure his purse was on him.

'I'll come with you,' Tristan offered.

'No, you stay here. You have a family and it's Christmas, Tristan. You've done enough. If I don't make it back in time, make sure Mother's ball is a success.' He was fairly sure he wouldn't make the Christmas ball.

'You're going that far, are you?' Tristan queried in low tones.

Julien nodded. 'I'll go as far as I have to. I owe her an apology.' And the protection of his name if she was still willing to take it. It seemed like the only thing they were good at was betrayal. This time it was he who had betrayed her.

Julien saddled his horse with instructions to have him picked up at the livery later and set off as fast as he dared for town on roads that were icy. He tried not to think of Aurelia covering those three miles on foot in the early morning cold. He tried only to think of the next step, which was catching the eleven o'clock train to London and from there, the next train that would get him to Yorkshire, or at least close. Aurelia had gone home, although she wouldn't stay there. She'd gone to get her horse and then she'd be off again. He'd lose her if he didn't get to Moorfields before she left.

The village was bustling with Christmas celebrants, mainly those who'd come to town on the early train to join Reverend Thompson's advent service before shopping. With just two days before Christmas Eve, people were in the holiday spirit and eager to see the fair and prettily decorated windows of the High Street, eager to spend coins on sweets and small gifts. Ordinarily, Julien would have been happy to see the crowds, but today, the crowds meant he had to struggle to get a space on the Christmas train, which ran an abbreviated schedule due to it being Sunday.

He had to settle for standing room only on the train. Aurelia would have been on the first train back to London. She had a two-hour head start on him. He wouldn't know how much that meant until he saw the train schedules to the north. If she had to wait a while for a northbound train, he might be lucky enough to catch her in London.

He had no such luck in London. London was, in fact, downright unlucky for him. He could not tell which option Aurelia might have taken to get north. Had she waited for a train that took a more direct route with fewer stops or had she taken the first train north that took a more circuitous route out of fear that someone might catch up with her before the direct train could leave? By someone, Julien meant her father. She knew her mother wouldn't come and she would not think he'd come.

Julien opted for the last direct train north instead of an earlier train that made more stops. His train left at three o'clock and would arrive in York a little after six, barring any difficulties. Then, he'd have to make a decision: try to find a post chaise that would take him to Moorfields in the dark or take a room at an inn and head to Moorfields in the morning, hoping she would still be there.

The weather made the decision for him. York was freezing and there was no post chaise to be had for love or money willing to brave the Dales in the dark and the ice until morning. He found a quality inn, ate a hearty meal and fell asleep in his clothes, hoping he wouldn't be too late.

It was shortly past six when Aurelia arrived at Moorfields. The big Gothic-style manor looked dark and deserted. There was no life to it, which came as a surprise. She paid the driver and lifted the heavy lion-headed door knocker, waiting for a servant to answer. She was fully prepared to throw herself on the mercy of the Americans who'd rented the place for Christmas for the space of a night, just long enough to pack some things, get Elspeth and go. She looked over her shoulder, as she had been doing all day, for fear her father would divine where she'd gone and come after her. But if no one was behind her now, she'd be safe until morning. No one would get from York to Moorfields this time of night in this freezing weather.

She knocked again and stamped her feet against the cold. Still no answer. She trudged to the stable block, where a light flickered in the upstairs garret, home to the grooms. 'Hello!' she called out, stepping into the warmth of the stable. In the depths, a horse nickered at the disturbance. Boots sounded on the stairs.

'Milady! What are you doing home?' Whit Tyler, the

head groom, came into view, pulling on a jacket. She'd caught him at supper, no doubt, and the end of his day.

'Where is everyone at the house? The Americans? No one answered when I knocked.' She strode the aisles, going directly to Elspeth's stall, the horse looking up as she approached, recognising her voice.

'That's a bad business, Milady,' Whit said. 'The Americans got bored so far from a city. The village was too rustic for them. They decamped last week to a town house in York to celebrate Christmas with some new friends they made on the trip over.'

'Where are the servants?'

'A bit of a mutiny, if you must know. They felt no reason to stay on until the Earl returned. Felt they were entitled to a bit of a holiday themselves since there was no one to look after and no one to know better as long as everyone was back in their places a few days before January the seventh.'

'I see.' Aurelia stroked Elspeth's nose and breathed in the horsey scent of her. After a day on the run, a sleepless night filled with tears and emotions, there was peace here with her horse, in the stable. She did see. The staff felt no particular loyalty to her father. Salaries had not been paid on time and there'd be no Christmas bonuses this year, ostensibly on account of the family being gone for so long over Christmas. But everyone knew the real reason. The Earl of Holme was rolled up.

'I am sorry it's not much of a homecoming, Milady.' Whit scratched his balding head. 'Did you travel all this way alone? Do your parents know you're here?'

'Yes, to the first, no to the second. I don't mean to

stay, Whit. It's a long story. I suppose, like the servants, I've simply had enough. I've come for a few belongings and Elspeth. If I tell you any more, you'll be obliged to share that information.' She smiled. 'Thank you for staying. The horses would have starved.' A thought occurred to her. 'Are you the only one at the stables?'

'Ollie stayed, too. The two of us can look after the horses fine.'

She nodded. 'Things will get better here, Whit. My father did secure a loan and there will be a new estate manager to ensure things stay right.' She paused, dreading the idea of going up to the dark, big house, and sleeping there alone in the cold. 'Do you think I could sleep here tonight in one of the grooms' beds?' Based on Whit's calculations, there wouldn't have been a fire lit in the hall for over a week. The place would be freezing.

Whit left her to go fix up a bed and she pressed her head to Elspeth's. 'It's been a day, girl. But I am here now and we're both going to be safe.' Julien was going to be safe, too. She would be as far from him as she could be. She wouldn't be a tool to be used against him any more.

It was the first time today she'd allowed herself to think of him. One of the boons of being on the run was that it consumed her thoughts and demanded her attention. She had no energy or time to spare for reliving the pain of last night, the horrible words they'd said, tearing apart their hard-won happiness. But it had to be done. She could not allow Julien to marry her, to tie himself to the dysfunction that was her family, her father. It would be a bottomless pit that would suck him down like it had sucked her mother, like it was sucking her, costing her everything, including the man she loved and the life she truly wanted.

He had hated her yesterday for refusing him. Would he come to understand that her actions hadn't been motivated by hate or a desire to hurt him? She'd left before dawn *for* him. To protect him. It had felt wondrous to know the depths of his love, to be loved. She'd not lied when she'd told him that being with him was the first time she'd ever felt truly loved for herself, not her title, or what fortune she might have possessed once upon a time.

She didn't want to see that love ruined and eroded after dealing with her family over a lifetime. He deserved better than that. She had to trust that he would come to see that, to understand that eventually he would thank her for it even though she knew it would hurt for a while, because she hurt.

'I love him, Elspeth,' she whispered to the horse whom she'd told a lifetime of secrets. 'And he loved me. It was the most wondrous feeling in the world. Now it's over.' For good this time. A tear trickled against her horse's face. Not even the magic of Christmas could change that. She'd had her second chance and she'd lost him.

Chapter Twenty-One

The luck of the season was with him. Julien found her in the Moorfields stables the next morning, after rousing a post chaise driver at the earliest possible moment and making the rather long trip out into the countryside, hoping each mile of the way that he wouldn't be too late, that she'd still be there. The weather was clear today, which worked both for him and against him. If he could travel, so could she.

Now that he'd found her, he took a moment to savour the sight of her, dressed in boy's breeches that showed off the curve of her hip, the firm, round derrière that usually hid beneath her skirts, an oversized shirt and boots, a golden braid hanging down her back as she tacked up a beautiful chestnut. Elspeth. He was in time, but only just barely. Another hour's sleep would have seen his cause lost.

'Aurelia,' he called her name softly to announce his presence without startling her or the horse and to let his tone suggest that he did not come in anger.

He watched her hand freeze on the bridle strap and she turned slowly. 'Julien.' The wariness suggested she thought he'd come to harangue her further. He never wanted the woman he loved to have reason to look at him like that again. 'What are you doing here?'

'I've not come to scold or to drag you back under duress. I have come to apologise.' Julien cut straight to the matter in the hopes of giving her assurance. 'But what I really want to do is hold you, to prove to myself that you're safe and well.' He realised it was true. There were words that required saying, but they paled next to the need to hold her, to feel her in his arms and know she was not lost to him.

'Perhaps talk first.' She gestured to a groom working in the stalls. 'Ollie, can you take Elspeth to her stall. I need to speak with this gentleman.' Then she looked around, unsure.

'Perhaps we could go upstairs, a hay loft will do,' Julien suggested. 'I rode past the house and saw that it was empty.' And dark and cold. He could not imagine a more foreboding place. He certainly couldn't imagine growing up there.

'That's a long story, but I do have a hayloft available, although I don't have anything to offer you to drink or eat.'

He shook his head to indicate food and drink were of no import. 'I only want to see you, Aurelia.' He let her lead the way up to the loft, warm and redolent with the bales of winter hay. They settled, each on their own bale. She was being very careful to keep her distance, he noted. Perhaps that was a sign of how thin the thread of her control was. Perhaps it, like his own control, would snap upon contact, sweeping reason away with it just when it was needed most.

'How did you know I'd be here?' She twisted strands of hay together to give her hands something to do, another sign, he thought, of her upset. Aurelia was usually so lively, so confident.

'I listened to you. If one listens, everything becomes obvious. The breadcrumbs were all there, all I had to do was put them together. You told me your father regularly holds Elspeth against you, and you told me how you would go away the first chance you got, to live free with your horse.

'I should have listened to you better yesterday, but I didn't. You weren't refusing me. You were trying to protect me the only way you knew how. Tristan helped me see that. Now, I need to help *you* see that you don't have to do this alone. You don't have to live life alone and you don't have to manage your family alone.

She nodded slowly, thinking over his words while he waited impatiently for a response. He'd come all this way and now he just wanted it to be over and for her to be with him again. They would sort the rest out. As long as they were together, nothing was insurmountable. But she'd not had the advantage of the hours he'd spent on the crowded trains to think through the possibility that he'd come for her, that he'd *want* to find a way through this.

'What happens next, then, Julien?' she said at last in quiet, subdued tones that spoke of weariness, but gave no hint to her emotional reaction. Julien's heart sank. He'd hoped for better.

'In a perfect world, you tell me I'm forgiven, you throw yourself in my arms and we take advantage of the hayloft,' he said, only half-joking.

'This isn't a perfect world. I can forgive you, Julien. I owe you one on that account at least. Our ledgers will be balanced. You'd like that. Settled accounts.' She smiled, to make it clear she didn't mean it cruelly, but that she understood how his mind worked. 'But what does it change?'

'You're talking about your father.'

'Yes, he will wreck our happiness. I can't bear to watch that, to watch you come to hate me.'

'Because you love me.' The acknowledgement that came with hearing himself speak the words out loud moved through him with ferocity, intensity. *She loved him.* He wasn't in this alone.

Her eyes were shining dangerously bright. 'Yes, because I love you, because I've always loved you.'

'You've never said the words.' But she hadn't needed to. He knew, hadn't he? It was there in her kisses, in her smile, in the gifts of her body, in her laughter, even in this misguided attempt to protect him.

'Saying the words makes it real, Julien.' And real things had leverage, real things were always used against her. Real things could be lost.

'You won't lose me, Aurelia, not again. I thought foolishly and behaved foolishly the other night.'

'Yes, you did.'

Was that a bit of humour with the scold? Julien wondered. Was the icy reserve thawing a bit at last? 'Marry me. Like we planned. Let us have the life we have imagined for ourselves. I can have that life with no one else— I want it with no one else. I've come all the way to Yorkshire to tell you that. And to remind you that your father doesn't get to steal your happiness.'

'You want to try?' There was disbelief in her voice as if she couldn't fathom being wanted after this latest debacle.

Julien chuckled. 'I don't think marriage is something we just "try." I think it's something we *do* and we don't stop doing it, we don't stop loving or trusting each other because things get hard.'

'Those are difficult things to accept when one has never had them,' she said shyly.

'You have them now, with me. Always. I will not make the mistake of doubting you again.' His heart burned as he looked at her, in hope for the future he saw in her eyes and in anger for all she'd been denied and the damage it had done. But he would change that, day by day, until she knew without reservation that she was safe in his love.

She came to him then, wiping away her tears, letting him take her in his arms, but the kiss was all hers, long and sweet and full of promise. 'I'm sorry you had to come all this way,' she murmured.

'I'm not.' He laughed as they tumbled into the hay.

'You will be, though.' She looked up at him with solemn blue eyes. 'You missed your mother's Christmas ball. The pantomime is tonight and you'll miss that, too. The costumes were going to be fabulous.'

He picked a piece of straw from her hair and levered himself up on one arm. 'Will you be sorry to miss it? They were your costumes, after all.'

'Not nearly as sorry as I am to take you away from all that you worked so hard to provide. You love Christmas with your family and I ruined that for you. You're here and...well, just look at this place. It's empty. The renters didn't even want to stay.'

Julien thought for a moment. 'But you like it here. Didn't you tell me you wanted to be home for Christmas? That you'd dreaded being away?' As an outsider it was hard to understand her attachment to a place that looked so full of foreboding and he told her so.

She laughed. 'I dreaded leaving Moorfields because I feared seeing you. Most of all, I worried if I wasn't here, there wouldn't be any traditions. My father doesn't lift a finger to put on the Christmas rituals—that falls to me. But I relish the opportunity to care for those whom my father neglects all year. There are no servants at the house because they know my father can't pay their wages and there will be no bonuses.' She sighed. 'Moorfields has no soul, not like Brentham Woods.' He could tell the admission hurt her, that she'd wanted more.

'I think you're wrong. I think you're its soul and it just needs to be awakened.'

She reached for his hand. 'You say the sweetest things, Julien. Maybe some day. What we ought to do now is get you back to York, get you on a train and get you home at least for Christmas Eve.'

'I don't think that's the plan at all. I intend to spend Christmas in Yorkshire with my wife before returning home to celebrate with my family.'

His wife. The words warmed her, touched her deeply, overwhelmed her. 'You mean to marry me here? Now?' What a wondrous thought, something she'd not dared dream of yesterday. 'Surely you want a big wedding with your family there. We need time to plan something appropriate to your station. You're a viscount now.'

'No, we don't need any of that,' he argued. 'Besides, *you* are my family as well and we've seen how transient plans really are. We spent the month planning the perfect Christmas in Hemsford and we won't be there to see it. Maybe that's because Christmas needs us here at Moorfields.'

'Christmas at Moorfields? Julien, that's not possible,' she sputtered. 'There's no time.' It had taken weeks of careful planning to arrange the Christmas festivities in Hemsford. He couldn't expect to pull something like that off here with just a day and a wedding on top of it.

'I say differently. We have all we need. I have a special licence in my coat pocket. There's a church in the village and you very likely have a wardrobe full of beautiful gowns that will suffice for the occasion. We'll open up Moorfields tomorrow afternoon for Yule festivities and we'll wed that night on Christmas Eve, catch the Christmas mail train on the twenty-fifth and be at Brentham Woods for supper. We live in a marvellous modern age. We might as well take advantage of it.' He was smiling broadly, but his words were in deadly earnest. He meant to do this, she realised. *For her*. Because he understood how desperately she needed it.

Still, there were practicalities that could not be overlooked. 'What about food, Julien? What will we serve our guests? I can't possibly bake enough in the time we have.' But this obstacle, too, was nothing to him.

'We'll take a leaf out of the London hostesses' book and bring the food in. I am sure the village baker would like to make some extra money and the village butcher, and even a few who wouldn't mind acting as footmen for an evening. Perhaps we might even find a fiddler or two. But we have to get started. It's already the twenty-third and there's a lot to do, including you changing clothes.' He helped her to her feet and she brushed the hay dust from her breeches, his body vibrating with a contagious energy that set her pulse racing with excitement.

'Are you sure we can do it?' she asked before they climbed down from the loft. What Julien proposed was exhilarating, but also likely impossible when one thought about it.

Yet, she could hear Elanora's words once more. *'Let Julien handle it. He can turn nothing into something.'*

'Doubter,' he scolded with a tease. 'I mean to show you, Aurelia Ripley, that Christmas is where you are, who you're with and it is absolutely what *you* make it.'

One person could make so much difference. When that one person was Julien Lennox, the impact was magnified tenfold. She'd not realised the extent of his power, how he wielded that power subtly through the simple act of listening to people, encouraging them and always looking for the possibility. 'There are no obstacles,' he told her as they exited the butcher's shop in Moorfields village. 'Only opportunities.'

She laughed up at him, enjoying herself thoroughly. 'You're certainly making plenty of those today.' Their shopping expedition had taken on a life and routine of its own as she accompanied him from store to store in the little High Street of the Moorfields village. She would introduce him as Julien Lennox, Viscount Lavenham, and he would take the visit from there, discussing the shop and business with the shopkeeper, offering an idea here and there. There'd been the discussion of gingerbread with the baker, who'd not thought of selling Twelfth Night Cakes with a prize hidden inside.

Such discussions were followed by an order for foodstuffs to be brought to the hall tomorrow for the Yule celebration and, Julien would add proudly, a celebration of their wedding. Hearing Julien say it sent a thrill through her every time she heard the words.

She was going to be his wife.

Not just the new Viscountess Lavenham. In truth, she hardly spared a thought for the title. Her thoughts were all for the man she watched in the shops.

The shopkeepers offered their congratulations, their eyes lighting up as Julien paid in advance for the goods and pulled out additional pound notes to clear the Earl's accounts. 'I believe everyone should start the year with a clean slate.' He'd wink at the shopkeepers, who agreed wholeheartedly. Julien had asked her to make a list of the debts before they'd set out and put it to memory. Business and bills concluded, Julien would then place a separate amount on the counter and say quietly, privately, 'This is from the both of us, from our family to yours, for your own Christmas celebrations or whatever you might need so you can start your own year in the clear.'

The chandler, from whom they'd purchased candles for the table and the fireplace mantel, had actually wiped away a tear and Aurelia had found the need to wipe her own tears when the chandler had confessed he would use it for medicine for his sick child. At which point, Julien had put another note on the counter.

'When we started this venture,' she said solemnly as they stepped outside the store, 'I thought it was for me, but that is only a very small part. This Christmas celebration is for them.' She let out a shaky breath. 'It makes me grateful and ashamed. Grateful, because you are doing what I could not and these people deserve it. But ashamed because I've been able to do more over the years and that my father did less.'

'*We* are doing this,' Julien insisted. 'I need your introductions and it is clear that they adore you, that they understand you've done your best. I may be giving them funds, but I am still asking for a large task from them. They wouldn't bother to do it for a stranger. But they'll do it for you. It is their wedding gift to you.' He raised her hand to his lips. 'Our gift to them is the promise of better times and the restoration of the Christmas spirit. This is a new era for Moorfields.'

They made two more stops, one at the confectioner's and the other at a toymaker's whose face beamed when Julien bought nearly every toy he had: wooden whistles, balls and hoops, dolls and drums to be delivered by wagon up to the big house early tomorrow morning. 'Thank you, Milord. Toys need children and children need toys at Christmas. This year, the harvests were poor and with the economy the way it is no one has had much extra to spend on a toy.' And the man had suffered as a result, collateral damage to her father's erratic land management.

'We have a new land steward,' Julien told the fellow.

'Good times are coming.' And Aurelia's heart swelled with pride at this man who would soon be her husband.

'You're so sure and you pass that on to them, you give them hope. Don't you ever doubt?' she asked as they drove back to the house, a few of their purchases piled in the little wagon bed. Most would be arriving tomorrow morning. 'When was the last time you were ever nervous over something?'

Julien chuckled and she thought she detected colour in his cheek. 'Just a week ago when I made love to you for the first time. I wanted it to be good for you.'

Now, she was the one blushing. 'It was. But perhaps you were nervous because you need more practice,' she suggested coyly. 'Maybe when we get home, you'd like to practise a bit more?'

'Do you think we have time? We have a party tomorrow and a wedding,' he joked, but there *was* a lot to do and just the two of them and Whit and Ollie to do it—sweeping the hall, moving furniture so that the hall was ready to receive its guests.

'Whose idea was it to have a party and a wedding all on the same day?' she scolded, cuddling close against the cold.

'Well, on second thought, practice *does* make perfect,' he relented playfully. 'We'd best practise this afternoon. We might be too tired tonight.'

And so they did.

A good idea it was, too. Aurelia yawned, falling into bed slightly before midnight beside Julien who was just awake enough to wrap his arm about her waist and pull her close. The hall had been decorated for the American guests, but there'd still been plenty to do and they had done it. Moorfields was ready for Christmas and she was ready for her new life. She'd had a glimpse of it today and it was good.

Chapter Twenty-Two

Life was good. Better than good. It was grand. This would be a Christmas neither he nor Moorfields would forget. Julien stood at the front of the candlelit church as people shifted from the Christmas service into the wedding service. It was late, nearing midnight. When the Christmas bells rang out, he would be a married man, a happy man.

It had been a day of joy, the perfect celebration to lead up to this celebration on the year's holiest night of love. He and Aurelia had been busy from the moment they'd risen until the moment they'd been driven to church in a festively decorated gig, the partygoers following them down, carols on the air.

What a whirlwind it had been, with food arriving mid-morning and being laid out along with Moorfield's best plate. Aurelia had outdone herself, overseeing that laying out: gingerbread on silver platters, candies in cut-crystal jars, long tables set with white cloths and china. 'What's the use of having such nice things if no one sees them? If they're just gathering dust?' she'd told Julien, sailing past him as he supervised the unloading of more wagons.

When he'd returned inside, the great hall had been transformed as it might have looked in more medieval times, offering guests a night of food and fun out of the cold. The guests had arrived in the early afternoon, the men to trek out with him and cut the Yule log, the children to play the games Aurelia organised for them—snapdragon, apple-bobbing, blind man's bluff—the women to sit and talk, enjoying being the hosted ones instead of the hostesses. When the men returned, log in tow, there'd been the grand ceremony of presenting it to the master of the house, in this case, the lady of the house, and it had been lit to great applause.

Dinner foods were brought out to replenish the already groaning tables, the fiddlers struck up dancing tunes and the hall was filled with merriment, the men clapping him on the back and giving him marital advice as if he were already one of them. Then it was time and, for Julien, the evening took on the cast of a more sober joy as he discreetly went upstairs to change his clothes. He'd bought a dark suit in town and, if it lacked the finesse of a Bond Street tailor, it was certainly cleaner than the clothes he'd left Brentham Woods in two days earlier.

Now he was here, awaiting Aurelia's 'arrival.' She and the ladies had stepped out at the end of the Christmas service, mostly so she could come back in and walk down the aisle. A newly made friend winked at Julien from the front row and Julien smiled. This was not the wedding he'd imagined. The one he'd imagined had been in Hemsford with Reverend Thompson presiding and

Tristan at his side, his parents in the front row instead of a friend he'd just met hours ago.

But he was coming to discover his imagination might have been limited. He never could have planned a wedding like this. He supposed that was the whole point. He could not have planned a Christmas like this if he had a year to do it and it was better than anything he could have conceived.

The church door opened and there was whispered exclamations as Aurelia stepped inside, wearing her green velvet, a bouquet of evergreen and holly in her gloved hands. Her hair had been taken down and brushed. He smiled—now he knew what they'd been doing. On her head she wore a wreath of mistletoe. Perhaps in honour of their first kiss. He felt his smile tremble with an unlooked-for burst of emotion. Despite all the fun and busyness of today, she'd thought to wear meaningful symbols of their love, private messages of the promises they'd make each other.

At the altar, he took her hand and leaned close. 'My mistletoe bride,' he whispered at her ear. 'You look stunning, Aurelia.' No Bond Street gown or French silk could have looked finer. She looked like Christmas and love.

The ceremony was short. Julien preferred that it was. He wanted to kiss his bride and when he did the Christmas bells in the belfry rang out and the congregation cheered. His bride's cheeks were wet with her joy as he led her out into the Christmas night where they were surrounded by well-wishers who'd spent the day with them and the most important night of their life.

'Happy?' He squeezed Aurelia's hand as he helped

her into the gig. 'Do you mind? I think they might follow us home,' he whispered, glancing at the villagers gathering around the gig.

'Throw them some silver pennies.' She laughed. 'They might leave us alone. It's an old tradition.'

Julien laughed and stood tall on the gig. 'Christmas pennies, for all!' he called out and tossed a handful or two or three in the air. They did the trick. He was allowed to go home and make love to his wife on the best night of the year and the first night of their life together.

'They're here! Uncle Julien is here!' Alex's loud cheers preceded them into the hall of Brentham Woods, at dusk on Christmas Day.

'So much for the element of surprise,' Julien said wryly as he and Aurelia stepped inside. He had a moment to take it all in before the family swarmed them in the hall. It had felt different this time, coming up the drive to Brentham, seeing the calming lights in the lace-curtained windows. This was truly his father's house now. He had his own house, his own family with his bride beside him. The circle was full. He had the closure he'd come home to seek. Or nearly so.

The family had just sat down to supper and now they spilled out from the dining room with exclamations of excitement. 'Julien!' His mother hugged him and turned triumphantly to his father. 'I told you he'd be here for supper.' Then, noticing that Aurelia's parents hadn't moved forward to hug her, his mother embraced her with all her characteristic warmth. 'It's good to see you as well, my dear.'

Julien took Aurelia's hand. 'We would have come sooner, but we had a bit of business to take care of. We were married last night, at Moorfields in the stone church in the village after the service. Everyone, may I present to my family, for the first time, my bride, Viscountess Lavenham, Aurelia Lennox.'

This was met with unbridled celebration. His mother was hugging Aurelia again. His father was clapping him on the shoulder, Tristan was holding him tight in a brotherly hug of bear-like proportions and Elanora sighed with misty eyes. 'A Christmas Eve wedding, Julien. It's perfect.'

He smiled at Elanora and his brother. He'd nearly forgotten. 'It's your anniversary today, what is it? Four years now?'

At his side, Aurelia laughed. 'It's fitting, then, that two men who love Christmas as much as you two do have Christmas brides.'

Elanora looped her arm through her new sister-in-law's. 'We will be able to celebrate together every year.'

Julien caught a glance from Tristan and the brothers exchanged a look. How wondrous that their wives would be friends, that the two women held each other in genuine affection, what a grand promise life held. In time their children would grow up together, play together, run the fields together, ride their first ponies together, fish in the same rivers their fathers had fished in.

Tristan wrapped an arm about his shoulders. 'I know what you're thinking, Brother,' he said in low tones and Julien smiled.

'I'm thinking here's to Christmas futures.' His eyes might have been wet with a little sentiment but it wasn't quite time to give in to that yet. There was one more item to settle.

He turned to where the Earl and Lady Holme stood apart from the group. Their distance was a bittersweet sign. Aurelia was a Lennox now. She had a family that loved her, that would embrace her as she was. She did not need them and whatever they passed off as love and affection. 'Do you not wish to greet your daughter and congratulate her on her marriage?'

His own father had the discretion to usher everyone else back into the dining room. Julien gave him a nod, which promised they would join them shortly. His business with Holme wouldn't take long. He'd already made his terms. He merely needed to remind Holme of that.

Her mother came forward and hugged her tight. Perhaps the Earl had not allowed her to come forward earlier. The sight tugged at Julien's heart as did her words. 'You must have been a beautiful bride, I wish I could have seen you. I've dreamed of your wedding day for so long.'

'It would have done your dreams proud, Milady,' Julien swiftly intervened lest the woman make Aurelia feel guilty about the speed of the wedding and its rather non-traditional aspect. 'When Aurelia looks back on her wedding day, it will be with joy. She was surrounded by the spirit of the season, the villagers she's known her whole life and we opened Moorfields' doors for a Yule celebration the likes of which I don't believe they've ever seen.'

That pointed comment was meant for the Earl.

'It's not your place,' Holme huffed. 'You may have given me a loan, but Moorfields is not yours, nor will it ever be.'

'No,' Julien said coolly. 'But it is Aurelia's home as long as you're alive. It is her obligation and her pleasure to make everyone feel welcome there. Or perhaps you've forgotten the symbiotic relationship that should exist between tenant and landowner, each having a duty to the other?

'Out of honor for that symbiotic relationship, as a wedding gift to your daughter, Holme, I paid the merchants what was owed them. I do not expect to see that level of debt accrued again. It's not good for the local economy nor for your reputation among them. If there is debt, it will negatively impact the conditions of our loan. Likewise, I know you and Lady Holme will want to offer Aurelia a wedding gift as well. That gift will be the safe and immediate delivery of Elspeth to my new stables. If anything happens to that horse before her delivery, I will foreclose on the loan. Send Ollie with her.'

'Ollie?' Holme looked baffled, or perhaps overwhelmed.

'He's one of your grooms. I will add that to the list of tasks I've assigned you at Moorfields. Learn your servants' names.' Julien gave a polite smile. 'Tomorrow, after the Boxing Day gifts are delivered, my wife and I will depart for my home. Lady Holme, you are always welcome there. I am sure my bride would delight in your support as she sets up our house. You could always accompany Ollie. The choice is yours.'

'Now see here, Lavenham,' Holme sputtered. 'You go too far.'

'No, it is you who went too far and now that is done.' Julien offered his arm to Aurelia and led her into Christmas supper where he was surrounded by the people he loved most: Alex crawling on and off his lap, showing him his new carved horse, baby Violet dribbling on his jacket, Elanora regaling them with the success of the pantomime at Heartsease and his mother's news of the Christmas ball. This was exactly where he wanted to be, just as last night in Yorkshire had been exactly where he wanted to be. Because Aurelia was beside him. Because love changed everything.

'You're happy to be home,' Aurelia whispered as he lit their way up to bed in his old chamber hours later. 'I can see it in your smile. It was worth the mail train to be here.'

He stopped before their chamber door. 'If home is where you are, then, yes, I am happy to be here. As long as I am with you, I will always be home for Christmas.'

Epilogue

December 25th, 1854,
four years later

'Jamie, slow down, lad, before you trip over something and fall,' Julien gently chided his energetic three-year-old son who came barrelling down the stairs on Christmas morning.

'But I smell sausage! Yum!' he cried as Julien intercepted him and swung him around.

'No sausage until Mama is down,' Julien cautioned. 'But maybe this will do until then.' He slipped the boy a gingerbread biscuit and watched his son's eyes light up at the unexpected treat. 'But don't tell Mama,' he whispered. 'It will be our secret. You know how she is about sweets before breakfast.'

The little boy laughed and Julien set him down, his heart filling with love for this wondrous creature who was his son. His son! It had been three years since he'd first held Jamie in his arms and the thrill never grew old. He woke each morning thinking how blessed he was to have a child. Aurelia's child.

'What shouldn't you tell Mama?' Aurelia's not-quite-awake voice spoke from the stairs where she was carefully making her way down. 'Are my men keeping secrets?' she teased.

'Mama!' Jamie cried. 'There's sausage! I can smell it!'

Aurelia forced a smile for Jamie's sake, her gaze meeting his over Jamie's head. 'Yes, my dear, I smell it, too.'

Although not with the same enjoyment, Julien would wager.

Julien went to her and took her arm with solicitous concern. 'Steady now. Is your stomach bothering you this morning?'

She laughed. 'Always. You know how it is in the early months. But never fear, I'll be ravenous by noon, once the family gets here.'

She gave him the soft smile that never ceased to melt him.

'Shall we tell them the news today?'

Aurelia was three months into her second pregnancy and it had been the best early Christmas gift Julien could have imagined.

They reached the bottom of the stairs and Jamie wrapped his chubby toddler arms around his parents' legs in a hug that encompassed them both.

Julien picked him up. 'Do you think you'll have a brother or a sister this time next year?'

'A pony!' Jamie laughed and Julien exchanged a look with Aurelia.

One had to be careful in what one said around children, even little ones. Cousin Alex, who was six now, was getting a pony for Christmas and there'd been a lot of talk about it between the adults in the past few months.

'That is not one of the options.' Julien tickled the little boy's belly. 'Do you want a brother or a sister for a playmate?'

Jamie screwed up his face in hard thought before declaring, 'One of each!'

Julien laughed and Aurelia swatted him playfully on the arm. 'That's easy for you to laugh at. You're not the one having them.'

He leaned in and kissed her cheek in response. 'Since your stomach is queasy, why don't we do presents first and breakfast second? Cook can hold it back for a while.'

'Presents *now*? Yay!'

Jamie squealed and Julien set him down to let him run to the Christmas tree room ahead of them. There would be more presents later, when the cousins came, but Christmas morning was just for them, the three of them, soon to be four.

'How long have you been up?' Aurelia asked as they trailed behind their son. 'The pillow was cold when I woke.'

'Since six,' Julien admitted, taking her arm and looping it through his. 'You know how I like a moment's time to reflect on Christmas Day. I love the chaos of Christmas, but I also like a moment of quiet to give thanks for you, for Jamie, for what I am able to do for others, for this home you've made for me.'

That time was important to him. December was an exceedingly busy month for him. He was the head of the Hemsford Village Improvement Society. That meant he'd been in charge of the Christmas fair, which continued to expand as attendance continued to grow. The days leading up to Christmas had been hectic with the pantomime and the ball. This year had been Jamie's first pantomime. He'd played a small pixie and Julien thought his son had delivered his one line with aplomb.

Of course, December wasn't his only busy month. He'd also been busy designing a summer market programme that would bring people to Hemsford for the fresh produce and splitting his time between London and Hemsford.

Thanks to the trains, gone were the days of spending the year in London due to work. He was able to work from his home and go up to the main office every few weeks. He loved being on hand to see to his estate, his community and his son. There was nothing more rewarding than being an active father involved in his son's childhood...unless it was riding down the drive and seeing Aurelia's lamps shining in the windows of Meadowlark Hall, which was what they'd chosen to name the place, in honour of the birds that sang in the morning at the promise of each new day. Those lamps were a symbol of their love, leading him home.

Jamie was waiting for them expectantly in the Christmas tree room, eyes wide as he studied the tree draped in its colourful winterberry garland.

Aurelia tugged at Julien's arm. 'Just a moment,' she whispered, halting in the doorway. 'I just want to look at him. I want to make a mental picture of this moment, of his little face turned towards the tree, his eyes full of wonder. Before he loses it.'

He squeezed her hand, knowing that she was thinking of other Christmases filled with less joy...the Christmases of her childhood.

'He won't lose it, Aurelia,' Julien said confidently. 'I never have.'

Julien gave her a moment and then went to his son, kneeling down beside him, a hand at his back. 'Do you see the star atop the tree?' This was a new addition. 'Do you know what it stands for?'

'For Bethlehem and the three wise men,' Jamie recited proudly.

Julien tousled his hair. 'Yes, for the three wise men,' he affirmed. 'It gave them guidance, showing them the way. It also gave them hope that they would find their way. Today, it does the same for us, my boy. The star is a reminder of hope for ourselves, and hope for the world, which it sometimes desperately needs.' He tapped his son's chest with a finger. 'Hope isn't just a Christmas thing, Jamie. Hope is for all year and it lives inside each of us.'

Jamie looked down at his chest. 'In me, too?'

'Most definitely in you. You are all your mama and I hoped for. Every time we look at you, we are reminded of hope. You are hope, just as your brother or sister will be hope to us, too.'

The boy probably didn't comprehend half of what he was saying, but Julien felt it was important to say the words anyway. He and Aurelia wanted their children to grow up knowing how deeply loved they were. Love bred confidence and security.

Aurelia settled on the sofa, rubbing her stomach and smiling at them.

Julien reached beneath the tree for a box and handed it to Jamie. 'Why don't we start with your gift for Mama?'

He wanted his son to learn early that giving was the greater joy.

Jamie solemnly took the little box over to his mother and curled up beside her on the sofa while she lifted the lid. Jamie had been so excited about it, Julien had worried the little boy would blurt it out before Christmas.

'I made it myself, with Papa and Uncle Tristan's help,' he announced as she lifted up a whittled wooden heart strung on a green ribbon. 'I carved it myself, with…' He grimaced and turned to his papa. 'What's the word, Papa?'

'Supervision!' Julien chuckled, enjoying the scene on the sofa very much.

'Supervision, Mama,' Jamie said. 'Look, there's words, too. Can you read them? It says *love* on this side of the heart and *family* on the other. Do you like it? I burned the letters on to the wood myself.'

'I love it.'

She pressed a kiss to her son's blond head, her eyes shining as Julien caught her gaze. She was the bravest woman he knew. She'd chosen him, chosen their love, at the expense of leaving behind her family for a new life, a life she deserved.

'Now, it's your turn, dear boy. What shall you open first?'

Delightful chaos ensued as Jamie opened his presents, exclaiming gleefully over each one, followed by Julien's favourite part of the day—the time between the opening and exclaiming and breakfast—a golden half-hour when he could sit on the sofa with his wife and watch his son play with his new toys beneath the tree, thoroughly engrossed.

'Are you happy, my love?' He raised her hand to his lips.

'You know I am. Happier than I ever dreamed I could be.' She smiled.

'I am sorry your mother isn't here,' Julien said quietly, knowing that was on her mind, as it always was at Christmas.

Each year, Lady Holme had been invited and each year there'd always been an excuse. Julien had even offered to go up and travel down with her, in case pressure from the Earl was preventing her from leaving.

Aurelia glanced at the star atop the tree. 'Perhaps next year, when she has two grandchildren to meet. I keep hoping.'

Her parents remained one difficulty they'd not yet conquered. She'd not seen her mother since Boxing Day four years ago. But Elspeth had arrived safe and sound soon after her father's return north and Julien's conditions had kept her father in check. The Holme estates were thriving, Moorfields had become self-sustaining under Julien's appointed steward and Aurelia enjoyed the long letters from Whit about the state of the village. Julien had promised the village better times four years ago and he'd delivered on that.

'Perhaps if we have a girl we'll name her Hope.' Julien smiled at his wife. 'For all the things yet to come.'

'I'd like that.' She kissed him softly, whispering, 'Happy Christmas, Julien. I love you. Now, off you go to play with your son.' She laughed. 'I know you've been wanting to get your hands on those tin soldiers since we bought them.'

Julien gave her a mock salute and did as he was told. Because if there was anything he liked better than sitting beside his wife on Christmas Day, it was playing beneath the Christmas tree with his son.

He gave the star a quick glance as he scooted beneath the tree and made a silent wish in his heart. *Please, let it be like this. Always.*

* * * * *

*If you enjoyed this story,
why not check out these other
captivating reads by Bronwyn Scott?*

Cinderella at the Duke's Ball
The Captain Who Saved Christmas

*Or let yourself get swept up in her charming
Enterprising Widows miniseries*

Liaison with the Champagne Count
Alliance with the Notorious Lord
A Deal with the Rebellious Marquess

HARLEQUIN
Reader Service

Enjoyed your book?

Try the perfect subscription for Romance readers and get more great books like this delivered right to your door.

See why over 10+ million readers have tried Harlequin Reader Service.

Start with a Free Welcome Collection with free books and a gift—valued over $20.

Choose any series in print or ebook.
See website for details and order today:

TryReaderService.com/subscriptions